Domini
was ~~nearly unbeatable,~~
but almost frightening in its intensity.

From the covert glances she'd received and the way his hand had casually covered hers at various points of the evening, she'd say the feeling was mutual. Just like her bra size, Jake McDonald was definitely a triple D—dangerous, distracting, and now she could add, debonair. It was a good thing she wasn't in the market for romance. Otherwise she'd be in big trouble.

Jake took a step and closed the distance between them. "You feeling what I'm feeling?" Now Dominique's throat went dry. His touch was like fire, scorching hot. Jake's face broke out in a confident grin. "Yes, you're feeling it."

"Look, Jake. I've already admitted that I find you attractive. But I don't have time for or interest in a relationship."

"Neither do I."

"Oh, so you just want to hit it and quit it?"

Jake's smile widened. "Basically. We're both adults here and I don't know about you but for me . . . it's been a while. I'm attracted to you. You're feeling me, so . . . why not?"

Also by Zuri Day

Lies Lovers Tell

Body By Night

Lessons from a Younger Lover

What Love Tastes Like

Lovin' Blue

Heat Wave
(with Donna Hill and Niobia Bryant)

Published by Dafina Books

Love in PLAY

ZURI DAY

Kensington Publishing Corp.

http://www.kensingtonbooks.com

DAFINA BOOKS are published by

Kensington Publishing Corp.
119 West 40th Street
New York, NY 10018

All Kensington Titles, Imprints, and Distributed Lines are available at special quantity discounts for bulk purchases for sales promotions, premiums, fund-raising, and educational or institutional use. Special book excerpts or customized printings can also be created to fit specific needs. For details, write or phone the office of the Kensington special sales manager: Kensington Publishing Corp., 119 West 40th Street, New York, NY 10018, attn: Special Sales Department, Phone: 1-800-221-2647.

Dafina and the Dafina logo Reg. U.S. Pat. & TM Off.

First mass market paperback printing: December 2011

ISBN-13: 978-0-7582-6000-0
ISBN-10: 0-7582-6000-8

10 9 8 7 6 5 4 3 2 1

Printed in the United States of America

*Football hero, everybody going got a football
hero, hero everywhere
He may be a rough and tough hero but
He's my lover and I love him a lot.
He's the guy on the winning team
He's got get up and go, oh, oh, my hero. . . .*

Author Unknown

ACKNOWLEDGMENTS

A big hug and thank you to my nephew, JaJuan Turner, the athletic director at Holy Name Catholic School in Kansas City. Your insight and suggestions made Jake's character and the sports scenes come alive! To copy editor Brenda Horrigan and as always to my cheerleaders: the oh-so-fab editor Selena James and my awesome agent Natasha Kern. We've done it again, ladies! Take a bow. . . .

1

"Mom, we've got a new coach!"

"Uh-huh," Dominique Clark absentmindedly replied, barely hearing her eleven-year-old son. Her mind was on a zillion other things: the upcoming model shoot, the rapidly approaching magazine deadline, her lovable gay assistant who'd just lost his man and therefore his mind, and right now the fact that there was nothing in the refrigerator to cook her son for dinner. Moments like these made this thirty-eight-year-old magazine executive feel that she was a much better career woman than she was a mom. It also made her value Tessa, her nanny/housekeeper who was out sick, all the more.

"Justin, you want McDonald's?"

"Yes!"

"Okay, let's go." As Dominique walked to the car, she texted one of the editors to ask about the article on being fat, fit, and fabulous. *I wonder if we've heard back from Sean Combs's people about buying the back page.* She sent off a quick text to the advertising manager as well.

All the while Dominique clicked BlackBerry keys, her son continued to prattle. "Did you hear me, Mom? We got a new coach! And he is *so* cool. He's big and tall and can run really fast, and he used to be a professional football player like for real though, Mom, like in the NFL. He played for the Oakland Raiders, Mom. The Raiders . . . my favorite team! Mom!"

"Justin! What?" Dominique buckled her seatbelt, put the car in drive, and headed for the fast-food-lined boulevard less than ten minutes from her comfortable San Fernando Valley home.

"We got a new coach!"

"That's good, baby," Dominique said, reaching to click the hands-free and answer her ringing cell phone. "Hello?"

"He hasn't called! I waited all day, just knowing that he would have left a baby-I-made-a-big-mistake message on my home phone. And that bastard didn't call, Miss Dom." Reggie fairly screeched the nickname he almost always used to address his boss. "He didn't call!"

"Reggie, you have got to calm down!" Dominique ordered in a quiet but firm voice. It was clear that her assistant, Reginald Williams, was no better now than before what she thought had been a success-fully calming talk. "If a man can walk away from you, let him leave," she'd admonished. Now, here was Reggie in a Boyz II Men moment making it so hard to say goodbye to yesterday.

"You're only upsetting yourself while the man who can't see your value and is therefore unworthy is off playing kissy face with some new dude." Reggie's cries began in earnest. *Okay, that probably wasn't the best thing to say.*

"Mom, you passed the McDonald's!" Justin cried.

I don't have time for two kids right now! Yet many times that's how Dominique felt when it came to her and Reggie's relationship, that she was the mother he never really had. She made a right, did a quick U-turn and headed back to the Golden Arches.

"Reggie, look, I'm sorry that you're feeling so badly and I know you need to talk, but I have to go. Why don't you take a nice, long soak and try and take your mind off what's his name. We'll talk tomorrow, okay?" Silence. Dominique remembered Reggie's last breakup and how some designer suits became cloth confetti thanks to his skill with sewing scissors. "Reggie, don't even think about doing anything crazy like going over to that man's house or out with your instigating friends. I need you bright and early tomorrow and the day's going to be a beast. We'll both need to be on top of our game."

"I don't know if I'll be in tomorrow," Reggie lamented between sniffles.

"Don't start with me, Reggie!"

"I can barely breathe, Boss." His voiced had now dropped to a raspy whisper.

Dominique pulled into the drive-through and rolled down her window.

"I want the number three, Mommy!"

"Welcome to McDonald's. May I take your order?"

"I gave that man everything. Every part of me," Reggie emoted, and then began crying again.

"I'm sorry you're hurting," Dominique replied.

"Hello, are you ready to order?" The question crackled through the drive-through speaker.

"Mom, I want the number three with a strawberry shake instead of soda."

"Just two weeks ago he sang "I'll Always Love You" and said I was his soul mate!" Reggie held out the word like he was Don Cornelius in a *Soul Train* flashback.

Reggie's lost his mind and now I'm getting ready to lose mine!

"Welcome to McDonald's. May I—"

"Hold on a minute," Dominique barked into the speaker.

"Mommy, I want a—"

"I heard you, Justin." Dominique threw the words over her shoulder. "Reggie, I'll call you back."

Three hours later, Dominique sat back against the headboard of her king-size four-poster, canopied bed—the one she'd had shipped from Europe after seeing it in a magazine. Her home definitely was her castle, a fact that had been very important to this former South Central projects-dweller when she'd become able to afford a place of her own. This abode was understated elegance with a little opulence sprinkled throughout. Her bed wasn't simply a place to sleep, it was a masterpiece—a place to be seen sleeping. It was made from rare pommelle sapele lumber, shrouded in silk, and draped with a politically incorrect chinchilla spread. Dominique had purchased this bed to celebrate her release from what she vowed would be the last nonproductive relationship of her life. She'd further vowed that no man would sleep in this bed unless he was "the one." She sat there surrounded by photos slated to be

included in a future *Capricious* edition, with several
articles to read and approve. In this age of technol-
ogy, Dominique still preferred to read the work in
paper form, feel its weight in her hands, and use a
red marker to highlight and comment. Glancing at
the clock, she eased reading glasses away from her
face and rubbed her eyes. Then she reached her
hands to the heavens and gave her five-foot-nine,
175-pound frame a good stretch. She'd been up
since six and now it was almost eleven. The long day
had held few dull moments. She chuckled, recalling
how her son had gone on and on about his new
coach at school. *What was his name? Jack? Jason?*
Whatever they called him, Dominique was glad that
her son liked this new guy. Justin was an intuitive
judge of character and didn't take to just anybody.
Good male role models were just what her son
needed. Dominique often felt guilty at the lack of
such men in her son's life. She kept planning to get
him involved in some type of mentor program, or
a Boys & Girls Club, somewhere where he could be
around strong men who looked like him. She
wished his uncle could be more of an example, but
her brother had not handled life well and had seen
his nephew less than a dozen times in the last five
years. Thankfully, her sister's husband, Aaron, was a
good man and an example to Justin, who spent
time in their Inglewood household every weekend.

And then there was her other son, Reggie. *What am
I going to do with that drama queen?* After returning
home from the drive-through she'd called him,
refused to let him wallow in his own misery, and
threatened him to within an inch of his life if he
wasn't gracing the desk in front of her office by

nine AM. Dominique couldn't remember when her and Reggie's five-year relationship had gone from boss-employee to friends (or mother-son depending on the day or circumstance). But at various times he'd been the girlfriend she needed to talk to or the brother she never really had. Dominique remembered how heartbroken she'd been to find out that her last lover had dipped his hands where they didn't belong. Reggie had been a comforting presence throughout that fiasco and Iyanla Vanzant, yoga, white wine, and buffalo wings had helped her heal. *I was probably too hard on him,* she belatedly thought regarding Reggie's predicament. *He was crazy about that man.* But the publishing industry was relentless, giving no quarter to breakdowns and broken hearts. Reggie Williams would just have to put on his big-girl panties. They had a deadline.

Dominique finished her work, turned off the lamp on the stand next to her bed, and slid down between luscious Egyptian cotton sheets. She adjusted the pillow under her head and snuggled the body pillow against her stomach. For a moment, more like a split second, she wished that there was someone there to wrap his arms around her, to knead her tight shoulders, or to hug her spoon-style. Dominique quickly replaced thoughts of a man with plans to have Reggie schedule a massage. Better to pay somebody to put their hands on her body, she figured, than take chances with a man who could grab ahold of her heart again and break it.

2

Jake McDonald cut a commanding presence as he walked out of the back door of Middleton Prep, crossed a lined asphalt racetrack, and stepped onto the grassy football field behind the school. At six five and 275, he stood out everywhere. Even without the height and solid build, his well-groomed head, smoldering brown eyes, luscious lips, and sparkling dimples would ensure that he got noticed. Jake McDonald was a triple threat—looks, talent, and personality. He'd been special his whole life.

"Coach Mac! I'm ready to play!"

Jake laughed and playfully slapped the shoulder of the energetic boy who'd become his shadow since the first day of practice a week ago. When he'd been hired as athletic director, boys like the one standing before him were the reason he'd also stipulated he be the football coach as well. So that he could change lives. He'd liked Justin Clark right away, had seen a bit of himself in the child's eager, searching eyes. Just as Jake stood out in life, Justin stood out on the elementary school football field. Tall and big for his age, he was also one of the few boys of color at this award-winning suburban private school, where the annual tuition was more than some folks made in a year. He'd heard from other teachers that Justin was academically sound, but it was his talent on the football field that made him popular. Jake had gleaned from school records that Justin had brought home the gold in that region's punt, pass, and kick competition and that kind of talent, along with his smarts and ready, infectious laugh, would help Justin Clark go a long way.

Jake blew his whistle, rounding up the team from various parts of the field. The assistant coach, who was also the offensive coordinator, ambled over as well. Twenty-five boys dressed in a mixture of shorts, sweats, gym trunks, and T-shirts made a sloppy circle around Jake, giving him their undivided attention.

"All right, team. These first practices are going to be all about conditioning, so get ready to run—sprints, routes, Oklahomas. And that's after you drop and give us 100 push-ups, 250 crunches, and 100 squats." Jake ignored the chorus of moans and groans, and continued. "And, since your verbal reaction tells me that what we've planned is not enough, we're going to divide up into offense and defense to work on a few basic techniques." Jake put his hand to his ear and listened. You could hear a mouse pee on cotton. "That's more like it. Guys, if we want to be number one then we've got to put in the work! Practice, heart, and attitude is what it takes to rise head and shoulders above the competition. We've got to come hard or go home. Are you with me?"

Twenty-five heads nodded and for the next two hours tried to give Jake McDonald and the other coaches everything they had and then some. Jake was impressed and let the players know how much he appreciated their hard work, which, of course, only made them want to work harder.

"How does it feel?" The assistant coach, Shawn Gallagher, moved the folders from a chair in front of Jake's desk and plopped down.

"How does what feel?" Jake asked, handing Shawn a bottled water from the mini-fridge before sitting behind the desk.

"Being a god."

Jake snorted.

"Coach, Coach!" Shawn mimicked, his green eyes sparkling. "The boys love you, man, especially that Clark kid."

"Aw, well, what can I say?" Jake drawled, straightening invisible lapels. "I'm the man."

Actually, it had been a difficult time of adjustment when Jake retired from the NFL eight years ago at the ripe old age of thirty-two. He'd experienced an unexpected bout of fame and team-withdrawal—one moment he was part of a family whom thousands adored every Sunday, and the next moment he was sitting in his home gym minus the cheerleaders and the roar.

Shawn took a swig of water. "I noticed somebody else who wants to play on your team."

Jake raised an eyebrow. "I hope it's that Burnett kid. I know his mind is set on basketball, and his father is pushing him to just concentrate on that and track, but I think that he'd make one heck of a running back."

"It's not just his dad; Alvin isn't interested in football. But I'm not talking about him."

Jake looked up from the player chart he'd been studying. "Then who?"

Shawn's smile widened. "The new fourth-grade teacher."

"The tall brunette with those long, sexy legs?"

Shawn nodded.

"She's gorgeous, but I don't think she's interested in me. I saw y'all hanging out before the meeting started, and her looking at you goo-goo-eyed."

Shawn was a red-haired, green-eyed heartthrob with an infectious smile and charming personality everyone loved. "I wish, man," he said. "Our conversation before the meeting was friendly chitchat. But *during* the meeting she was looking at you. Which is just as well, since I think Taylor might throw a few penalty flags if she caught me flirting with a colleague."

Jake laughed. "Your wife might have a problem with that? You think?" A reminder pinged on Jake's computer. He clicked on his calendar. "Damn."

Shawn stood. "Forget about a hot date?"

"Hardly. It's this Hollywood educational benefit where I'll rub shoulders with celebrities and influential movers and shakers . . . maybe rustle up a few deep-pocketed sponsors for our program."

"That's definitely your arena, man. I'm not the black-tie type."

"Me either," Jake said, putting away the folder and reaching for his duffel bag and keys. "But duty calls."

3

Dominique ran her hand discreetly over her abdomen as she stepped into Hollywood's W Hotel's great room. Having grown confident in and comfortable with her plus-size figure years ago, she still thanked God for the body shaper that smoothed, toned, and highlighted the curves that flowed in all the right places. Her freshly done twists accented the high cheekbones in her otherwise round face and her auburn hair with gold tones sparkled under the light of the chandeliers. In this room of size twos, Dominique felt good about how she looked. She went to black-tie events all the time.

So why is my stomach fluttering?

Was it because of the stress of a deadline a week away, Reggie's continued depression, or the fried catfish with jalapeño cornbread she'd had for lunch? No matter, *Capricious* rarely missed a PR opportunity and tonight's event benefiting education was one that would get major press. When solicited last year, Dominique and the board had immediately agreed to be one of the night's sponsors and she'd also agreed to provide complimentary subscriptions to one hundred lucky student winners. In an age when girls under sixteen were having plastic surgery and a size 10 was considered big, the magazine's brass felt it more important than ever to tout their message: beauty comes in all shapes and sizes, and in every *Capricious* magazine! So even with a looming deadline and the knowledge that she shouldn't stay long, Dominique had braved an hour of LA traffic to show her support.

Secure that she was a walking ad for "fat, fit, and fabulous," she looked around, recognized the organizer whom she'd lunched with last month, and headed in her direction.

Someone tapped Jake's shoulder. He turned and saw a TV host he'd known for years, a beautiful blonde who was the ex-wife of one of his NFL buddies. They'd just started to chat when he saw someone else—a statuesque African American woman gliding across the room, her chin slightly tilted as she scanned the crowd. Her form-fitting copper dress showed *pow* out to here and *bang* out to there and as if that wasn't enough to make a brothah's mouth water, those thick, shapely calves would definitely do the job. *Dayum! Who is that?*

"Jake, did you hear me?"

"I'm sorry, Madison, what did you say?"

"I was asking if you'd seen my ex lately. I heard he got divorced again, and quite frankly I'm worried about him."

Jake answered Madison's question but later that night if someone had offered him a million dollars

to do so, he couldn't have repeated what he said.
Big and natural wasn't normally his type, but there
was something about the woman who commanded
the room, as she'd walked through, it that touched
his soul in a deep, almost primal way. Maybe Shawn
was right. Not about the fourth-grade teacher but
about what he'd suggested the previous week—that
Jake get back into the dating game. Jake hadn't
dated seriously since relocating to LA a year ago. So
maybe he did need to pull out the Big Mac skills and
make a play. And maybe he needed to do so tonight.

Later, Dominique sat chatting with those on each
side of her, enjoying the delicious second course of
lobster bisque. The president of the foundation
hosting the benefit had just done the welcome and
an award-winning actor had delivered a succinct
and humorous speech, and then underscored his
belief in the importance of education with a check
for $100,000. Several honor roll students from vari-
ous districts—both privileged and at-risk—gave
short speeches on what education meant to them,
followed by a pop singer's rousing performance of
her latest hit single. Other well-known speakers
graced the stage and awards were given. By the time
a short, fifteen-minute film had ended, Dominique
had finished her main course. She looked at her
watch and decided to skip dessert. Having made an
appearance and secured a few cards for future interviews and ad campaigns, she felt it was time to go.
    She said good-bye to her tablemates, including
the event's organizer, and during a lull in the program Dominique stood to make her move. Walking

alongside the wall and trying to be as inconspicuous as a woman who stood six foot two in heels could be, she kept her eyes downcast as she made her way to the double doors leading out of the room.

"Next on the program," she heard as she was midway to her destination, "is one of the NFL's shining stars, a man who knows firsthand how getting an education can change a life. Ladies and gentlemen . . . Jake McDonald."

The audience applauded and, thankful for the noise and distraction, Dominique quickened her pace. She was almost to the doors when she heard his voice.

"Thank you, and good evening."

The voice was deep like still waters and sweet like molasses. She'd reached the door, but turned to see the being from whom this captivating voice had emanated. The flutter that she'd felt earlier that evening returned full force and a little squiggle went from navel to nana in nothing flat. She was a sistah from the streets who could play it as cool as an ice cream float, but *Oh. My. Goodness!* The man's very presence seemed to touch her even though he was on the other side of the room. He easily filled the tall, *really tall,* dark, *really dark,* and handsome, *really handsome,* bill . . .

But it was more than that.

Dominant. That's the word that came to mind when she looked at him. And then, in a heartbeat, a few other words filtered in as did remnants from the ain't-had-none-since-dog-was-a-pup conversation she'd had with Reggie the other night, when both had had probably one too many glasses of wine. But if she was going to do what she and Reggie had discussed, it would be with someone like the chocolate candy now commanding the room. For an instant their eyes locked, and held. The squiggle became a throb that caused Dominique to clench muscles that hadn't felt action in months. She exited the room on shaky legs, walked across the lobby, and handed her ticket to the valet.

She thought of him. On the forty-minute drive home, while wrapping up work with returned phone calls and e-mails, and while taking a shower. Oh, especially then. Afterwards she performed her nightly ritual of getting in just the right position to welcome slumber—head pillow positioned just right, body pillow snuggled against her stomach. Eventually, finally, Dominique went to sleep. And dreamed of still water and sweet, sticky molasses.

4

"All right, guys, listen up." Jake's booming voice demanded quiet, and in a moment he had all of the eleven-year-olds' undivided attention. "The first game of the season is always a very important one. But that doesn't mean that you shouldn't have fun. I want all of you to do your part, do what we practiced, and we will be successful." Various expressions, from curious to excited, anxious to confident, showed on the boys' faces. "We have to want it more than they do," Jake continued. "It's our heart that separates us from everyone else, because we want it more." He looked into the eyes of each teammate and noticed that Justin's gaze kept shifting from him to the bleachers just behind him. *It's a big day; probably looking for his father.* "Don't try and play outside yourself. Be you, do you, and win or lose, just be sure you've given it your all."

Justin raised his hand. "But Coach, I thought winning was everything."

"Winning is better," Jake replied. "But giving your all is best. Any more questions?" Jake looked around the circle and when none of the other boys spoke up, he placed his hand in the middle of the circle. The boys piled their hands on top of his. "Who are we?" he demanded.

"Hurricanes!"

"What do we do?"

"Tear it up!"

"How do we play?"

"Hard!"

"What do we have?"

"Heart!"

"Then get out there and—"

"Get it done, work it out, tear it up!"

"That's what's up. Now, one, two, three!"

"Hurricanes!"

The boys ran onto the field. Justin glanced up to the stands once more and then turned to join his teammates near the fifty-yard line. Jake, who'd been watching Justin out the corner of his eye, grabbed his shoulder as he ran by. "Is your dad coming?" With a hand still on Justin's shoulder, Jake turned and scanned the stands, which were fairly crowded considering this was an elementary school football game at eleven o'clock on a Saturday morning. When he heard no answer, he looked back at the student he thought might actually have potential in the NFL. "Justin?" For just a moment, he saw something raw and very familiar in the boy's eyes.

"My mom," Justin replied, pulling his eyes away from the stands and looking at Jake. He pasted a wide smile on his face, totally unaware that Jake had already seen the pain it covered. "We're gonna win today, Coach," he said with confidence.

Jake squeezed his shoulder and gave a wink. "Let's go to work."

Dominique looked at her watch as she found a parking spot in the crowded lot. *Geez! Are all of these people really here to watch some kids catch a pigskin?* Her heart dropped. She knew she was late, and hoped that she hadn't missed too much of the game. Football is all Justin had talked about since school began. It had been like pulling teeth to get him to talk about subjects near and dear to *her* heart—math, science, and geography, for instance. The only thing he talked about was his beloved new coach. "Coach did this," or "Coach said that." He'd been just two or three comments shy of getting on her last nerve. Yet as she walked across the parking lot thinking of these dinnertime conversations, Dominique realized that she hadn't seen her son this happy in quite some time.

"Through hail, snow, sleet, rain . . . we are the Hurricanes!"

Dominique walked through a short tunnel and entered the stadium, hearing chants led by cheerleaders wearing purple and gold-colored uniforms. She looked around and even though she'd missed much of the first quarter, she was still surprised to see that the stands were almost filled to capacity. It seemed as if the entire school's population and half the neighborhood had come out for this debut game. Belatedly, she realized that her work gear might not have been the best choice for wear—that her fitted purple dress, large shawl, and three-inch heels may not fit in with the rest of the parents or other spectators. These high-powered executives, soccer moms, and trust-fund babes hid their riches behind jeans, khakis, and diamonds worn like inexpensive glass. But since the office was where Dominique was heading as soon as the game clock ran out, followed by an early dinner with a potential freelance writer, hers was a professional look. Dominique shook away the slight discomfort of looking out of place, and the memories that went with this feeling, and began climbing the bleacher steps. She was so focused on finding a seat that she didn't see the pair of eyes that had watched her like a hawk from the moment she entered.

Jake worked hard to focus on the pad in front of him, filled with various offense and defense formations that he was reemphasizing to the team. But the *x*'s and *o*'s paled in comparison to the *pow!* and *bang!* of ample assets that now sat perched on a row near the top of the stands, at the fifty-yard line. He'd never thought to see her again, the woman who'd almost disrupted his speech the week before when she'd chosen the moment he reached the podium to make her exit. *What is she doing here?* She looked as glamorous in the stands today for a game of sixth-grade football as she had at the five-star hotel black-tie event. And, as then, she took his breath away.

"Coach Mac?" Assistant Coach Shawn brought Jake back to the present and the first game of the Middleton Hurricanes' football season.

Jake forced his eyes away from the woman who was as pretty in purple as she was in copper and back to the matter at hand. *And what is that? Oh, yeah, right, coaching, football, and how to win this game.*

"As I was saying," he continued, pointing to the clip-board he clutched in his hand. "Ends, tackles, we've got to close up those holes, stop giving their half-back that two-foot-wide lane to run through." Jake deliberately turned his back to the stands and fo-cused on the circle of eager faces looking up at him, depending on him to help them win their first game of the season.

At first, Dominique could have sworn she was seeing things. When she'd finally settled herself on the plastic bench and looked out onto the field in search of her son, she hadn't been prepared for what caught her eye at once—broad shoulders, big chest, and a butt that looked hard and firm even crouched down as it now was surrounded by eager players in helmets, shoulder pads, and cleats. A fluttering began, eerily similar to what had occurred when she'd gone to the benefit and about the same time she made this observation a thought dawned that Dominique was hard-pressed to ignore. *No . . . it couldn't be.* But it was.

This is the man Justin has been talking about? That hard piece of chocolate candy is my son's coach? Before Dominique could wrap her head around that possi-bility her cell phone rang. Unable to hear the call amid the yelling fans, she hurried off the bench and away from the noise. It was Reggie, telling her that the finicky actress who was to be their next cover story had suddenly pulled out. This news led to sev-eral more calls and about a dozen texts. By the time Dominique returned to her bleacher seat, it was the fourth quarter and the score was 21–7. She hoped she hadn't missed Justin doing something spectacular and was happy to see that her son's team was in the lead. She wasn't too sure how happy she was that her eyes kept being drawn to the big handsome man prowling the sidelines—his arms crossed, eyes focused on the field, barking orders to men and boys who seemed more than happy to obey them. His was a formidable presence, she admitted, and she almost convinced herself that the only reason she kept staring at him was because he was too big and tall to miss. If it weren't for the flutters in her stomach and the squiggles several inches further south, she would have almost been able to believe that lie.

How long has it been since you've felt this way? Dominique couldn't remember. Justin's dad had been her college sweetheart, but Leland Clark had never caused the flutters that she felt now. When it came to her ex-husband and his many infidelities, she'd been more likely to feel heartburn or indigestion, and after the painful divorce, followed by Leland moving out of state and basically abandoning his son, all Dominique felt was extremely pissed off. It had taken her a while to get back into the dating game, and after a few blind dates and a very brief stint of online dating she'd met Kevin Patterson in a coffee shop near her sister's house. A few short months later she imagined spending the rest of her life with him. Justin adored him as well and if it hadn't been for the fact that an observant bank manager contacted Dominique regarding her account, and activity described as "suspicious," he might still be in her life, stealing her money along with her heart.

A roar from the crowd brought Dominique out of her musings. She looked up to see the entire team run onto the field, congratulating their mates on a well-played game. It only took a few seconds of scanning to find Justin. Like his coach, he stood head and shoulders above most of the other kids. *They almost look like* . . . Dominique cut off the thought, refusing to entertain fantasies. She'd vowed not to seriously date anyone until Justin graduated high school. He'd been young when Leland disappeared and rarely mentioned his father, but he'd grown attached to Kevin, who'd treated Justin like a son. She'd felt badly about ending their relationship so abruptly and completely but for Dominique there had been no other choice. She'd learned from painful experience that the only thing worse than a philanderer was a thief.

"Mom!" Justin's voice cut through the buzz in the crowd.

Dominique stood and waved back at him.

Justin waved for her to join him on the field.

Lord have mercy, Justin, please don't make me come and stand next to that man. Dominique had purposely kept her eyes on her son and away from the massive hunk of fine standing next to him. *Coach Mac.* Dominique remembered the name Justin had repeated ad nauseum. *Jake McDonald.* The name of the ex-NFL football star introduced at the benefit flitted into her mind. As she tried to calmly make her way through the crowd to where her son stood she remembered something else—how long it had been since she'd scored a man, been touched down there, or drawn a penalty for holding. Her mind was dead set against it, but her body wanted to be tackled and pinned down by the man now melting her with his eyes.

5

Jake's eyes darkened, even as his expression remained unreadable. *Damn! The woman I haven't been able to get out of my head for over a week is Justin's mother?* Jake was at once upset and elated. He thought he'd never see her again and thought that for the best. The night of the benefit he'd mentally revisited Shawn's dating suggestion several times and finally decided that he didn't have the time or inclination for anything serious. The way his heart vibrated at the sight of this woman made having a fling out of the question. *What is it about her anyway?* She wasn't even his type and she certainly looked nothing like the wife he'd lost five years ago. Jake preferred model-thin, soft-spoken women who wouldn't question his lead. This woman walked liked a person with authority, someone used to being large and in charge. Just like him.

"Did you see it?" Justin enthusiastically asked.

"You were great, baby!" was Dominique's vague response. Between the phone calls, text messages, and staring at the coach's massive physique, she hadn't seen whatever her son was talking about, or much of the game, period. She turned with hand outstretched. "I'm Justin's mom, Dominique Clark."

"Jake McDonald." He enveloped her large hand in his even larger one, one set of chocolate orbs boring into the other. Sparks flew. Heat spread. Dominique quickly released his hand.

"But did you see me?" Justin again inquired, bouncing on the balls of his feet.

Dominique glanced at Jake, who saw the subdued look of panic in her eyes. "Everyone in the stands saw your touchdown, Justin," he smartly replied. "*Both* of them," he added, his eyes fixed on the mom who'd obviously missed her son's heroic feats.

Dominique's gratitude at Jake's save of face quickly turned to chagrin. If she didn't know better she'd think she was being judged. So she didn't see Justin being chased down the field trying to beat a group of boys across a line of chalk. *So what? Who does this man think he is?* All of what she did—the long hours, stress-filled days, and lonely nights—was done so that her son could have a comfortable life and an assured future. Nobody was going to make her feel guilty about that, no matter how fine that "nobody" was.

She pointedly gave Jake her back as she turned to speak to Justin. "How about we celebrate with a thick gooey pepperoni pizza before I go to work?"

Justin looked over at Jake. "Um, I can't eat that kind of pizza."

"Why not?" Dominique frowned, as she looked from Justin to Jake and back again.

"Coach says it's not healthy."

Dominique cocked her head at Jake. "Oh, does

he now? And does Coach also offer to feed you what he believes you should eat?"

Jake's eyes narrowed slightly as he eyed Dominique's luscious mouth. He didn't like the attitude coming out of it and knew just how he wanted to shut it up. It had been a long time since he'd had a woman. Too long. His manhood twitched at the thought of the one in front of him bringing him out of his six-month slump. Impulse replaced rationale. Straightening to his full six foot five, Jake responded. "As a matter of fact, I do, Ms. Clark. Lunch. My house. In two hours."

"Can we, Mom, please?"

"Oh no, honey," Dominique quickly answered, the thought of being behind closed doors with this testimony in testosterone bringing on the squiggles and flutters again. He looked even finer up close, his authoritative air getting on her nerves even as it aroused her. "Thanks, Mr. McDonald, but we couldn't impose. Besides, I have dinner plans for later this evening"

"It's Jake, and it's no imposition at all. And we'll keep it light so that you'll have an appetite for your date tonight."

So you assume I have a date, huh? Dominique saw no need to correct this thought.

"Please, Mom! Coach Mac can really cook!"

"How do you know?"

"He brought us cookies the other day."

Now it was Dominique's turn to raise a skeptical eye to Jake. "Cookies? You mean the kind with loads of sugar, butter, and other unhealthy ingredients?"

"No," Jake said. "The kind with agave sweetener, unbleached flour, raisins, nuts, flaxseed, and other"—

Jake paused, giving Dominique's ample body the once over—"healthy ingredients."

"They were delicious, Mom!"

I bet he is. "If you say so."

Jake looked up to see Shawn and a couple parents heading in his direction. He reached into his jacket, pulled out a card, and gave it to Dominique. "Call me in half an hour to get my address." He walked off without waiting for a reply.

An hour later, Dominique was still trying to come to grips with Jake McDonald and the effect he had on her. He was an attractive man to be sure, but that wasn't the only thing that made her heart race. His confidence was sexy and that he could cook, a total turn on. He was, in a word, dangerous. In two words, a dangerous distraction. Dominique needed to focus. Besides the cover-story drama with the per-snickety actress, there was a vengeful board member who'd recently reminded her, in so many words, that he was just waiting for her to mess up, and through all of this, Reggie's malaise over his lost love continued. With a plate this full, she didn't have time for a supersized extra like Jake McDonald, even though just the thought of seeing him again made her mouth water. *I'll call and politely decline.* With that thought firmly in mind, Dominique reached for the phone.

"Hello."

His voice brought to mind hot chocolate, sticky buns, and other forms of decadence. "Jake, it's Dominique."

"Hey, Nick."

Immediately, Dominique copped an attitude. To everyone except Reggie, who called her Miss Dom, and her family, who called her Nikki, she was Dominique. No shortcuts. No other exceptions. "I do believe I introduced myself to you as *Dominique* Clark."

"You did, but that's a mouthful." Jake paused and let that unexpected double entendre hang in the air. "So may I call you Nick?"

Dominique's jaw tightened even as her lower body squirmed. "I prefer Dominique."

Another pause and then, "All right, then. Dominique."

She loved the way his voice caressed her name. *And had its timbre gotten deeper, lower?* One thing had definitely moved. The now-familiar flutter in her stomach had eased its way down to her smoldering cootchie. She needed to end this madness now! "Jake, I really appreciate your offer but—"

"I've just put the food on, enough for three people. Don't even think about cancelling on me."

Justin, who'd been playing his Xbox, ran over to where Dominique sat on the couch. "Is that Coach Mac? I'm hungry!"

"Yes, Justin, now put on your shoes so we can go get you something to eat."

"Where," Jake asked. "A fast-food restaurant? Are you really going to pass up a home-cooked meal for that junk?"

Why did he have to hit the nail on the proverbial head? His assessment was so accurate that Dominique couldn't even be mad. "We weren't going for fast food," she said, changing her mind on the spot from a drive-through to a sit-down establishment where the meal wasn't delivered quite so . . . quickly.

"Where were you going?"

She barely hesitated. "Red Lobster."

"Mom, I hate lobster!"

Dominique had answered with the first non-fast-food place that popped in her head. *Dangit! I should have said Sizzler.* "Okay, baby, we'll choose another place."

"What you'll do," Jake responded as if he were talking to his squad, "is write down my address and come over so that your son, and his mom, can have a nice, home-cooked meal. Something I have a feeling is a rare occurrence." Before Dominique could formulate a sufficiently sarcastic response, he continued. "If what I'm saying isn't true, you won't be offended." Once again, Jake had rendered speechless a woman who normally got the last word. "Good. Here's my address. See you in twenty to thirty."

It was actually forty minutes when Dominique arrived at Jake's place, just so she could show him who was in control. At least that's what she told herself as she walked up to the well-landscaped residence less than fifteen minutes from her own home. She'd been surprised to learn he lived so close to her. The area wasn't exclusive but it was expensive, especially on a teacher's salary. *What other surprises do you have in store for me, Mr. McDonald?*

6

"You're late." A perfectly decadent frown marred Jake's stoic face.

"Does that mean dinner's cancelled?"

Jake and Dominique eyed each other silently. He took in the fact that she'd changed from her hip-hugging purple number to an equally tantalizing warm-up outfit: a baby-blue color that kissed her mahogany skin in a velvety-looking fabric that he instantly wanted to touch. Even this casual outfit was completed by a pair of three- or four-inch pumps. *Does this woman always wear heels? And does she always look this sexy while doing so?*

Jake wasn't the only one battling temptation. Dominique noted the black cotton button-down shirt stretched to capacity over a chest *magnifique,* with a light sprinkling of hair at its opening just waiting to be rubbed. His arms were large, and thick veins rippled across his forearms and hands. Unlike many men his size, Jake's stomach was flat, and the shirt tucked inside a pair of well-worn jeans hugged his body the way Dominique longed to do.

"Guys, I'm hungry." Justin eyed the adults as one who'd reached the end of his patience. "Are you going to stand there staring at each other all day or are we gonna eat?"

"Watch your mouth, boy," Dominique admonished.

Jake stepped away from the doorway and gave Justin an affectionate slap on the back. "Food's almost ready, Justin. You played good today, worked up quite an appetite, I reckon."

Dominique smiled at his choice of words. It reminded her of something her grandfather would say. "You reckon?"

"Ha! In fact, I do. That's a little bit of 'Bama seeping through. It's where my family is from."

"Really? My grandparents were from Alabama, too. What part?"

"Birmingham."

"Mine were from Huntsville."

"Good. That way we don't have to worry about being cousins."

"Why would we have to worry about that?" Dominique asked. She and Jake had navigated to the kitchen while at Jake's suggestion Justin had plunked himself in front of a massive flat screen in the living room.

Jake reached the stove, turned around, and allowed the desire that he'd felt for her since the beginning to show in his eyes. "I think you know why." He lifted the lid on a concoction of chicken, onions, peppers, and sauce, and leisurely stirred it.

Dominique swallowed. The fluttering that only happened when Jake was in the vicinity went out of control. "Okay, I'll admit it. I find you attractive."

"I'll admit that about you, too."

"And that there's definitely a spark between us."

Jake stopped stirring and turned. "Is a spark all you feel?"

"But this situation would simply be too complicated," Dominique continued, ignoring his question. "You're my son's coach. I'm not looking for a relationship and . . ." The rest of the sentence was silenced by Jake's full lips connecting with her equally thick ones. It was a wisp of a kiss, the merest meeting of flesh. But the sensation was like magic, potent and filled with the promise of more to come.

"And I think it's time to eat," Jake whispered, once he'd ended the chaste yet powerful kiss. "Justin! Come grab these plates and set the table."

It took less than thirty minutes for Jake, Dominique, and Justin to demolish a delicious meal of chicken tacos and spicy vegetable-laden brown rice. He'd used organic this, fresh that, and free-range the other but Dominique had to admit that the dinner was delicious. Conversation flowed as easily as the sparkling pomegranate juice that accompanied the meal. Justin was all ears as Jake shared stories from his NFL glory days, and Jake showed genuine interest as Dominique gave an overview of life in magazine publishing. When she looked at her watch and noted the time, Dominique truly did not want to leave. But staying was not an option.

"Jake, your healthy *home-cooked* meal was quite tasty. Our magazine is big on touting the benefits of good nutrition and I realize I've been lax on incorporating this fact into my own life. Thanks for the reminder."

"Can I come over here tomorrow, Coach Mac?" Justin asked. "Your food is *good*."

Inwardly, Dominique flinched. Nothing like a child to keep it real and diss his mother's cooking skills—or lack thereof—in the process. "Boy, don't be ridiculous. You can't expect your coach to cook for you every day."

"But he likes to cook!" Justin implored.

"Yeah, but I've got work to do," Jake said, once again coming to Dominique's rescue. "Like studying tape on next week's rival. Y'all played well today but don't think that every game will be as easy to win as that one. This next team is going to bring it. Y'all better be ready to give it right back."

Jake and Justin continued to talk as they walked to the door. Dominique was glad for the idle chatter, for the chance to rein in the emotions and hormones that had been roiling all evening and to think of an appropriate "so long, farewell" to end their stay. She'd covered it well, but Dominique's attraction to Jake was not only undeniable, but almost frightening in its intensity. From the covert glances she'd received and the way his hand had casually covered hers at various points of the evening she'd say the feeling was mutual. Just like her bra size, Jake McDonald was definitely a triple D—dangerous, distracting, and now she could add, debonair. It was a good thing she wasn't in the market for romance. Otherwise she'd be in big trouble.

The three reached the front door. Justin grabbed his mother's keys and ran out to unlock the car.

"Thanks for the attention you're paying Justin," Dominique said as she and Jake stood in the open doorway. "He needs good male role models in his life."

"And you think I'm one?" Jake took a step and closed the distance between them. One step more and her generous breasts and his solid chest would make their acquaintance.

Dominique barely breathed. "Yes."

Jake's eyes narrowed and his long, thick tongue flicked out to moisten suddenly dry lips. "You feeling what I'm feeling?"

Now Dominique's throat went dry. She placed a foot on the porch before Jake stopped her with a hand on her forearm. His touch was like fire, scorching hot.

Jake's face broke out in a confident grin. "Yes, you're feeling it."

"Look, Jake. I've already admitted that I find you attractive. But I don't have time for or interest in a relationship."

"Neither do I."

"Oh, so you just want to hit it and quit it?"

Jake's smile widened. "Basically. We're both adults here and I don't know about you but for me . . . it's been a while. I'm attracted to you. You're feeling me, so . . . why not?"

Dominique's back was ramrod straight as she faced him, her heels bringing them almost eye to eye. "Because my goodies are worth more than a damn chicken taco, that's why not!"

And before Jake had time to formulate an answer, Dominique was gone.

7

"What's wrong, Mom?" Justin noticed his mother being uncharacteristically quiet on the drive home.

"Nothing, baby. Mommy just has a lot on her mind."

"Is it Coach Mac?"

"No!" *Yes.* "Why would you say that?"

Justin shrugged, totally unaware of the field of dynamite into which he navigated, and in which his mother was trying to prevent an explosion. "You and Coach were looking at each other funny, and then you didn't want to leave his house."

Dominique's head whipped around. *Is this my son or a psychic sitting beside me?* "What do you mean I didn't want to leave?"

"Y'all kept talking when you got to the door. I think you like him."

"Justin Demetrius Clark! Don't you ever let me hear you say something like that again! Is that clear?" Belatedly, Dominique realized she might be over-reacting and went back in for damage control. She loosened her death grip on the wheel. "What I mean, baby, is that I do like Coach Mac, the way friends like each other. The way you and your friend Alvin or your new teammate, Travis, get along."

"Dag, Mom. What way do you think I mean?"

This potent question shut Dominique right up and if it hadn't, the caller ID showing on her ringing phone surely would. She pulled into her garage as she answered. "Yes?"

"Still thinking about me?"

"Ha! So on your resume is a job titled 'comedian.'" Dominique remained in the car while Justin bounded into the house. "Either that or you're exercising that overly confident professional athlete's swagger."

"Am I wrong?"

"Obviously, since you think you can melt a woman's panties with a single glance or a single meal." The fact that Dominique's va-jay-jay could at this moment be renamed "the burning bush" was, in her mind, beside the point.

"Dominique, I need to apologize for what I suggested earlier. I stand by my belief that two grown people should be able to do what they want without strings or ties, but I didn't mean to offend you."

"I may have overreacted a bit as well," she quickly countered. "Two consenting adults can do as they please."

"Then with that out of the way, why don't you come over?"

"Excuse me?"

"You heard me. And you know you want to. There's no way you didn't feel what I felt when we were together earlier."

"What exactly did you feel?"

"Hum. I can show you better than I can tell you. Now quit playin' and get over here."

The phone clicked in Dominique's ear, signaling the end of the call. The only thing worse than hearing his hang up was the fact that she didn't get to punch off first. Mr. Big-Baller-Shot-Caller was feeling pretty sure of himself and obviously he was used to having women fall at his feet. *If you don't stand for something, you'll fall for anything.* That's what Dominique's mother, Anita, would say right about now. And if there was one thing Dominique Clark didn't fall for, it was the okeydoke, or one who assumed too much. She had entertained her share of egotistical, successful men who thought they were all that and a winning lotto ticket. Most of the time she'd found out that their overblown egos were covering up an underwhelming endowment. The last thing this big girl needed was a little . . . anything. *Just another reason not to even get this started.* Dominique figured she was just the one to stand up to Mr. Jake McDonald, and let him know that as hot and handsome as he was, he was a temptation she could resist.

Later that night Dominique returned home to an empty house. Tessa had left the place spotless and she'd dropped Justin off in Inglewood to spend time with his cousins. Dominique looked at her watch: 9:30. After flipping through the movie channels and finding nothing to catch her interest, she decided to put in another hour or so of work. She'd just showered and settled herself in the middle of her king-size bed with photos and articles surrounding her when her text message indicator beeped.

Too scared to visit me without your son as a chaperone? Really?

Dominique failed in her efforts to keep a smile from her face as she typed in a reply. Please. Don't flatter yourself. She waited for his text, and was only mildly surprised when, instead, her cell phone rang.

"Hello."

"Dominique, it's Jake."

Still water and sticky molasses. "I'm not afraid of you."

"I believe that. You have no reason to be afraid of me. I'm as harmless as a fly."

"Like the one in the movie starring Jeff Gold-blum?"

"Who?"

"Never mind." Dominique forced the smile from her face and turned serious. "Listen, Jake. There are a million reasons why we have to keep this relationship strictly professional . . . and platonic."

"Name three."

"One, of course, is my son. I don't intend to introduce any more temporary men into his life."

"That's fair, but what Justin doesn't know won't hurt him. Two?"

"Two . . . I'm not interested in you."

"Whoa! Way to pierce a brothah's ego, baby."

"Just keeping it real, darlin'. I'm focused on my career right now, and on raising my son."

"Another one of those career women," Jake mumbled. He preferred more homey and less driven women, the way his mother had been, and a couple of his sisters-in-law were. They were content to take care of home. That's the kind of women he found attractive. Wasn't it? The way he kept trying to make a case to the contrary, one couldn't tell. "I don't buy that you're not interested," he continued. "But let's move on to number three."

Dominique stifled a sigh. "Do you really need more beyond these first two I gave you?"

"I guess not. But I'm bored tonight. Humor me." When seconds passed without a response, Jake asked his question again, with a bit more bass and sexy to his voice. "What's the third reason?"

Dominique shifted in a bed that suddenly seemed to have too much room for just her body alone. "Three is . . . well . . . it's late." *Yes, that sounds good!* "Any invitation after ten is just a booty call."

At the word "booty," Jake almost groaned aloud. Visions of Dominique's plump rump had plagued him ever since he'd followed her to his front door. After a couple seconds, he responded. "What if I told you what would happen if you came over?"

"Do you really think it would make a difference?"

"Let's see." Jake then proceeded to tell Dominique what he had in mind for their late-night rendezvous.

"My answer," Dominique stuttered, even as her nipples remained hardened by his words, "is still no." She mentally kicked herself so hard, a headache set in.

"What about tomorrow?" Jake persisted.

"I have to work tomorrow."

"On a Sunday?"

"It's a photo shoot with a busy actress, the only open date on her calendar, and I need to be there to hold her hand."

"Working seven days a week, Dominique? Where is the balance in that? You're focused on your job and on Justin. Who's focused on you?"

Nobody was, but she was less than pleased to be reminded that outside of work she had no life.

"Let me take you out to dinner tomorrow night."

Because he didn't have school on Monday, Justin was spending an extra day in Inglewood. Dominique couldn't remember the last time she'd been taken out to dinner, let alone the last time she'd spent time in the company of a desirable man. "I'll think about it."

"I have a feeling you do too much thinking. What time would you like me to pick you up?

This man is relentless! A part of her was appreciative of this fact. She liked that someone else was in charge and making decisions for a change. "What restaurant do you have in mind? I'd prefer to meet you there."

They chatted for a few more moments before Dominique ended the call. *What have I gotten myself into?* That was the first question that came to mind when the heat of her libido had cooled and sanity returned. *You'll soon find out* was the devil's response, vying with the just-say-no angel on her other shoulder. She went back and forth between wanting to jump Jake's bones right now and cancelling the dinner date she'd just made. As sleep overtook her, she still hadn't decided. But one thing was for sure: Jake's description of what he wanted to do to her had definitely whetted her appetite.

8

"Baby! I've met a man!" Reggie waltzed into Dominique's office carrying two large lattes. They'd decided to meet at the office to check over a presentation for the following day before riding together to the Malibu photo shoot.

So did I. "Oh, really?"

"Yes, honey, and that no-good two-timing a-hole I've been crying over for the past month is now in my rearview mirror!" Reggie paced the room as he described his latest love interest to Dominique, the one he'd met the previous night and with whom he'd awakened with this morning.

"I'm happy for you, Reggie. But be careful. You tend to jump first and ask questions later. And while I'm not trying to rain on your parade, this sounds like a rebound romance."

"Rebound, he-bound, what does it matter? I'm in *love*, sistah. I'm not hurting anymore!"

"Love doesn't happen in twenty-four hours. You're in lust, *sistah*. But hey, whatever floats your boat." Dominique took a sip of her coffee and tried to squelch her ire. Her lack of sleep from the previous night's restlessness had nothing to do with Reggie. "Besides the presentation and the shoot, is there anything else on the agenda?"

"I know what needs to be on *your* agenda." Reggie sat and crossed his designer-clad leg as he muttered this answer.

"I heard that, Reggie."

"No disrespect, Miss Dom, but it's true. You've been snapping at me for a while now and while I'm not trying to get all up in your business, I'll bet you ten to one that that attitude is all because nobody is on dick duty."

Dominique looked over her reading glasses at Reggie's sincere face. In the time that he'd been her assistant, their relationship had definitely gone from strictly professional to professional *and* personal. The lines had begun to blur during his second year at *Capricious,* when she'd broken up with Kevin Patterson. Reggie had been an excellent listener and had often provided the comic relief that this time in her life sorely needed. Her executive position and busy schedule were more conducive to associates than friends, so aside from her mother, Anita, and her sister, Faith, there weren't many people whom she felt comfortable confiding in. But her love life, or lack thereof, wasn't a topic she wanted to share with her mother, and with Faith having just experienced a painful miscarriage, she didn't want to burden her sister either. Still, Dominique needed another opinion and, right now, Reggie was her only other choice.

"I met someone, too," she began in a casual tone.

"When?"

"Yesterday."

Reggie became even giddier than his impromptu romp in the hay had left him. He slapped her arm before sitting back with a big smile on his face. "Do tell."

"I met him at Justin's football game."

"One of the parents? You met a single father?"

Dominique shook her head. "The coach."

Reggie whirled around in his chair. "All right now. You go girl. I like those athletic types myself. Quinn plays tennis."

"Quinn?"

"My new man!"

"Well, help me keep it straight, Reggie. You never mentioned his name."

"Girl, trust and believe, his name wasn't the least bit important last night."

"Ha! You're a skank."

Reggie laughed. "Thank you, darlin'. I appreciate that compliment. But we're talking about you right now." After a few seconds of silence, he continued. "So, spill the beanie wienies!"

"His name is Jake, and he's an ex-NFL player."

"Ooh, a manly man. Those are the best."

"If you say so."

"I definitely do. What does he look like?"

"He's . . . attractive. Tall . . . dark, handsome . . ."

"How tall?"

"At least six foot four, maybe five."

"Girl," Reggie responded, drawing out the word. "That's a guaranteed extra long all-beef frank, hold the ketchup and the mustard, okay?"

"Speaking of condiments," Dominique said with dry sarcasm, "he's also a good cook."

"Hm . . . to know that then, he'd have had to be in your kitchen or you would have been in his. Do tell some more."

"It was nothing, really. After Justin's game he invited us over for chicken tacos that he made from scratch using fresh ingredients, a salad, and this spicy rice that was really delish."

"Shut the front door! You mean he can fix *your* meal and then you can be *his* meal? That's what I'm talking about!"

Dominique pointedly ignored Reggie's sexual innuendo about the man who'd invaded her thoughts since first seeing him a little more than two weeks ago. The intense feelings she felt for a virtual stranger made absolutely no sense. But denying them was equally crazy, which is why she felt so torn. She wasn't in the emotional position to give her heart to anyone and logistically wouldn't be able to do so for another six years, after Justin graduated high school and left home for college. That's when she'd be able to once again focus on herself, and love.

"He invited me out to dinner tonight, but I'm going to cancel."

Reggie didn't even try and hide his chagrin. "Why?"

Dominique sipped her coffee, answering thoughtfully. "He seems like a nice enough guy, but the timing sucks. I'm not interested in a relationship right now and have never been able to handle casual encounters. Going out with him would be pointless because nothing can come of it."

"You want to know what I think? Good," he hurried on before she could answer. "I think you should keep an open mind, Miss Dom. Not saying that anything serious has to develop out of anything. But would it really be so bad to go out to dinner every now and then, take in a movie or hit the dance floor every once in a while? Put your cards on the table and let him know that you're just interested in friendship . . . although with a man such as the one you just described in close proximity your interest is sure to shift to something else before long. And I do mean long."

"Ha! Reggie . . ." Dominique shook her head, sure that anything she said would fall on deaf ears. She looked at her watch. "Let's get back to work. We need to leave in an hour."

After Reggie had left her office, Dominique reached for her cell phone. Certain muscles in certain places clutched as the image of the person she was getting ready to call wafted into her mind. *You mean he can fix your meal and then you can be his meal?* Dominique took a deep breath and punched the first three numbers. *Your interest is sure to shift to something else before long. And I do mean long.* She punched in the next three, her resolve waning. Then she remembered what Jake had shared with her last night, the things he had planned if she came over— the plans that included cold ice cream in a hot Jacuzzi with no bowl or spoon needed. Then another picture came to mind—the look on her son's face when she told him that Kevin had left and that he would not be coming back. She punched in the final four numbers.

Her heartbeat quickened as she waited for Jake to answer and she breathed a sigh of relief when his voicemail picked up instead. Even so, she couldn't stop the flutters as she heard his smooth, deep voice encouraging all who reached out to him to leave a detailed message at the sound of the tone. Dominique cleared her throat. "Jake, this is Dominique. I'm sorry, but I'm going to have to cancel on dinner tonight. I feel it better that you and I keep our relationship cordial, but professional, for Justin's sake. Thanks for understanding."

An unexpected wave of sadness came over Dominique as she hung up the phone but she quickly buried the feeling underneath a PowerPoint presentation. She was glad when the photographer called and said the actress had arrived and the shoot would begin earlier than scheduled. That sent Dominique into cram mode, which was just what she needed. And even with her mind crammed with all things *Capricious,* it wasn't enough to keep her thoughts off of one certain tall, sexy, smart man . . . and his all-beef frank.

9

Jake stood directly under the hot water from the shower spray, tired but satisfied after his workout. His normal routine was three workouts a week, but since laying eyes on a certain female he'd worked out almost every day. So far the barbells, crunch boards, push-ups, and bike riding had been only partially successful in releasing the pressure. The tension Jake was experiencing was the kind that only a woman could help release. He smiled at the prospect that tonight could be that night and Dominique Clark could be that woman.

A short time later, Jake was dressed and out of the gym. He'd checked his phone and saw a couple missed calls. But it was the area code 818 that had him smiling. Dominique had called and left a message. Wanting no distraction while listening to her sexy voice, he waited until he reached his car and settled in to listen. A few seconds into the message, disappointment replaced anticipation. Jake did not like what he'd heard and before the day was over he planned to make Dominique aware of that fact. Just as he began to hit redial, his phone rang. "Yeah," was his brusque greeting.

"Dang, man. Who pissed in your grits?"

Jake's twin brother's comment, a favorite one used by their grandfather, brought a slight smile to his face. "Hey, Johnny. Ain't nothing to it, man."

"Didn't sound like nothing to me."

"I'll be all right. What's going on?"

Jake should have known that he wouldn't be able to get away with the vague response. Jake, the younger brother by seventeen minutes, and his twin, Johnny, had been thicker than thieves since holding each other's hand in the womb. They were fraternal twins, but their looks and the differences of opinion in one important area are where the dissimilarity ended. In all other ways the men were alike—tall, good-looking, determined, successful. Jake and Johnny had two older brothers, Harold and Mike, and while it was a close-knit clan, the twins' bond was even more special. "I had a date cancel on me tonight," he responded, after a pause.

"Is that all? With the number of females lined up to sit in your presence, I'd think this a mere inconvenience at best."

"Should be, huh?"

"But . . ."

"But this one isn't like the other women. I don't know what it is about her but she's different."

"Different how?"

"Looks for one thing. You know how I've always preferred the slender, petite sistah . . ."

"Yeah, which I could never understand since you've been over six feet since you were sixteen years old." But if anybody had asked him, Johnny would have vouched for the fact that his tall brother and late wife, Robin, who had been shorter by twelve inches, had made the perfect pair. "So . . . what's the stats on this one?"

"Tall . . . around five nine, ten. Big-boned."

Johnny's shock reverberated through the phone. "A fat chick?"

"Yes and no." Jake closed his eyes, remembering soft velvety fabric hugging a vivacious body. "She's a big girl, but she's got curves in all the right places, breasts out to who and ass out to what . . . man."

"A big pretty," Johnny said, using another term passed down by the grandfather but mostly used by their dad to describe their mom before he passed.

"Brother, you don't even know."

There was a pause in the conversation as both men thought on similar things from different angles. "I tell you what I *do* know."

"What's that?"

"This is the first woman you've mentioned to me since Robin died. It's been over four years, bro. If this one is worth brooding over, she's worth going after."

Jake agreed, but a call from his older brother, Harold, followed by one to their mom, delayed Jake's call to Dominique. When he finally dialed her number, it went to voicemail. He wasn't surprised. In many ways, her actions reminded him too much of himself. He resolutely waited for her greeting to end, and then left his message. If he wasn't going to give her a piece of his body tonight, she was definitely going to get a piece of his mind.

* * *

Dominique rested a weary head against her plush, cherry-red leather office chair. *What a day!* It had been a long one, both excruciating and exhilarating at the same time. Her team had pulled off the miraculous, and it wasn't their first time. The cover shoot with Kirstie Alley had gone fabulously, making the crew wish they'd thought of her first instead of the temperamental no-show who'd been such a pain. And as if that weren't enough, she'd received an e-mail stating that up-and-coming actress Gabourey Sidibe, as precious as she was capricious, had agreed to be their cover girl for the June issue. They'd been working with her publicist for weeks and had finally gotten the official yes. A contented smile came to Dominique's face as she stretched and sat up. Her eyes widened as she looked at the time. Was it really seven o'clock? It was definitely time to go home!

As if to underscore this fact, Reggie bounded from the chair in front of her desk. "I sure hope we're done for the day, Miss Dom, because I gotta go."

"Yes, Reggie. It's a wrap. Thanks for your hard work. I'll remember this at the end of the year, when the holidays roll around."

"Thanks, Miss Dom. See ya!" Reggie pranced toward the door but stopped short when he reached it. "Wait a minute. Don't you have somewhere to go as well?"

Dominique shook her head. "I cancelled the date, Reg. But don't worry about me. I've got a long soak in a hot tub and a glass of wine with my name on it. Justin is still in Inglewood so I'm looking forward to some me time."

"If it were up to me," Reggie said, "you would be doing something more meaningful with your footloose-and-fancy-free evening."

"Then it's a good thing it's not up to you, huh? Now get on out of here before I think of more work for us to do."

Reggie shrieked and was gone.

Dominique laughed out loud as the door slammed. Reggie could be a handful but when all was said and done he was the best assistant she'd ever had—organized, pro-active, could sell snow to an Eskimo and make Scrooge smile. His background wasn't pretty but her assistant was proof that one could take life's lemons and make lemon icebox pie. *You could follow my lead sistah-girl, and have some dessert yourself.* Dominique laughed again. "Get out of my head, Reggie," she said aloud, reaching for her cell phone in the process. She saw that she'd missed a call. Her heart skipped a beat when she read the number. *Jake.* She pressed the button to hear what he had to say.

"Dominique. Jake. Your gratitude is premature because not only do I not understand your cancelling our dinner plans, but I don't accept it either. You want to protect Justin and I respect that. But to accept my invitation knowing full well that you never intended to honor your word? That's just foul."

Dominique sat back in her chair. She wanted to be angry, but a part of her agreed with Jake. She never should have accepted the invitation in the first place and wouldn't have, had lust not clouded her thinking for a moment. She thought about calling him back and apologizing again, but what good would that do? Probably more harm than good, since hearing his voice seemed to always bring on flutters and squiggles and cause her kitty to go all meow meow and shit. He was obviously too through with her. And isn't that what she wanted? Dominique hit speed dial. Within seconds, the voice that could give her joy no matter the circumstances spilled into her ear.

"Mommy!"

"Hey, baby. What are y'all doing?"

"Watching movies. And Grandma's here, too."

"Mama's at Faith's house?"

"Uh-huh," Justin said. "And she brought snacks with her, just like at the movies."

"Snacks, huh? What kind?"

"Skittles, hot dogs, nachos, everything!"

Hm, wonder what Mr. Organic would think about that? Dominique chose not to dampen Justin's joy by pointing out how quickly he'd forgotten his coach's admonishment about junk food.

"I'm glad you're enjoying yourself, baby. Put Mama on the phone."

"Grandma, Mom wants to talk to you."

"Hey, baby." Her mother's voice was as soothing as Justin's, and Dominique hadn't missed that the same term of endearment she'd used with her twelve-year-old still applied when one was thirty-plus.

"Hey, Mama."

"You sound tired, Dominique."

"A little bit; I just left work."

"On a Sunday, Dominique?"

Dominique told Anita about the photo shoot.

"Baby, I know your career means a lot to you but you're working too hard. You need balance in your life."

Jake's words from the previous night rushed into her mind. In fact, Dominique surmised, he'd been taking up way too much of her brain space. Still, her mom's words echoed what he'd said. *Where's the balance? You're focused on your job and on Justin. Who's focused on you?*

"Don't worry about me, Mama. I'm finished here, and looking forward to a long, hot" . . . *Ball Park frank* . . . "soak in the tub when I get home."

"I do worry about you, baby. There hasn't been anyone meaningful for me since your dad left. I don't want my story to be your life."

"It won't, Mama."

"Are you sure? Because I haven't heard you mention a man in quite some time. I want you to be happy, baby."

"I am happy."

"Then I want you to be delirious with the kind of joy that can only come from having someone you love and who loves you back in your life."

"I have that," Dominique stubbornly continued. "His name is Justin."

"You know what I mean," Anita huffed. "And you'd better hear what I'm saying."

They talked a bit more, made plans for Dominique to join them for next Sunday's dinner, and then Anita told her she was leaving so that she could get home before it got too late.

Dominique picked up her briefcase, headed to the building parking lot, and pondered what both her mother and Jake had said about balance, being grown and doing what grown folk do.

There'd been one man after Kevin and the theft fiasco—Charles, the "tune-up" man. Dominique had met him one evening while at a restaurant, dining alone at the bar. He was an excellent dresser. That's the first thing Dominique had noticed about him. He was also a businessman from Miami who travelled to Los Angeles two to three times a month. He'd approached her seeking companionship when he was in town and she'd agreed. Their dinner, movie, and concert dates quickly turned into him fine-tuning her feminine flower during his brief stays. He even occasionally accompanied her to magazine events.

Charles never met Justin, and Dominique never met any of his family. According to him, he was a lifelong bachelor with no interest in marriage or kids. And even with all that they had in common— successful careers, love for fashion and the arts, and a penchant for fine dining—his declaration suited Dominique just fine. Or so she'd told herself. She had labeled the arrangement perfect: private and unobtrusive. Then one day about a year ago she'd received a phone call. It was Charles, calling off their relationship. His reasons had been vague but one day the truth smacked her in the face, courtesy of Google. On a whim, she'd put his name in the search engine and got back a wedding announcement for her troubles. The *Miami Herald* article in the society section came complete with wedding photo: him and a twenty-something socialite, the daughter of prominent doctors. Dominique Clark convinced herself that she didn't care and, in classic Clark (Kent) fashion, had gone into the phone booth otherwise known as the *Capricious* office and made *Superwoman* her middle name. Always a hard, focused worker, she'd become even more so: accepted a board position of a local charity and agreed to be the consultant for a nonprofit organization's online magazine. From morning to night her hours had been filled but her bed—from then to now—remained empty.

Dominique reached her home but sat in the driveway with the car idling. She wasn't ready to go into her big, empty house and even emptier bed. So she headed toward her favorite spot back up on the boulevard. It wasn't quite Cheers, but she ate there often and everyone at this cozy Italian establishment knew her name.

Frankie greeted her at the bar and poured her favorite Chianti without her asking. She requested a menu and after ordering an appetizer settled into the comfy bar chair to shoot the breeze and dish the dirt with the guy who seemed to know everything that went on from one end of Ventura to the other. Within minutes she'd finished half her Chianti and ordered another, threatening to max out her two-drink limit before her food arrived. The wine, cozy setting, and friendly camaraderie between her and Frankie had Dominique more relaxed than she'd been all day. So she was totally unprepared for how her body froze up seconds later when a heavy hand squeezed her shoulder and a flutter-causing voice whispered in her ear.

"Well, well," Jake murmured, his breath like a hot melody on her ear lobe, sending a chorus of fire throughout her body. "Fancy meeting you here."

10

Dominique let out a shaky breath as Jake came from behind her to slide on to the next bar seat. "Jake."

He didn't respond but instead waved over Frankie and ordered a beer. He looked at her, his expression unreadable. Was it anger? Disgust? Disappointment? Hurt? Dominique couldn't tell, so she took another sip of wine and waited for the lambasting she felt was sure to come.

Jake eyed her again before taking a long swig of his brew. He placed the glass on the table, ran a strong, thick thumb over the condensation formed outside it and then leaned back in the chair. Eyes boring into Dominique's, his voice was deceptively soft, his question simple. "Why?"

Dominique lowered her eyes, grateful to the waiter who chose this moment to deliver her clams and mussels sautéed in a creamy tomato broth. The aroma wafted up to her nostrils but Dominique's appetite had fled along with all the excuses she'd used to cancel the date. Now, with Jake's sincere, questioning eyes boring into her, she was asking herself the same thing. Why did she cancel her date with this handsome, intelligent, interested man? "I don't know," she finally murmured, feeling nothing like the bold, confident woman who oversaw a multimillion dollar publication. Now she felt like the teenager and young adult she used to be—insecure, unsure, and vulnerable. She pushed memories of that woman to the background, determined to express exactly how she felt. At the very least, he deserved her honesty.

"Jake, I can't be clearer than I've already been. My attraction for you is undeniable but when it comes to establishing a relationship this isn't a good time for me. That's the beginning and the end of this story because I've never been good at casual romps in the hay."

Jake nodded thoughtfully. "Your food's getting cold."

Dominique had forgotten all about eating. Mentioning romps in the hay had immediately conjured up an image, making her hungry for a different kind of meal altogether.

Jake reached over, plucked a clam from Dominique's bowl and sucked it from the shell into his mouth. She watched in rapt fascination, the intimate act of his eating from her bowl escalating the sexual tension. He chewed the tender morsel and licked his lips. "Tastes good; you should try it."

Thankful for the distraction, Dominique picked up the soup spoon and sipped the tomato broth. With the first taste of it, infused with garlic, lemongrass, and thyme, her appetite was reawakened and she sampled more of the dish.

At this same moment, the waiter reappeared. "Can I get you anything, sir?"

"Yes," Jake replied. "A table." Dominique looked up as Jake confidently continued. "Corner booth if you have it. We'd like privacy."

Dominique didn't comment or resist, but rather silently followed the waiter to a small booth at the back of the room. The red candle flickering against the stark white linen created a romantic ambiance. Jake stood back to let Dominique slide into the booth and when she sat at the end, expecting him to sit opposite her, he shook his head. "Move over, I want to sit beside you."

Usually, Dominique was the one giving orders yet, without a word, she acquiesced to his demand. The waiter brought over the appetizer he'd reheated, along with Jake's calamari order. He then took orders for their entrées and left. Jake dug into the fried squid with gusto and for a couple moments, the two enjoyed the food and a companionable silence.

After both had demolished half their dishes, Jake wiped his mouth and sat back, his thoughtful eyes cast once again on Dominique. "What happened that has you so guarded when it comes to relationships?"

Dominique finished her bite, dotted her mouth with the linen napkin, and turned to answer him. "My last relationship ended badly," she began, deciding for once to let down her privacy barrier. For some reason she felt she could trust Jake with her truth, and she didn't exactly know how she felt about that. "He betrayed me, and I'll admit that it eroded my trust in men."

"He cheated on you?"

"Worse. He stole from me." At Jake's questioning look, she continued. "We lived together and had a joint checking account. Because of my demanding work schedule I was more than happy to let him take over the personal affairs. That's why it was a couple months before I knew what was happening, that he was regularly withdrawing money from my savings."

"But you just said joint *checking* account."

"I'd set this account up years before and when adding his name had never thought twice about the accounts being linked. It was a stupid and expensive oversight. But I was the only one who overlooked it. Kevin saw it, and took full advantage."

Jake placed a hand on Dominique's shoulder. "I'm sorry he did that to you."

"Yes, well, so am I." Dominique could have moaned aloud, so good was the light massage from these sure, strong fingers.

"Every man isn't like that, Dominique."

"I know, but that's only part of it."

"And Justin is the other part?"

"Yes."

Their entrees arrived, and for awhile the two ate in silence. "What about you?" Dominique asked, after she'd enjoyed a forkful of fettucini. "Why aren't you married or in a relationship?"

Jake finished his bite of grilled salmon and took a swig from his refreshed brew before answering. "I was married," he said, sitting back and seeing his past instead of the dark maple walls surrounding them. "My wife died. Over four years ago."

"I'm so sorry." When Jake remained silent, Dominique probed. "Was it an accident? If you'd rather not talk about it . . ."

"The first year after she died, it was about all I talked about." His voice was steeped in reflection. "She was only thirty-two years old. It seemed so unfair."

"What happened?" Dominique's voice was soft, nurturing, as she unconsciously placed a hand on his leg.

"Brain aneurysm from out of the blue. She woke up one morning complaining of a headache. At the time, I was head coach at a high school not far from our home near Oakland. I wanted to stay home with her, but she insisted that it was nothing, that she'd take a couple aspirin and call me as soon as she felt better. I never got the call."

"That had to feel terrible."

"It did. Of course, I blamed myself—"

"But surely you know that it wasn't your fault."

Jake shook his head. "That didn't matter. I still felt that had I been there she may have had a chance. As it were, her best friend found her. They'd planned a lunch date and Robin didn't show up. She called an ambulance right away and they worked on her forever but . . . it was too late."

"I'm so sorry for your loss, Jake," Dominique repeated. As much as she'd hurt from her partners' betrayals, she'd never had to endure anything like what he'd described. "It's understandable why you prefer to keep things casual."

"I never told you I preferred it," Jake corrected. "I told you that I wasn't necessarily looking for more than that. I enjoyed my years with Robin, enjoyed being married. I like steady companionship, having someone to come home to and confide in. I had enough of waking up next to anonymous bodies in my bed while playing in the NFL. But after a while that shit gets old, and you want a woman of substance." He turned his gaze on Dominique, looked at her lips for several seconds before raising his eyes to meet hers.

Dominique swallowed discreetly. "And you think that's me?"

"I don't know. But I'd like to find out."

11

Reggie's pacing threatened to wear out the plush white carpeting in Dominique's office. He was lamenting the fact that after enjoying a wonderful dinner, Dominique had turned down Jake's invitation for a nightcap at his house. "I just don't get it, Miss Dom. Pardon my French but you're a grown-ass woman with grown-ass needs. Ain't nothing wrong with getting a little loving every once in a while."

"I know . . ."

"Or a lot."

"You're right. But I get this feeling . . ."

"Where, in your cha-cha?"

"Reggie . . ."

"I'm just sayin' . . ."

"I get the feeling that if I slept with him it would be hard for me to keep my feelings and expectations in check. I think I'd want more."

"And what's wrong with that?"

"The timing, Reggie! I have to wait six more years, until Justin has graduated and is away at college. Then I can refocus on my personal desires."

"Why do you keep hiding behind that flimsy excuse? That didn't stop you from seeing the tune-up man. What was his name?"

"It doesn't matter." In this moment, Dominique regretted ever telling Reggie about Charles. If she hadn't, he wouldn't be able to use this oh-so-sensible argument right now. "Justin didn't know the tune-up man, didn't worship the ground that the tune-up man walked on. That's the difference." Dominique looked off into the distance. "I just wish the thought of him didn't turn me on so much."

"That's just it, girl. It's because you're thinking and not doing. Look, the reason why the attraction is so strong is because you're making him forbidden fruit. We always want what we can't have." Reggie came over to the sitting area where Dominique sat idly flipping through a magazine mock-up. He sat down next to her and stilled the flipping pages to get her attention. "Here's what you need to do. Call that man when you get home. Make a date to go over to his house as soon as possible. Screw that brothah's brains out and let him return the favor. Get yourself some sexual healing, girl. You won't be able to get him out of your mind if you don't."

"I'm afraid that I won't be able to get him out of my mind if I do!"

"Well, hell, if you can't win for losing at least be satisfied."

"Ha! You just might have a point." Reggie crossed his arms and gave Dominique a look. She acquiesced. "Okay, I'll think about it."

"Don't think, do." Reggie looked at his watch and noted it was time for their weekly Monday meeting. "I gotta go set up. Can I bring you more coffee?"

"No, thank you," Dominique answered. *Just bring me Jake.* She watched her well-dressed, never-without-a-man-for-long assistant prance out of the room and then she dove into the pile of articles waiting to be edited.

Lunchtime arrived and it felt as if Dominique had hardly made a dent in the day's agenda. She knew the reason—couldn't keep her mind on work. Every time she looked at a dark-skinned model, or saw a chocolate-brown piece of cloth for that matter . . . she thought of a certain well-defined face, containing lips she'd longed to kiss last night. She thought of the strong forearm and thick thigh on which her hand had rested, and the big chest on which she wished she'd placed her head. She remembered the story about his wife, the pain in his eyes that had accompanied it, and the determination she saw when he spoke of loving again. Immediately she thought of Justin, her go-to barrier where men were concerned but for some reason, in this moment, that hurdle was flimsy at best. Her head was telling her to stay away but her heart—and other body parts—were saying "Full speed ahead!" *Maybe Reggie's right,* Dominique thought, pushing away the article in which she'd read two lines in ten minutes. *Maybe I just need to do him and be done.* With renewed determination, Dominique picked up the phone but before she could dial out, Reggie stuck his head in the door.

"I forgot to tell you that your sister called."

"When?" Dominique asked, immediately thinking that something may have happened to Justin.

"Just about ten minutes ago, when you stepped away from your desk."

"Thanks, Reggie."

"Oh, and your two o'clock canceled. Said she's sick."

"Again?"

"I know. Drama." He rolled his eyes and returned to his desk.

Dominique quickly dialed her sister's number. "Faith, it's me."

"Hey, Sis."

"Reggie said you called. Is everything okay?"

"Yes, everything's fine. The kids are over at Mama's."

Dominique exhaled a relieved breath. "She'll bring Justin home."

"Physically, I've healed but emotionally . . . it's still touch and go." Faith had been three months pregnant when she miscarried what would have been her and Aaron's third child. It didn't matter that the embryo had barely been an inch long when she lost it; she'd loved it as much as twelve-year-old Michael and eight-year-old Alexis.

"It's going to take awhile, Faith. Don't expect too much of yourself."

"Aaron's been great. We know we'll get through it, just taking it day by day." The women were silent as they pondered the preciousness of life. "So," Faith said into the silence, "you're probably wondering why I called you in the middle of the day."

"Yes."

"It's about a friend of Aaron's and before you put your blocks up, let me tell you about him."

"Really, Faith—"

"He's a nice guy, Nikki," Faith argued, calling Dominique by the name that only the family was allowed to use.

"I'm sure he is but I'm not interested. And it's not for the reasons you think."

"Oh really? Then why is it?"

Dominique was grateful that Faith had brought up the subject of men. It made her feel it was okay to talk to her about Jake. "Because me and Justin's football coach had dinner last night."

"Who, what, when, where, why?" Faith gushed, running the words together the way they used to as hormonal preteens and teenagers about to share a juicy story. Dominique heard more joy in Faith's voice than she'd heard in a while, definitely since the miscarriage. "Well, don't keep me waiting, sister . . . tell me more!"

Dominique giggled and soon it was like old times when these sisters shared secrets about stolen kisses and school-boy crushes. Except for Dominique this wasn't your average attraction. The more she talked the more she acknowledged that what she felt for Jake didn't happen every day. For her it had never happened before. Not like this.

12

Dominique stood in front of the floor-length mirror in her master suite. She was looking at her fourth wardrobe choice, a streamlined blouse and pencil skirt that were precariously close to joining three other choices in the reject pile. *Why is nothing working for me tonight? Probably because I feel like a fricking teenager going on her first date.* She'd heeded her own desires and her sister's advice and called Jake. He'd been pleasantly surprised to hear from her and even though the second game of the season was tomorrow at noon, immediately accepted her invitation to get together tonight. She'd suggested meeting at his place, and this is where Reggie's advice came in. *Screw that brothah's brains out and let him return the favor.* She wanted to go over there, get her groove on, and get the lust for this man out of her system. "This is about two adults handling the business of being attracted to each other," she'd explained, after voicing her meeting choice. "I don't want or expect anything more." But Jake had insisted on making an evening of it, saying he'd pick her up at eight, and told her to dress sexy. Dominique took another look in the mirror and blew out an exasperated breath. The blouse and skirt weren't the look either. She walked to the dress rack in her large, walk-in closet. Her eyes fell on one toward the back that she'd purchased on impulse and never worn. "Of course!" she said aloud. *That one is perfect!* She quickly slipped into the silky number and pulled a pair of three-inch stilettos from the shoe rack.

As she stepped into them, Justin burst into the room with a football under his arm and a pack strapped on his back. "When is Grandma coming?"

"She should be here soon, Justin. What about your room? Is it clean?"

"Kinda." Then he fixed her with the big brown eyes and crooked smile that melted her heart and Dominique decided not to force the issue, even though she knew that looking under his bed would probably require searchlights and tracking equipment. When she told him to put things away, that's often where they got shoved. Many items weren't found until Tessa's weekly cleaning, only to sometimes be lost again in no time flat.

Justin watched Dominique put on her heels and walk over to her jewelry collection. "Where are you going?"

"Nowhere special, just out with a friend."

"Who?"

"Why are you being so nosy?"

"You know where I'm going."

"I'm supposed to; I'm the parent."

Justin watched his mother apply powder and mascara, and then cocked his head to the side. "Is it with Coach Mac?"

Dominique hid her surprise behind a spritz of Vera Wang. "Why would you think that?"

Justin shrugged. "Dunno. I really like him though. Sometimes . . ."

Further conversation was interrupted by the doorbell. Justin ran out to answer it and Dominique's mother, Anita, her nephew, Michael, and her niece, Alexis, walked through the door.

"You look nice," Anita said, after hugging her daughter. Unlike Dominique, Anita was of average height and on the slender side. The big-boned side of the family came from Dominique's dad. "Big date tonight?"

"No." Again, Dominique felt defensive. She knew she shouldn't. It was a perfectly legitimate question to ask, considering how she was dressed. But she'd sworn Faith to secrecy and didn't want to tell Anita about what Dominique knew would be a temporary dalliance. "I'm meeting friends for dinner."

"You're pretty dressed up," Anita said, eyeing Dominique from head to toe. "Must be *some* kind of friends."

"Where's Faith?" Dominique asked, to change the subject, though she knew the answer.

"She's at home, waiting for us. I told her I would pick up Justin since I was coming over here anyway."

"She all right?"

Anita nodded, with a look that let Dominique know that they would talk later when little pictures with big ears weren't around. "While I was at the doctor's I let the kids play at the mall. Michael took very good care of his sister."

Dominique looked at Michael. "Aw, isn't that nice."

Michael rolled his eyes, though one could tell he was proud of the compliment.

"How's the acupuncture going?" Dominique had been surprised when Anita had told her about a doctor who'd been recommended to help with back pain she'd suffered since being broadsided a year ago. Since then she hadn't worked, and was receiving disability.

"I can tell the difference, Dominique," Anita said, a big smile on her face. "I thought that short of a miracle I'd have to either endure pain or take medication the rest of my life. But my dosages have been reduced by half and I've started walking for exercise again."

"I'm so happy to hear that, Mama." Dominique hugged her mother.

"Speaking of happy, you give anymore thought to what I told you last week?"

Instead of commenting, Dominique reached for her son and gave him a hug. "Be good, baby. Don't give Mama or Auntie any trouble, no back talk and no fighting!" Michael and Justin loved each other like cousins but fought like brothers—mainly arguments, though Dominique had broken up a wrestling match or two. "Michael, Alexis, come hug Aunt Nikki."

Ten minutes after her son and family left, the doorbell rang again. Dominique placed a hand against her stomach to still the flutters. In her profession, she was constantly seeing attractive men. Justin's father was handsome. But her body had never reacted this way to anyone. Until now.

She walked to the door, opened it, and immediately wondered where the air went. Jake looked as he had the evening of the benefit—tall, confident, and sexy as hell. A bona fide fashionado, Dominique quickly took in the tailored black suit, stark white shirt open at the collar, and the effectively understated platinum jewelry. There was also a large spray of fragrant roses in his left hand, but their scent was not nearly as intoxicating as Jake's darkening eyes, square jaw, and plush lips. He licked them, and Dominique felt moisture that was not created by the Santa Ana heat. A need arose— sudden and powerful. A need to be touched, held, kissed . . . loved.

Realizing that not one word had passed between them, Dominique leaned against the door. "Hey, Jake."

Jake's eyes narrowed as he gazed at the alluring woman before him. He doubted she realized the picture she painted, wide hips and part of a luscious breast resting against the door, accenting curves so sharp she should have been required to wear a caution sign. Eyes darkened with desire, mirroring his own. Lips painted with a color evoking berries that he wanted to lick off. She was wearing another one of those form-fitting dresses, the kind that had him needing more room in the groin area of his slacks. A lot of oversized women wore black, but not this chick. This dress was tan with a subtle abstract design that caressed her thighs before flaring out just above the knee. Her muscled calves were shapely and the tall, strappy sandals minimized the reality of her size 10 feet.

"Hey, Nick."

Dominique fixed him with a look.

"Ms. Clark." Jake presented the flowers.

"Thanks, Jake. They're lovely. Would you like to come in while I put them in a vase?"

Without waiting for his answer, Dominique turned and walked into her living room. Later Jake would swear his blood pressure rose a notch as he watched her luscious backside sway from side to side encased in that soft, flimsy material that he felt he could tear off with one good pull—and wanted to.

Dominique walked over to where a collection of vases sat on a shelf, trying to rein in the fire that burned down below. Her legs were shaky, and it took a Herculean effort for her to casually reach for one of the larger vases to fill with water.

Jake's control wasn't as strong. Her butt cheeks winked at him with each step she took. They were like twin magnets, pulling him forward. When she turned around, he was right behind her. "You look good, Dominique."

Their bodies were separated by inches; his shaft grew by inches.

"Uh, you look good too, Jake." Dominique attempted to walk around him.

But no go. Jake reached out and grabbed her arm. "I want to kiss you."

By now, a light could have been turned on by the electricity flowing between them. "Maybe later," Dominique answered, surprised at the breathlessness of her voice.

"Maybe now," Jake replied.

He took one step, his thick, juicy lips hovering mere inches from Dominique's berry-colored ones. She closed her eyes and instantly was pulled into his arms. Their bodies melded together in perfect symmetry, as if they'd been designed for each other.

Jake wrapped his arms tighter around her, pressed a strong tongue inside willing lips, and deepened the exchange. Dominique sighed contentedly. The forgotten vase fell to the carpet as she wrapped her arms around combed wool and broad shoulders, drowning in spearmint-flavored mouthwash and musky cologne. Jake tilted his head and continued the assault. His tongue mimicked the act of lovemaking as his hands introduced themselves to Dominique's curves. They came to rest at the crest of her ample rear asset, and Jake groaned with pleasure. With his large hands and size fourteen shoes, he rarely experienced more than a handful. His wife had been five foot five and the few tall women he'd dated had been thin, where he felt he could lift them over his head with one hand. But now he realized what it felt like to have a whole lot of wonderful woman in his arms, a piece of plus-sized paradise on his hands. It was as if her body had been made for him, because when he pressed his hardening erection against her, it fit just right.

"Nick," he whispered into her mouth, as he slid a hand up her stomach and squeezed a juicy tit. He rubbed his hand across the silky fabric and was rewarded with the feel of a nipple hardening beneath his touch. Again, there was more than a handful for him to play with, and he longed to feel the weight of her loveliness bare and in his hands. Not able to hold back the suspense any longer, he slipped his hand inside the plunging neckline, flicked his thumb across a perfectly formed areola, just right for sucking. His mouth watered.

Dominique gasped. "Jake."

The sound was like a starter's gun at a sprinters'

race. Jake broke the kiss, reached for Dominique's hand, and walked them over to the off-white leather sectional that dominated the room. He pulled her down beside him, reclaiming her mouth, fingers reaching for her breasts to continue where they'd left off. Dominique was vaguely aware of caution lights and warning bells ringing inside her head, but so muted were they by the haze of desire that instead of pulling back, she reached forward, placed a hand on the chest she'd dreamed of a thousand times and ran her hand across his manly physique. Her hand lowered to a taut waist, and lower still. *Wow! Is this for real?* Jake ground himself against her hand. "It" was very real, and still growing. Something inside exploded, in both of them, and soon suit jacket, dress, pants, shirt, and shoes were scattered near the sectional. Lips and hands sought and found, squeezed, devoured. The language of love was the only one spoken. The moment was one unto itself, with neither player seeming to control their own actions. It was meant to be. This was going to happen, like an earthquake rumbling near the planet's core, or a volcano simmering in the depths of a distant cave— inevitable. Sensations tore through both of their bodies. They were on fire, like the volcano; shaken, like the quake. Jake positioned them horizontally and then stretched out on top of her. Dominique welcomed his massive weight, and spread her legs so that his shaft was nestled against her heat. She reached around and palmed the hard, round butt that she'd admired since day one, caught her breath as Jake sucked a hardened, lace-covered peak into his mouth. They rubbed their bodies against each other, hands moving, exploring, conducting one very serious get-to-know. It was as though Jake couldn't get enough of the feel of her as he turned them to the side so that he could rub his hand across the soft ripples along her stomach, over her ample hip, and around to the mountainous gluteus maximus that had put him in the trance that started this dance. He squeezed the soft, juicy cheek. His heart almost stopped right then. His shaft became even more engorged. Jake thought he'd burst and Dominique thought she'd die from anticipation. Taking the lead, she reached between them, gathered his massive weapon into her hand, and began stroking it.

"Do you have condoms?" she whispered.

Jake nodded, blindly reaching for the slacks that contained his wallet. Without breaking the kiss he retrieved them, blindly reached inside until he felt foil. "Let's go to your bedroom."

"No, here is fine."

Jake stopped and looked into Dominique's eyes. *What is up in your bedroom? Evidence of another man?* But the moment was too fragile and too beautiful for him to press further. Instead he pulled the T-shirt over his head. Taking his lead, Dominique reached behind her and undid her bra. Her girls came out swinging, begging for attention. Jake leaned over and once again claimed a round, hard nipple. He kneaded the other with his hand, rubbed it back and forth between his thumb and forefinger. Dominique stroked his massive manhood, tracing its mushroom tip through his cotton boxers.

Jake stood, and dropped his drawers. If this were a movie the moment would have warranted a special effect.

Dominique pulled off her panties. She rolled to

the side, exposing her butt, and Jake swore he heard Usher. *Oh. My. God.*

Jake handed Dominique the condom and she rolled it on his shaft as if his dick was a rare find in an art museum. In her mind it was damn sure a piece of work. "Ooh." She positioned herself on the edge of the sectional, her legs spread wide in silent invitation.

The feeling was exquisite as Jake slowly, purposefully, slid his massive girth inside her. Dominique spread her legs farther to accommodate his size but it still took a moment. When he'd finally settled his body fully against hers, he whispered one word in her ear. "Nick." Then he began stroking.

And to Dominique Clark it didn't matter that he'd called her by that name twice in one evening. She didn't care at all.

13

Jake and Dominique made fast love on the couch before she quietly took Jake's hand and led him upstairs to the master suite. There, Jake McDonald went where no man had ever gone before—to the king-size, four-poster canopied bed. The place reserved for "the one." He sexed her again and again and this last time the orgasm felt as though it began at her toes and shot clean through her cranium. Jake thought he'd never stop throbbing.

He pulled her into his arms and rubbed his hands over sweaty skin that was as smooth as a baby's bottom. "What just happened?"

"The earth moved," Dominique answered, too sexually satisfied to think of a clever, ambiguous retort. She'd been married to one man, lived with another, and partnered with a few others in her three-plus decades on earth. But never, ever, had a man rocked her world off its axis the way Jake McDonald had just done. Her cootchie still quivered from memories alone.

Jake's laugh was deep, knowing, spilling out like

the joy of a first place runner doing the victory lap. "I take it that you don't mind that the evening's plans changed."

Dominique turned on her side and spooned her behind against Jake's flaccid penis. "Do I look like I minded?"

Few words had been spoken during their one-hour lovemaking session. Aside from commands such as "spread your legs," "touch me there," "deeper," "more," and "harder," their bodies had done the talking. But now, in the aftermath, the lovers' haze lifted, Dominique realized that there were some pretty important issues they probably should talk about. Like the fact that even as mind-blowing and earth-shaking as the sex with Jake had been, there was no way that they could continue to see each other. She had taken Reggie's advice and screwed Jake's brains out. But obviously part of hers remained as she thought somberly, *This can never happen again.*

Before Dominique could get into full backpedal mode, Jake spoke. "I usually like small women." He felt her stiffen up and hurried on before she could interrupt. "But this," he ran his hand from her shoulder to her thigh, "all of this, is absolutely incredible." He leaned in to whisper into her ear. "The best I've ever had."

Oh, Lord, help save me from myself. Why did he have to go and say that she'd been his best? Now, she knew that he felt the exact same way that she did. What they'd just experienced didn't happen every day.

"I loved making love to you, Nick, I mean . . . Dominique."

"All right already. You can call me Nick . . ."

Jake smiled as he nuzzled her neck. "Nick, I love the way your body fits with mine, the way your breasts and booty are the perfect size for my hands. I love how when I hold you I'm holding something solid, something thick and meaty, juicy—"

"Are you talking about me or a steak?" Dominique drawled sarcastically, covering up the fact that his words were making her whole body smile.

"I love eating steak," he responded, his hands seeming unable to stay away from Dominique's lusciousness. "But you're even more delicious."

Dominique shook her head as if to clear the lusty clouds that threatened to once again settle around her. They needed to talk. She needed to explain that as wonderful as tonight had been, they needed to put it behind them. She took a deep breath, unwrapped herself from Jake's embrace, and sat up against the headboard.

Jake rolled onto his back, looked up at the ceiling but after a moment, joined Dominique in her seated position against the headboard. "What is it?"

Dominique sighed.

"Aw, hell. Is this when you deliver the 'Dear Jake' speech?"

Dominique looked over at the man who'd just made her nana applaud, and didn't miss how good and right he looked in her bed. "You made me see stars, several times. I'm not going to lie. But I think this is the moment we come back to earth and discuss what can happen in the light of reality."

Jake turned to her. "And what's that?"

Dominique sighed. "Nothing, Jake."

"Woman, what are you so afraid of?"

"I'm not afraid of anything."

"Ha. Yeah, you are. You're scared."

Dominique laughed at the streetwise way Jake pronounced the word, and worked hard not to correct his yeah as she would have done with Justin. Instead she simply repeated, "I am not afraid. I'm realistic."

"If that's the case then let's go with the flow, for real, and see where it leads us. You've made it very clear that one"—Jake counted on the thick, strong fingers that had played a concerto on Dominique's flesh—"you're not looking for a serious relationship. Two, you won't bring a man into your life or the house, tonight being the exception, because of Justin. Three, your career comes first. Four, a man can't wear the pants in your house because you've got them on—"

"What?" Even sitting in her king-size bed, Dominique's hand found its way to her hip.

"You heard me and don't even act like it isn't true. *You* wear the pants in this family. "

"In this family, I'm the only one who can."

"Point taken. But as the chief at your company and the queen of your castle, you're used to being in control. I get that." Jake took her hand, began tracing the lifelines on her palm and caused Dominique's heart to soften . . . a little, especially when he turned those big, brown eyes on her and looked at her so sincerely. "I'm just saying you can have all that," Jake brought her hand to his chest, "and this, too. You might find it hard to believe, but it had been a while since I'd been with a woman."

"I could tell."

"How's that?" Jake asked, though he knew the answer.

"The first round lasted less than five minutes."

Jake turned until he could lie with his head on her soft thighs. "I didn't hear you complaining."

"Short and sweet worked just as good as long and leisurely."

"I'm glad." Jake tweaked Dominique's nipple. "I love your breasts," he said, his voice almost reverent. "You know what I'm ready for now?"

Dominique felt familiar flutters as she anticipated his answer. "What?" she breathed huskily.

Jake sat up. "Food, woman. What do you have to eat in this house?"

Dominique thought of Jake's stocked kitchen and felt embarrassed. "Nothing you'd like," she admitted.

"Well, let's order in," Jake said, rising from the bed. "And include some ice cream, so that I can bring those sweet nothings I whispered the other night to life."

14

Brilliant sunlight streamed through the bedroom curtains left open from the night before. Dominique nestled closer to the wide hard back beside her before opening her eyes. Once she did, she sat up with a start. *Oh my goodness! What time is it?* Her head whipped around to the bedside clock: 9:45. Dominique gasped and then jumped out of bed, waking Jake in the process.

"What's going on?" he asked, his eyes barely opened. They'd "exercised" for most of the night, until almost four AM.

"I can't believe I've overslept!" Dominique hurried over to her sitting area and picked up the phone, thankful that she'd had the presence of mind last night to call Faith, have Justin stay over, and then have her sister drive him directly to school this morning. "Reggie, it's me," she said in a rush. "I'll be in the office in ten minutes."

"Whoa, slow your roll, Miss Dom. You didn't get my message?"

"No." Dominique allowed the simple response to

stand, not wanting to explain why she'd slept through the Black Eyed Peas' "Let's Get It Started" that served as her ringtone for Reggie's calls.

"Okay," Reggie responded, drawing out the word. "I'm glad you called because I just got off the phone with Emily. Looks like our fabulous senior writer's water heater broke and she's there with the repairman. I looked at your schedule and it was clear so I moved the Monday meeting to this afternoon. You might as well take your time on getting in here with this weather acting all crazy."

"What's up with the weather?" Dominique walked from her closet to the side of her window, carefully shutting the blind against her nakedness before peeking behind it to see outside.

"You can't hear all that rain pouring down? The devil is beating his wife."

"How do you know about that?"

"I grew up in the Midwest, Miss Dom, but my granny is as Southern as a mint julep. We all know that's what happens when it's raining while the sun is out. I looked at your calendar," Reggie continued. "That was the only time-sensitive thing on it this morning." Jake sneezed. Dominique frowned, imagining Reggie's smile. "If you'd like, I can move the meeting to tomorrow, forward your edits via e-mail and girl you can, you know, work from home. Anything important come up, I'll call you."

Reggie put a certain emphasis on the words *work* and *come up. He's not slick. That fool knows he heard Jake sneeze.* "Don't worry about the edits. I have work here. I'll check my e-mails and see you in a couple hours."

She hung up the phone and slowly turned to find

Jake's big doe eyes drinking her in. She was so used to sleeping in the nude and walking around her master suite naked that only now, by the heat in his eyes, did she think about her state of undress.

"What?"

"You're beautiful. Do you know that?"

Dominique suddenly felt shy. She walked over to the settee, picked up the satin robe thrown across it, and covered herself. "I do all right."

"I like running my hand through the twists in your hair. How long have you worn it natural?"

"I cut out my weave about three years ago. Was referred to a woman named Mati who specializes in locs and other natural styles. She changed my life. I'm thinking about letting them grow long."

"They're nice."

"Thank you." Again, that awkwardness, and now Dominique knew why. It was the compliments. She wasn't used to them, not on a personal level. Because of her position, people were often full of flattery. She always felt that wasn't as much about her as it was about what she could do for the person giving the compliments.

Jake sat up on the side of the bed. "Was that work?"

"Yes."

"So, you're kicking me out?"

Dominique smiled. "Don't you have to go to work as well?"

"I have to be there at noon."

"Then I suggest you get moving. I'm going to take a shower."

Fifteen minutes later Dominique stepped out of the bathroom, having washed away last night's pleasures, covered herself in scented cocoa butter, and decided that maybe spending a little more time with Jake wouldn't be so bad. She stopped upon seeing the empty bed and then sniffed the air. *Is that food I smell?* Dominique slipped on a silky kimono, placed her feet into the jeweled mules she wore around the house, and followed the scent. She was shocked to enter her kitchen and encounter what smelled like a home-cooked meal.

She walked over to where Jake stood stirring something on the stove, and looked over his shoulder. "Did you go to the store?"

"Didn't know what you had in your house, I take it."

"I don't cook much."

Jake simply looked over his shoulder at her and smiled. He placed a cover on the skillet and turned down the heat. "Can you handle watching the toast that's in the oven? I'm going up to take a quick shower."

A short time later, Jake and Dominique were sitting in her rarely used dining room, eating a well-prepared vegetable omelet, toast, jam, and juice.

"This is delicious," Dominique said, after finishing a hearty bite of the egg, peppers, and onion concoction. "I would never have come up with it."

"I'm not surprised," Jake replied. "Your kitchen is a haven for processed foods. I was surprised to find the frozen vegetables."

Dominique didn't answer, but rather thoughtfully chewed on her piece of toast. She didn't feel it necessary to share that her mother had left the frozen onion-pepper mix and a box of frozen Texas toast last month when Dominique had gone out of town and Anita had stayed in the Valley so that Justin wouldn't miss school.

"Justin is a growing boy, has a lot of potential in sports. Fresh fruit and vegetables . . . that's what he needs."

Dominique's fork stopped in midair. "I don't need any advice when it comes to raising my son."

"Maybe not," Jake calmly countered, placing the last bit of omelet into his mouth and finishing it before he continued. "But when it comes to raising a healthy teenager who's not overweight, has a low cholesterol count, and no signs of type 2 diabetes . . . you might consider making a few changes to your grocery list."

"Is that so?"

Jake nodded.

"And just how many kids do you have that makes you such an expert?"

"Right now? About twenty-five." Jake reached for his juice and leaned back in the chair. "Justin reminds me of me when I was his age, except I was heavier. Thankfully my natural athletic ability kept me from being dogged, and when I got serious about sports, the extra weight fell off."

"It will probably be the same for Justin."

"When I was twelve," Jake continued, "my father died from heart disease. He was only forty-nine. My favorite uncle died two years later, same thing. Very few men on my father's side lived past their sixtieth birthday. My college coach was big on diet being a major component to staying in shape. We had a team nutritionist, which was outside the norm back then. That's when I made the connection between my father's health, the stuff in our kitchen, and especially the stuff he'd grown up eating with our grandmother."

So that's why you're such a health nut. Her stance softened. "It had to have been devastating to lose your father at such a critical age."

"Yes." A shadow came over Jake's face as he remembered the man he'd worshipped. The day his mother told him that Jake Sr. was not coming home from the hospital remained the saddest one of his life. It also shaped the decision with which he still grappled. And no matter how he wished life were different . . . it was what it was.

"Thanks for breakfast, Jake," Dominique said into the silence. She rose from the table, reached for his dishes, and walked into the kitchen. Jake followed her and while making quick work of putting the kitchen in order, she shared a bit of her childhood— living next door to her grandmother in Alabama until the family settled in Inglewood when she was ten. Like Jake, she'd grown up eating pigs and cows from the rooter to the tooter, fried this and smothered that, and cream-filled, butter-laden desserts that made you want to slap somebody. Almost all of her extended family was fat, or big-boned to put it politely. After wiping up the playground with a girl named Beverly, she hadn't had to endure any more childhood taunts. She then told him about one of her first life-changing moments—when a teacher had encouraged her love of fashion and words. During a trip to New York, she was tapped to be a plus-size model. The magazine's circulation was small with the job paying Dominique around a hundred dollars but what that photographer's words gave her, money couldn't buy. He told her she was beautiful, and he said it as if he meant it. Her confidence soared. Back in LA, she focused on journalism, working at various newspaper and magazine offices and finally working her way up to senior editor. When the founders of *Capricious* came to her with their idea about a fashion and informational magazine geared towards plus-size women . . . she knew she'd been born for this job.

"You know what else you were born for," Jake asked, coming up behind Dominique and wrapping his arms around her.

Her breath caught in her chest at the unexpected gentleness of his touch. "What?" She turned around, wrapped her arms around his neck, her lips just inches from his.

"Good loving," Jake answered, brushing her lips with his.

"You think so?" Dominique murmured.

"I know so." With that, Jake swept up Dominique into his arms.

"Jake!" Dominique hadn't been picked up and carried anywhere since she was six years old, seven tops, and she couldn't believe that Jake was now doing so without breaking a sweat. He reached the couch, placed her down, and sat beside her, lazily caressing her back. Dominique nestled her head in the crook of his neck. She was a big girl, but next to Jake's even bigger frame she felt smaller, coddled. Dominique rubbed Jake's chest and tried not to think. Soon this little tryst would end and life would go back to normal. But for the next hour, maybe two, she would forget about everything but the man whose massive arms were around her and the evidence of his rekindled desire pressing into her flesh.

15

Reggie walked through the outer office of his boss's suite and stopped short. Was that humming he heard? He crept up to her door, and placed his ear against it. The humming continued until she got to the hook. Then the words spilled out. "You are the reason to love . . ."

"Well, somebody sure seems happy." Reggie waltzed into Dominique's office with the prerequisite lattes and a box of pastries.

"Good morning, Reggie."

"Don't stop singing on my account. I love me some Uncle Charlie." Reggie set Dominique's coffee on her desk before continuing to the table on the other side of the room. "What kind of donut do you want? I have glazed, chocolate, powdered sugar, or plain cake. Oh, and I threw in some bagels for those heifahs on a lifelong diet." When she didn't answer, he turned around. "Girl, you have got to tell me what happened to put that look on your face."

"What look?"

"Miss Dom, don't even try it. I asked you a question and you didn't even hear me."

"I was engrossed in this interview that Emily did with Kirstie. It's really good."

"Yeah. Right." *Humming and reading at the same time? Really?* "What kind of donut do you want before I take the rest to the break room?"

"Do you have a bagel?" Dominique asked.

Reggie frowned but said nothing. After handing Dominique a cinnamon-raisin bagel and taking the rest of the goodies to one of two break rooms, he returned to Dominique's office and plopped down in the chair opposite her desk.

"I need you to pull up all of the references on the Master Cleanse story," Dominique began. "Shoot me the abbreviated advertiser contact list and send these on to typesetting." She handed Reggie a folder. "They've been approved."

Reggie made notes on his iPad. "Your first meeting is in an hour."

"I know. Print out the notes from the last meeting and make sure the entire sales team is in attendance. I knew it wouldn't be long before a copycat publication reared its ugly head and I just got word that that's about to happen. We need to step up our game big time and lock in the advertisers that best fit our market." Dominique scanned her computer screen. "I think that's it for now."

"Uh, not quite, Miss Dom."

Dominique looked up. "What did I miss?"

"The part about what you did yesterday."

Dominique paused before admitting, "I took your advice."

"You got tackled by the coach?" Reggie asked, a large smile covering his face.

"Yes. We went into the end zone and now the game is over. Back to work."

"Yes, ma'am." Reggie stood, grabbed his coffee, and walked out of the room humming Uncle Charlie's Top 10 R&B hit.

The day flew by and Dominique was thankful for the busyness. Meetings about sales and editorial content, and phone calls regarding the imminent announcement of a competing magazine, had kept her thoughts off of the absolutely fabulous time she'd had with Jake—two memorable days that could not be repeated. Shortly before he'd left her house, she and Jake had another version of "the talk." Dominique reemphasized that, while the sex had been amazing, she didn't think it wise that they hook up again. This time, Jake had agreed with her, explaining that he was feeling her in more than a casual way and since she was adamant about not having a relationship, he'd acquiesce to her wishes. Dominique had told herself that she was relieved. Saddened, however, was a better description.

Reggie's voice broke into Dominique's thoughts. "Tessa is on line one."

"Hey, Tessa. What's going on?"

"I'm at school to pick up Justin."

"Is he all right?"

"He's fine. But he's not ready to leave. Something about his coach tutoring him in math. Do you know about this?"

At the sound of the word "coach," a rush of images

came to mind. She squashed them. That situation was over. "No, I don't. Is . . . the coach there?"

"They're just coming up from the practice field. Justin called earlier, but I didn't check messages until I arrived here at the school and didn't see him waiting for me."

"Okay, have him call me as soon as you see him. Never mind. I'll call you back."

Dominique ended the call and dialed Jake. As always, his voice did strange things to her body.

"I'm calling about Justin," Dominique said by way of greeting. "My nanny tells me that he's staying after school and being tutored by you?"

"We sent home an announcement that these free sessions would be available. Several parents phoned in, but that wasn't mandatory. When Justin showed up, I assumed you knew."

"Well, I didn't."

A moment of silence and then, "But you're okay with it, right?"

Dominique took a breath and released some control. "Of course. If you'll e-mail me the schedule, I can forward it to my nanny so she'll know what times Justin needs to be picked up."

"Will do. But I can drop him off tonight if you'd like."

"I won't be home, but Tessa will be there."

"That's cool. I need to run an errand in your area anyway."

"Okay. Thank you."

Five seconds passed. Ten.

"Is there anything else?" Jake's tone suggested

that there were definitely other things that he wanted to discuss.

Dominique got the feeling that tables, fractions, and equations were not among them. "No . . . that's all."

"All right then, Nick. I'll talk to you later."

"Good-bye."

After wrapping up the projects on her desk, Dominique headed out to a dinner meeting in Beverly Hills. After two hours of discussing a possible collaboration with an up-and-coming designer, she was more than ready to go home, take a hot shower, and fall into bed. The full day's schedule, not to mention a weekend with little sleep, had left her exhausted. She pulled into her driveway, noting Tessa's car, which was parked on the street. *She's such a godsend. I need to put buying a gift on my calendar.* Tessa's birthday was coming up and Dominique wanted to get something really special. When it came to her son, Tessa went above and beyond the call of duty. Her official titles were housekeeper and nanny, but she was more like a personal assistant, handling many responsibilities when Dominique could not. She acted much older than her twenty-four years and treated Justin like her kid brother. She'd been on the job less than two years, and Dominique already didn't know what she'd do without her.

"Hello, Tessa." Dominique entered the house, placing her briefcase, laptop and purse on the foyer table.

Tessa looked over her shoulder, her thick, black hair hanging down her back. She was a pretty young woman, short with dark olive skin and bright brown eyes. "Hey, Dominique."

"Thanks for staying late."

"No worries. It gave me a chance to reorganize the kitchen."

Dominique looked up from the mail she browsed. "Why would you have to do that?"

A mischievous smile touched Tessa's lips. "Go on in there. You'll see."

Dominique walked into the kitchen. Everything seemed to be in order, just the way she'd left it this morning. She walked over to the refrigerator, opened it, and stood stunned. It was fully stocked, but instead of the processed and prepackaged meals that would have resulted from her grocery shopping, the vegetable bins were filled with fresh fruit and green stuff, and the shelves held such foreign objects as yogurt, organic eggs, and almond milk. Next to her supply of diet sodas was an array of sparkling juices and what looked like processed lunch meat was actually tofu. *WTH?*

Still too shocked to examine her feelings, Dominique moved to the pantry. Inside the health fair continued: oatmeal, nuts, cans of organic beans and soups, wheat pastas and Italian sauces. She picked up a cereal box and noted that the "all natural" contents included flaxseed, and had been sweetened with honey instead of sugar. A scowl formed as reality began to dawn. *No. He wouldn't dare.*

"As you can see," Tessa said as she entered the kitchen, "Coach Mac went on a shopping spree before dropping off Justin."

He would dare.

"I've never seen a kid so excited about food in my life. Coach Mac—"

Dominique put up her hand, effectively cutting off Tessa's statement. She didn't want to hear about Coach Mac, she wanted to talk to his overpresumptive ass. Surprise, anger, guilt, and confusion roiled around in Dominique's head, making the formulation of sentences challenging in the present moment. She appreciated that Jake was helping her son and other students embrace math. Teaching decimals, fractions, and formulas was one thing—trying to come in and run her household was quite another. Surprise and confusion faded, while guilt took a backseat to the anger that propelled Dominique out of the kitchen and towards the purse that held her phone. She grabbed up the items she'd placed on the foyer table and with a quick good-bye to Tessa, headed up the stairs. She emptied her arms, reached for her cell phone, and sat down on her bed in a huff. As soon as her butt hit the plush, silk comforter, memories flooded in—memories that lessened her ire just a little, but did not deter her from the plan to speak her mind.

Flipping through her address book, she quickly found and tapped the desired number. Her chest heaved with indignation as she waited for an answer on the other end and as soon as it happened, she jumped right in. "Jake, this is Dominique. You've got a lot of nerve."

16

Jake had been expecting this call all evening. "Hello, Dominique."

"Who do you think you are buying groceries for *my* house?"

"A thoughtful man helping a friend who I know is busy but who just might grow attached to the idea of having real food in her fridge." Putting it that way, he hoped, might take some of the wind out of Dominique's angry sails. "From your greeting, I take it that you think differently?"

Though less angry, Dominique sounded firm. "I'm not used to things happening in my home without my knowledge. It would have been nice to get a call asking if this was okay."

"I'm not used to getting people's permission to do them a favor." Dominique remained silent. *She's really mad at me for stocking her fridge with food?* Jake took a breath and tried to see the situation from her point of view. "If what I did offended you, Dominique, I apologize. What started out as a casual conversation with your son, followed by a call from your assistant, led to what you now have in your kitchen."

"How so?"

"Justin asked what I was having for dinner and when I told him, he asked if he could come over to eat because he didn't have anything like what I was preparing at home. In the middle of this conversation, Tessa called to ask Justin what he wanted for dinner. When I asked if she could cook and Justin said yes, I offered to bring them some groceries over since I was stopping by the store anyway. If your son had had his way you would have twice as much stuff as you found. There's a reason parents don't like to take their kids to the grocery store."

"That's for sure."

"So . . . how was your day?"

And with that question, they found themselves on the phone for over an hour. They'd agreed that their interaction would be limited to the very occasional phone call and seeing each other at Justin's games. Yet now, roughly twenty-four hours since they'd said this, here they were on the phone catching up on each other's day. There was something about this exchange that felt comfortable and intimate and, as if Dominique had just realized this, she said she had to get off the phone.

"It's been a long day, Jake, and I should be going. Thanks for the groceries. I know you meant well."

"You're welcome, baby. And I know we've agreed not to but . . . I'd sure like a Nick fix right about now."

* * *

The next morning, Dominique didn't need the alarm clock to awaken her. She'd tossed and turned for most of the night. Was it really only three days since her world had gotten turned upside down? She showered and dressed and when she went downstairs, Tessa was already in the kitchen, preparing breakfast.

Dominique joined her. "You're here early."

"Morning, Dominique. Yes, I promised Justin I'd arrive in time to make him breakfast."

"Since when did my son become the boss?" In spite of herself, Dominique reached for a strip of the crispy turkey bacon beckoning her from the oil-absorbing paper towel.

Tessa shrugged. "When Jake brought in the groceries, he was telling Justin about the importance of breakfast, and I overheard their conversation. He says that people who don't get the proper morning nutrition are those most likely to gain weight." She shrugged again. "So I decided to make his breakfast and help myself in the process. No worries, Dominique. I'm not looking for extra pay or anything." She stopped and looked at Dominique. "Should I fix another plate?"

Dominique looked at her watch. Since she'd gotten up early, it was another thirty minutes before she usually left for work, another hour before her first appointment. "Sure," she said, walking over to the island and pouring herself a glass of orange juice. "Why not?"

Justin came downstairs a few minutes later. "Hey, Mom. Coach Mac says breakfast is the most important meal of the day. He brought us all of this food, the good stuff he calls it, and told me that I could only eat the yucky stuff one day a week." This revelation was emphasized by Justin sticking a forefinger up in the air. "Coach Mac is great, Mommy," he continued without missing a beat or taking a breath. "He taught me this trick to help me remember fractions and wouldn't let me use the calculator but it was okay because I got the answers right anyway but then he showed me how to get the answers with the calculator, too. Coach says I'm really good at math. Do you like math, Mom?"

"That was never my strong suit, honey. English and social studies were more my thing." Dominique paused, surprised at how much she was enjoying the tasty, honey-sweetened oatmeal and the pre-school conversation. She'd never given much consideration to what had become the morning routine. She usually kissed the top of Justin's head, which was buried in a bowl of sugary cereal, before rushing out the door. That's if she got up in time. Fourteen-hour days and late-night social obligations often left her not seeing her son until after school. Still, she tried to make sure they spent at least an hour or two of quality time together every day and after picking him up at Anita's on Sundays, they always spent the rest of the day together. The shared activity was usually Justin's choice. Yesterday, they'd gone to a dinosaur exhibit before eating way too much ice cream at their favorite shop—his number one choice for yucky foods. They'd ended the day at the movies and then Dominique had stayed up half the night for the work the romp with Jake had interrupted. She'd always considered her and her son's relationship a good one. They were close, and had always been the center of each other's universe. Dominique wasn't sure how she felt about the invasion of a planet named Coach Mac.

17

Jake looked up as a knock sounded on his office door. "Come in."

"Hey, Coach."

"Shawn. What's up, man?"

"What's with the closed door?" Shawn asked, walking into the room and moving a pile of papers before taking a seat.

"Phone call," Jake said, offering no further explanation. Truthfully, he welcomed Shawn's interruption. The conversation with his older brother, Harold, had given him some things to think about.

"I've been watching the Spartans tape," Shawn continued, referencing this week's opponents. "They've got some heavy-hitting linebackers and the quarterback has real talent."

"Tony Pinelli?"

Shawn nodded. "Yeah, but he has a tendency to drop his arm right before releasing the ball. The observant tackle will know exactly when he's ready to throw."

"I noticed that, which is why I want to work with

the defense on a particular maneuver and maybe force a few turnovers."

"Good idea."

"Are we still going with the same offense as last week?"

Shawn nodded. "Pretty much. "I think we should focus on the passing game, move Schumacher to the tight-end position. I'm going to run Justin through the receiver drills as well."

Jake nodded. "Good move. He's a big boy but he's agile as all get out, can catch a ball and move down the field in a hurry. Opponents will never see these trick plays coming."

The two men were joined by more coaching staff and the strategizing session continued. Practice went great and while the boys were boasting their undefeated season, Jake warned them not to get cocky. For them, he explained, the hard work was just beginning.

Once he left work, the real challenge began for him as well. He fired up his SUV and navigated the city streets by rote, his mind back in the office and on the conversation he'd had with his brother.

"It was just a date, man." Jake laughed to further convey to his older brother how unimportant his night with Dominique had been, even as he silently kicked himself for even bringing her up. All of his other brothers were married, happily, and had kids. They'd not been as scarred by their father's death as Jake had been. And there was little if anything about one brother's life that the other brothers didn't eventually know about.

"Keep telling yourself that," Harold replied, not buying Jake's casual act for a second. "But it sounds like much more than that. What's her name again?"

"Dominique." As Jake said it, a warm, fuzzy feeling rose up inside him.

"Tell me about her."

"She's the editor of a magazine for full-figured women, some bougie executive gig in which she's obviously in control."

"It wouldn't happen to be *Capricious*, would it?"

"As a matter of fact, that's it. How do you know about it?"

"Man, Mary grabs each issue out of the mail and reads it like the Bible." Mary, Harold's wife, could cook southern cuisine like nobody's business. Which was part of the reason this couple and their children were all overweight. "I must admit that while in the bathroom I've even picked it up a time or two. Come to think of it, one of my favorite articles was about big and tall NFL dudes."

Jake's interest was immediately piqued. "Who was in it?"

"Michael Oher, Brian Waters, Will Shields, Mario Williams, Nick Fairley, cats like that. Large, in charge, and playing the field." Harold laughed, remembering the catchy phrase that had pulled him into reading not only that article but most of the magazine. "Good stuff."

He could understand Michael Oher of *Blind Side* fame, but Jake squelched the urge to ponder the obvious: *Why not me?* Instead, he used this oversight as further fuel to distance himself from the woman who'd haunted his dreams since the day he'd laid eyes on her.

"What does she look like?" Harold asked.

"Not my type at all," Jake quickly replied. "Don't get me wrong, she's fine, but she's a big girl, wears her hair natural . . ."

"Oh, so she's not the silicone-injected, weave-wearing babe with whom you mostly keep company?"

"That's a low blow, bro."

Harold chuckled. "Maybe, but remember I've met more than one of your bimbo attractions. Need I remind you about the chick you brought to Mama's seventieth birthday party who came to the pool—"

"In a thong," Jake sighed. "No, you didn't have to remind me about something that I'd thankfully almost forgotten. Those women all knew the score, that it was just a casual dalliance, nothing more."

"But Dominique isn't casual, is she?" When Jake didn't answer, Harold continued. "Look, man, Robin was a wonderful woman, but it's been almost five years. If you're trying to find someone like her . . ."

"I'm not."

"Are you sure?"

"Positive. What Robin and I had was special and will always be very dear to my heart. But the last thing she'd want is for me to go through the rest of my life alone and unhappy. I loved her, and I've grieved her, but it's time to move on."

"Well, that said," Harold continued, "maybe you've finally met the woman with whom you can move on."

18

"Ooh, girl, I don't know about this sports stuff." Reggie adjusted the shoestring tie that he'd apparently decided to bring back into fashion all by his lonesome and swiped nonexistent dirt off of his duly purchased cowboy boots before exiting Dominique's car. "I might get so excited that I break a nail."

Dominique laughed. "You're too much drama, Reggie. Remember, this is the grade-school league, not the NFL. I think your nails will be just fine."

Reggie commented on everybody and everything as the two navigated the steady stream of parents, students, and neighborhood Hurricanes supporters filing into the stadium for the third game of the season. Dominique was appreciative of Reggie's constant chatter. It kept her mind from being continually focused on seeing Jake for the first time since the previous weekend's lovefest.

As they reached the bleachers, Reggie poked Dominique in the side. "Miss Dom, please tell me what that child is wearing."

Dominique's eyes immediately went to the woman

who'd captured Reggie's attention. She was hard to miss, dressed in white skintight pants, body-hugging top, and thigh-high boots. She looked dressed more for an eighties throwback party than an elementary school sporting event.

Dominique shrugged as she sat. "Maybe the white is symbolic of a hurricane . . . you know, the wind, water . . ."

"Miss Dom, that outfit is more symbolic of the aftermath!"

Dominique laughed, the warm, throaty sound spilling over the packed crowd. While checking her e-mails and texting, she continued being entertained by Reggie's commentary, totally unaware of a pair of smoldering eyes that kept darting in her direction.

Soon, Reggie poked her again. "There he is, Miss Dom!" He pointed toward the group of players dressed and running from the locker room to the sidelines. "Your son looks ready to play in the big leagues."

Dominique smiled and waved as she caught Justin's eye. Reggie was right. Justin did look rough and rugged outfitted as he was in football gear. And was it her imagination or had he grown a couple more inches in the last month? Her little boy was growing up, fast. In a few short years he'd be gone. Dominique batted back unexpected tears and a wave of melancholy. Since he'd been born, Justin had been her anchor. While men, jobs, and circumstances came and went, her son was the constant in her life, her primary focus for eleven years. Dominique watched him warm up with the other boys: jumping jacks, push-ups, and short sprints. *How will my life look once he's spread his wings and left the nest?*

Her eyes drifted from her son to the sidelines where Jake, surrounded by assistant coaches and other personnel, held a clipboard in one hand and marker in the other. He was scribbling, pointing. What he was explaining Dominique could only guess. Whatever it was must have been important as Jake had the men's undivided attention. He had hers as well. Dominique watched his gestures, remembering how skilled were the fingers that had massaged even as they'd explored and become familiar with every inch of her five-foot-nine frame. Her body warmed as she watched him talk, remember how good those lips felt . . . everywhere. She scanned his back, buttocks, thick strong thighs, and her hands longed to do the same. She'd willed herself not to think about what could not be, at least not now. But there was no denying the facts and the fact was . . . she missed him.

Jake prowled the sidelines, his eyes riveted to each play. He clapped, cheered, scolded, and encouraged his players, even as he worked to keep his mind off of the person dominating his thoughts, the woman who'd had the nerve to show up at the game with a date! As if by sixth sense, he'd looked up just in time to see her climb the bleachers with what looked like a man plucked from the Bill Pickett rodeo. It was the twenty-first century. What dude wore a shoestring tie these days? Still, a wave of jealousy had swept over him, especially when the man had touched Dominique's arm and guided her into the bleachers before taking the aisle seat. The man was about six feet, on the slender side, and looked like he spent a considerable amount of time in the mirror. *Just like her to want a pretty boy, a little eye candy on her arm.* Jake had never felt so possessive, not even with his former wife. But in seeing them, Jake had the urge to walk over and throttle the dude, the man who had the nerve to mess with his woman. *My woman?* Jake admonished himself, pushed the thought aside, and refocused on the game. *Mine.* The thought returned with fervor, it would not be denied. Because that's what Dominique felt like to him—his woman. He sighed with the impossibility of it all.

Jake's and Dominique's thoughts about each other diminished under the Saturday sun and a fourth-quarter score with the Spartans leading by three. The Hurricanes were less than two minutes away from experiencing the loss Jake had warned them about. This was sixth-grade football but by the tension in the stands you couldn't tell. Nails were chewed and muscles tensed as if this were the play-offs and money was on the line. Dominique's eyes were glued to number twenty-one.

"Black cat straight!" Jake shouted out the call. Players scrambled into position. Shawn winked at Jake, who gave a curt nod in response. All of the players on the bench stood in solidarity as the active players took their places on the field. The opposing team's fans shouted with ferocity, trying to shake the concentration of the Hurricanes' quarterback. The offensive and defensive lines crouched into position, running backs traded places, centers ferociously looked each other dead in the eye.

"Two, zero, one, one, hike!" The center flicked the ball into Kareem Alexander's capable hands. Kareem's father had transferred him over to Middleton specifically because Jake coached there. Observing his natural throwing talent, Jake had moved him from running back to quarterback. Would the move pay off?

The running backs shot down the field with defenders hot on their trail. Justin hung back for a moment, and then with a quick shimmy shake, he shot past his defender. Towering over the other boys, he ran straight down the field, looked back, and held up his hand. Kareem nodded and cocked his arm, firing the perfectly spiraling ball in Justin's direction. It was a bit high but Justin leaped up and made a one-arm catch. He came down almost thirty yards from the goal line as the Panthers' safety rushed over to make the tackle. They collided but Justin, easily the bigger of the two, spun in the opposite direction and avoided being pulled down. The crowd was on its feet, holding their breath as the clocked ticked down to under a minute.

Dominique, who'd forgotten that she cared nothing for football, was on her feet with the rest of the crowd. "Run, Justin!"

Reggie chimed in beside her. "You go, boy. You better work!"

The referee's arms shot up as Justin crossed into the end zone. Touchdown!

The crowd roared their approval as the boys on the bench ran onto the field to hug their teammates. There were still thirty-nine seconds on the clock but the game was as good as done. Dominique joined several of the other onlookers, especially

parents, making their way towards the field. She
waved frantically to get his attention, ready to help
her son celebrate his fantastic run. Her boy looked
good! Through the maze of helmet pats and butt
swats he saw her, smiled, and waved back. She
waited for him to run over and into her arms but he
passed her with obviously another destination in
mind. She turned to see where he was going, just in
time to see him run into Jake's open arms. Stepping
back, Jake placed his hands on Justin's shoulders,
his look intense as he spoke. Justin stood stock-still,
nodding occasionally. Dominique's heart clenched
as she observed what almost looked like a father-son
moment. She watched as Justin took off his helmet,
threw it near the benches, and fell in step beside
Jake, who walked the length of the player's benches
congratulating the boys. She stood rooted to the top
steps as other parents moved around her and down
onto the field. Jake looked up and saw her. Their
eyes caught and held.

"Miss Dom, girl, you'd better go and get your
chocolate treat," Reggie whispered, gently pushing
on Dominique's back.

Dominique shot a look over her shoulder. "Behave."
Yet Reggie's words had propelled her feet forward
and she went down the five short steps to the field
below.

Justin saw his mom and waved her over to where
he and Jake were standing. Keeping her eyes on the
light of her life, she reached him and pulled him to
her for a big embrace. "You did good, son," she said,
her eyes shining.

"It was Coach Mac," Justin replied, still animated
from the come-from-behind victory. "He devised

the play and it was awesome, perfect, happened just like he said it would. Right, Coach?"

Jake gave Justin a playful punch. "If you say so," he answered, his eyes never leaving Dominique's face.

"It was a good game, Coach," Dominique said, finally acknowledging him. *The boys played almost as good as you look.* The flutters came calling in spite of her resolve.

"Thank you." *Will you help me in an after-hours celebration?* his expression seemed to say.

There was an awkward, tension-filled silence.

"It was good," Reggie added. "But I can't believe how you make these little boys beat up on each other. So violent!" He held out his hand. "I'm Reggie Williams, Miss Dom's assistant."

Jake shook Reggie's hand, a smile dancing across his lips. "Jake McDonald." He raised his brow. "Miss Dom?"

Before either Reggie or Dominique could respond, other parents and players surrounded Jake and the current that had run between the lovers was broken. Dominique stepped back, waiting for Justin to say good-bye to his teammates. She knew Reggie was getting antsy, since he was due to meet Quinn at the Kodak Theatre.

"Time's a wastin', sistah," Reggie said, looking at his watch as if reading her mind.

"I know you've got to go. Justin!"

Justin ran over. "Mom, the team is going over to Coach's house. Can I go? Please?"

"How will you get home?" Dominique asked, remembering what had happened the last time she'd stepped over the McDonald threshold.

"Coach will bring me."

Dominique walked over to where Jake stood, politely interrupting the sports talk on the Hurricanes loosely resembling a team in the Pac-10. "The boys are going to your house?"

Jake's dark, unreadable eyes bore into hers, before moving lower to her mouth and back up. "Yes."

Dominique swallowed. "If Justin will call me, I'll pick him up."

"You're not far. I'll bring him home."

"I don't want to be a bother."

Jake scanned her body again. "No bother."

Dominique's triple Ds heaved as she worked to calm her nerves. *What is it about this guy that frazzles me so?* Straightening her shoulders and tilting her chin, Dominique responded. "Fine." But was it, really? Because at the thought of Jake McDonald in her home, the flutters started again.

19

Dominique watched television without seeing a thing. Before Justin got involved with football it was a rare Saturday that would find her home at this hour. Usually after working until seven or eight on Friday nights, she would join any number of the editors or other magazine staff and unwind around a piano bar, jazz quartet, dinner, and drinks. Concerts, theater, fundraisers, sporting events—her life was kept busy with invites to some of the best that Los Angeles had to offer. Saturdays were for sleeping in before putting in a good four to five hours at the office. But when it came to Justin and his love of sports, she'd made a decision to sacrifice her Saturday mornings during football season and involve herself in her son's passion. She thought that it would bring them even closer than they were already. One thing was for sure, it was definitely bringing him closer to his coach.

Hearing a set of keys in the door, Dominique rose from an inclining to a sitting position, smoothed out

her caftan, and muted the TV. Justin burst through
the door, a laid-back Jake following behind him.

"Mom! I helped cook!" Justin ran over and sat
next to Dominique. "Coach Mac made pizzas."

"Pizza?" Dominique asked, casting a doubtful
look at Jake. "That junky food?"

Justin shook his head. "No, these were healthy.
We had a choice of sausage or pepperoni, and they
were good!"

Dominique looked at Jake with the same quizzical expression. "Pepperoni?"

Jake lowered his eyes, and sat on the recliner opposite the sofa. Clearly, there was a p-word on his
mind all right and it wasn't a pizza topping.

Dominique picked up the vibe and try as she might,
she couldn't seem to control the order of things. One
minute the three sat there talking, or mostly listening
to Justin rattle on, and the next minute Justin announced that he was going to his room to watch
movies. Just like that he, Dominique's human buffer,
was gone. The quiet—and Jake's stare—were unnerv-
ing. Dominique resisted the urge to pick up the
remote and unmute the TV. Refusing to feel uncomfortable in her own house, she pulled on her big-girl
panties and smiled at Jake.

"Thanks for entertaining the teammates and bringing Justin home."

Without saying a word, Jake stood, walked over and
joined Dominique on the couch. "You're welcome,"
he murmured, wrapping his arms around her.

"Jake . . ." Anything further coming from Dominique's lips got swallowed in his kiss—soft, languid,
then growing in intensity. His tongue remembered
every crevice of her mouth, his hand ran up and

down her arm, before settling on her silk-covered thigh.

Dominique felt as if she were drowning and didn't want to be saved. Her arm wrapped around Jake's neck, slid across the broad expanse of his back and back to cup his face. The gentle act intensified Jake's flame of desire. He moaned and leaned back, pulling Dominique into his arms. With her lying across him, he was able to grab hold of her plump, meaty booty. He ran a hand up her back, and a shiver shortly followed as Dominique felt herself becoming wet and Jake becoming hard. Then she remembered. Justin was upstairs and she was downstairs with a man in the house—something she swore would never happen again.

"Wait, stop," she said breathlessly, struggling to release herself from Jake's embrace and put distance between them. Her body immediately felt his absence and there was no doubt in Dominique's mind that in his arms was where she wanted to be. But this wasn't about her. This was about Justin. Jake had to go.

"I'm sorry, Jake, but this isn't happening. My son is upstairs and I'm down here doing something I swore would not happen until he left home—entertaining a man."

"I'm not just some man, Dominique. I'm your son's coach and tutor. And quite frankly, though we've only known each other a short time, I thought I was a little more than just a man to you. I thought I was your friend."

"That's just it, Jake. That you are involved with my son on a professional level is why our relationship needs to stay professional . . . and platonic."

"That's bullshit."

"Think what you will, but it's what I've decided."

The air crackled and in the silence, muted sounds from the upstairs TV were heard. Thoughts of Justin entered both of their minds—in different ways, for different reasons.

Dominique was remembering what Justin said once Kevin, her former partner, had left their lives. "It's okay, Mommy. It's just you and me."

Jake was remembering what Justin had shared with him on their drive over. "Coach Mac, you're awesome. I wish you were my dad."

20

Dominique checked to make sure she had everything before leaving her master suite. It was going to be a long day. On top of the time she and Reggie would spend at the office, she had the undesired task of having dinner with a couple of the board members who'd come from overseas for a meeting the following week. She was especially not looking forward to after the meeting, when she'd be home alone, but was determined not to think about that until later. She'd get to work, drown herself in all things *Capricious,* and pull Reggie into the office to keep her laughing. After another melancholy, near-sleepless night, she needed his humor as much as his daily delivery of their favorite lattes.

As she walked down the stairs, Dominique heard Tessa in the kitchen with Justin beside her, chattering away. At the last step she stopped and listened.

"Coach Mac has a *real* theater and after we made pizza we went into the room and watched video of our game."

Dominique could hear Tessa placing dishes into the washer. "Sounds like fun."

"It was! Coach Mac is so smart. I told you about the touchdown, right?"

Tessa laughed. "A few times, Justin."

"Well . . . that was Coach Mac's idea. He knew they wouldn't be paying attention to me because I'm big. They wouldn't expect me to be able to catch or run fast. Coach says it was the same for him when he was my age. And he went to the NFL! I'm going to play pro ball too, just like him."

"What's his name?"

"Jake McDonald. But we have to call him Coach or Coach Mac."

"Who'd he play for?"

"The Raiders. He was their star defensive end for almost nine seasons. He used to crush 'em . . ."

Justin kept talking away but Dominique no longer heard him. The Hurricanes had won their fourth game and, once again, Justin had been one of the shining stars. She leaned back against the wall, trying to process how deep her son's feelings were where his coach was concerned and statements he'd made about him. *Mom, we've got a new coach! He played for the Raiders . . . my favorite team! You and Coach Mac were looking at each other funny. I think you like him.* And especially what he said just now. *I'm going to play pro ball too, just like him.* Those last three words echoed in her ear as Dominique crossed the foyer and entered the kitchen. *Just like him.*

"Hey, Justin!" Dominique walked over to the island, placed down her briefcase, and enveloped Justin in a big hug. "How's my baby?"

"Mom, come on. I'm too big for you to call me that. Coach Mac—"

Dominique put up her hand, demanding silence. She took her son's chubby cheeks in her hands, noting that he was becoming a man before her very eyes. "I know you value his opinion, but when it comes to this mother's love for her child, I don't care what Coach says. You'll *always* be my, baby. Got it?"

Justin delivered that lopsided grin that Dominique just loved. "Yes, ma'am."

Dominique picked up her briefcase and purse. "Tessa, Faith should be here around five."

"No worries, Dominique. I hope your mother feels better soon."

"Looks like a twenty-four-hour bug and, as usual, she really wanted to see her grandbabies. But we couldn't take any chances on their getting sick." Dominique felt her mother being under the weather was a blessing in disguise. Faith hadn't gotten out much since the miscarriage. A drive to the Valley would do her good, maybe help get her back into the swing of life. Dominique made a mental note to ask Faith to join Aaron and Michael if they came over next week to watch Justin play.

Dominique kissed Justin again and was out the door. All during her ten-minute drive to work, she thought about him. And Jake. A smile tickled the corners of her mouth as she remembered the previous week and how happy Justin was to have made the winning touchdown, the look of pride that had shown in Jake's eyes as Jake spoke to her son, and the camaraderie between the three of them as they discussed his winning play. If she allowed herself to dream, Dominique would imagine many more times being enjoyed by the three of them. But as Dominique entered the luxurious surroundings of the magazine for the full-figured, fit, and fabulous, she had no time for dreaming. Her head was nowhere near the clouds and her feet were firmly planted in the realities of *Capricious* magazine.

Ten hours later, Dominique gratefully entered the confines of her car. The dinner had been the torture she'd expected, with the bane of her existence, François Deux, picking at details that didn't matter and making suggestions that made no sense. It was all she could do not to curse his scrawny ass out and if it weren't for Solveig Ericksson, the statuesque Swedish board member whom she both liked and respected, Dominique may have done just that.

Her phone rang, and the first name that came to Dominique's mind was Jake. She looked at the caller ID and instead saw her sister's number. "Hey, Faith."

"You're not going to believe what happened," Faith responded by way of greeting.

"What?" From the sound of Faith's voice whatever it was couldn't be good.

"I'm so mad at Michael and Justin I don't know what to do!"

Dominique's heart rate increased with the volume of Faith's ranting. "Girl, calm down and tell me what's going on." She'd reached her home but instead of pulling into the garage she turned off the engine as soon as she pulled into the driveway.

"I caught our sons looking at porn."

Dominique's mouth dropped open. "You have got to be kidding."

"I wish I was." The two women were silent a

moment as Dominique absorbed what Faith had just told her. "They'd asked if they could watch TV in Michael's room. I said yes and once they'd gone upstairs, I started preparing dinner. When I went up to get them, I was surprised at how quiet it was in the room. Then I eased open the door and found out why."

"They were watching videos?"

"Nikki, that's about the only reason I didn't totally lose my mind about this—that it was pictures they were viewing instead of a movie. But the pics were bad enough: naked women in provocative positions, some engaged in acts of self-pleasuring. I'd never seen such a mess in all my life and I'm thirty-five years old. Aaron is just as mad about it, even though he admitted it was his fault."

"How so?"

"Last year when we got the computer for Michael, I'd asked him to set the parental controls. He got called out of town for work that same week and evidently forgot all about it."

"Faith, I'm just shocked. I didn't know Justin was even thinking about stuff like that yet. He's only eleven!"

"But he'll be twelve next month and Michael turns thirteen in two. If there was any doubt our little boys are not so little anymore . . . here's the proof."

Dominique sighed audibly, reaching toward the ignition. She started the car and backed out of the driveway. "I just worked a ten-hour day, mostly for his ungrateful behind. The last thing I want to deal with tonight is this mess. But I'm on my way."

"Sister, it's getting late. There's no need to

come over tonight. I've already put the boys on restriction—took Michael's computer and Justin's handheld games. Aaron gave them a good talking to as well. Justin is sleeping on the pullout in the living room and tomorrow's trip to the Long Beach Aquarium is cancelled. They're feeling the heat from their wrongdoing. Tomorrow will be soon enough for you to come and add your fuel to the fire. You work too hard, Nikki. Sounds like you need your rest."

Just as Dominique ended the call, she found herself about two minutes from Jake's house and had the immediate urge to drop by. Calling Leland would be useless, and that's even if she was able to get through his insecure fortress of a wife. She loved her brother-in-law to death, but wasn't sure if Aaron's soft-spoken nature would provide the long-term deterrent she felt her son needed. But Jake could. Dominique felt sure of that. She stopped in front of his house and, seeing lights on in the living room, picked up her phone to call him. The last thing she wanted to be was an unexpected interruption.

"Jake, it's Dominique."

"Nick. I'm surprised to hear from you on a Saturday night . . . with us remaining platonic and professional and all."

"I'm outside your house and need to talk to you. May I come in?"

A long pause ensued before Jake responded. "Baby, nothing about me has changed since I last left your house. You can come in here if you want to . . . but talking will be the last thing on my mind."

21

Dominique hesitated only briefly before opening her car door and stepping outside. She refused to acknowledge the feelings Jake's last statement had evoked in her heart and elsewhere. This visit wasn't about her and Jake, Dominique told herself as she rang Jake's bell. This was about her son.

She tried to remember that as Jake opened the door and filled the space with hard, dark chocolate wrapped in a ripped white tee and gray jogging pants that rode low, exposing the trail of hair with which Dominique was all too familiar. She blinked and forced her eyes back up to Jake's face. The look that met her made her blink again.

"It's about Justin."

Jake stepped back and let her in, barely resisting the urge to wrap her in his arms. He was perturbed that his body reacted to her so strongly, not to mention that today, other than work, she was just about all he'd thought about. He followed her into the living room and when she sat hugging one end of the black leather sectional that dominated his front room, he sat on the other end. The worried expression on the face of one of the strongest women he'd ever met gave him cause for alarm. That she'd said it was about a kid he was fond of and a star on his football team increased his worry.

"Talk to me, Nick. What's going on?"

Dominique launched right in, relaying the story that Faith had shared. Halfway through the replay, she couldn't sit any longer. Her heels clicked a staccato side note on the polished hardwood floor. "If he weren't too big to spank, I'd wear him out," she concluded. "My son will not grow up being a pervert!"

Jake watched as Dominique retook her position on the sectional sofa, noted how what she'd described had frazzled her nerves. He knew that he'd have to tread carefully as much as he knew it was a road he'd have to go down. "What are you going to do?"

Dominique looked at Jake. "That's one of the reasons I'm here, to see what you would do. He's grounded for sure, and I'll have to remove his computer until I'm satisfied the proper controls are in place. I'm tempted to threaten him with losing the ability to play football if this happens again."

"Not a good idea."

"Why not?"

"Why would you tie this to his football dreams?"

"As a strong deterrent, that's why! I plan to nip this in the bud."

Jake snorted and shook his head.

"What? You don't think I should?"

"You don't want to know what I think."

Dominique turned and crossed her arms. "Maybe not, but tell me anyway."

"I think you're making too much of this." As if to

underscore this panic that Dominique had fully embraced, Jake leaned back on the couch and began flipping through the magazine he'd been reading when she arrived.

"My eleven-year-old son is viewing porn and you think I'm overreacting?"

"Yep."

Never at a loss for words, Dominique was temporarily speechless. "So," she began once she'd found her voice, "you think I should do nothing, act as if what he did was okay?"

Jake placed the magazine on the ottoman and closed the space between him and Dominique. "I think," he said, moving behind her and massaging shoulders that were tighter than drums, "that you need to understand the dynamics of a growing male. Wet dreams, hard-ons, jacking off, and sexual preoccupation are all a part of coming into manhood." Jake's hand moved from Dominique's shoulder and began to massage the base of her neck. "In looking at those pictures online, your son was simply satisfying a natural curiosity. Are there other ways of gaining this education? Of course. And that's where your reaction comes in. You can either use this as a teachable moment or you can punish him and close the door on your awareness of this part of his life. Because, trust me, he won't stop doing whatever he's doing. He'll just learn how to effectively hide it from you."

"It's obvious you don't have kids," Dominique retorted, even as she relaxed under Jake's expert ministrations. "I'm not down with all of that modern-day psychobabble. There are some things a child just does not do. I was hoping that you'd perhaps cosign my position, but I guess that was wishful thinking."

"You guess correctly. I'm not going to tell a boy to stop doing what comes naturally. I actually empathize with your son," Jake continued, running a strong thumb up the length of Dominique's spine before massaging her arms and the top of her head. "I want to focus on what comes naturally, too."

"Well, I'm not having it," Dominique insisted, though her mind was now less on Justin and more on the effect Jake's fingers were having on her body. And even though she didn't for one minute agree with him, and was upset that he wasn't more supportive of her point of view . . . she still didn't leave his house until morning.

22

"Justin, I'm very disappointed in you." Dominique spoke to her son for the first time since they'd gotten in the car five minutes ago and begun driving back to the Valley. She glanced over at him and then back on the road. "What were you thinking?"

Silence.

"Justin, I'm talking to you!"

Justin shrugged. "I don't know."

"That's because you weren't thinking!" Dominique sighed, still unsure of exactly how she was going to deal with the situation. When she'd arrived at Faith's house, they'd had a little powwow—her, Faith, and the boys. Aaron had reiterated his position before leaving to play golf. Justin's answers had been similar then: head nods, shrugs, and monosyllabic grunts. Michael admitted that it had been his idea to look at the pictures—something Faith learned he'd done with other friends on a number of occasions. "Everyone does it," he'd insisted.

"Everyone but Justin," Dominique had replied.

"And you," Faith quickly added, glaring at Michael.

Dominique had left shortly afterwards with a head-hanging Justin in tow. He'd barely looked at her at all since she'd stepped in Faith's house and even now kept his eyes fixed out the window.

"Son," she continued in a softer voice, remembering Jake's words and deciding to take a snippet from his point of view, "I know you're growing up. It's natural to be curious about girls and . . . that sort of thing. But you need to go about it in the right way and looking at Internet porn sites is definitely not it. Sex is about more than body parts. It's about love and respect and a woman's value. Do you understand what I'm saying to you?"

"Kinda," Justin replied after a pause. "But I don't understand why looking at pictures of naked girls is so bad."

Oh, brother. This is going to be harder than I thought. "Because looking leads to thoughts that you are not yet equipped to deal with, skews your view of women and your idea of what is and isn't beautiful. And worse, it can lead you to trying to take advantage of some little girl, maybe even getting her pregnant."

This got Justin's attention. He turned to her with widened eyes.

"That's right," Dominique continued, recognizing an opportunity to instill fear when she saw one. "Are you ready to be a father? Not be able to play football because you have to work as hard as you see me work to support you, to take care of your own child?"

"No," Justin whispered, his brow furrowed in thought.

"Well, that's what looking at those types of pictures leads to . . . fatherhood." Dominique knew this statement was a stretch but she hoped it was an effective deterrent as well.

After a long pause, Justin asked, "When do I get back my video games?"

"When you've had time to think about what I said, and why your actions were not okay. You think a week is long enough for you to do that?"

Justin squirmed in his seat. "I already thought about it!" he whined.

"And what is your thought?"

"That I shouldn't have looked at the pictures."

"Because?"

"Because you think it's nasty."

"Not because I think, Justin; because it is." Dominique's next thought made her clench the steering wheel. "Justin, have you and Michael done more than look at pictures?"

"No," Justin quickly replied.

"You've never looked at videos?"

"Uh-uh."

"Are you sure?"

"Yeah."

"What?"

"Yes."

"Because if I ever find out that you've watched those types of movies, you'll have graduated high school before you get your games back."

After deciding that in addition to his video games, television and the computer would also be off-limits for a week, Dominique stopped by the mall so that Justin could find a book to read to fill the downtime after homework was completed. They then drove the short distance to a gourmet store where she picked up veggies and a roasted chicken. Once home,

Justin went straight to his room and after a dinner in which Dominique had never seen her child so quiet, he retired for the night.

Although hardly sleepy, Dominique decided to call it an early night as well. She showered, put on one of her favorite gowns, grabbed her work, and climbed into her haven—her four-poster canopied bed. She tried to bury herself in editing, but her thoughts simply were not on it. Instead she was questioning her decisions regarding her son. *Did I do the right thing by taking away his privileges? Is a week too long? Not enough time? Should I have just taken the games and left the TV?* The only choice she was absolutely certain about was the computer that she was taking to work tomorrow so that Reggie could set the controls. Dominique could type eighty words a minute and Google from here to eternity but when it came to setups and functions she was totally inept. Hopefully Reggie would help ensure that at least on his home computer, Justin would have absolutely no access to pornographic sites. *He won't stop doing whatever he's doing. He'll just learn how to effectively hide it from you.* Jake's sober warning drifted into Dominique's mind, and not for the first time. But how could she have let this slide without some type of reprimand? As if to answer the question, her cell phone rang.

"Hey, you," Jake murmured after Dominique had answered. "How'd it go today?"

Dominique released a sigh, glad to turn her mental monologue into a dialogue. "Honestly, Jake, I don't know."

"What happened?"

She relayed her conversation with Justin. "I've

never seen him so quiet and as soon as dinner was over he went to his room."

Jake let what Dominique had told him sink in. "Leave him alone," he finally said. "He'll be all right."

"Yes, but will I?" Dominique moved the papers surrounding her and walked to the loveseat in the sitting area of her master suite. "Justin and I have always been close. I'm all he has."

"Where's his father?"

"In Philly, preoccupied with an insecure, clingy wife and new family."

"Does he see him?"

"Once or twice a year. But those two weeks in the summer and whichever holiday is convenient is hardly what bonding is made of. When we first divorced, Leland was more active in his son's life. But after his marriage and the birth of their first son together, things went downhill. His current wife does nothing to encourage the relationship but I don't blame her. Leland is his father and no one should be able to talk a man out of taking care of his own child's needs."

"So he doesn't pay child support?"

"He does, but it's not money Justin longs for. Emotional closeness and physical involvement is what he needs. I used to think I could be both mother and father to my son, but boys need their fathers."

"So have you called him about this?"

"No."

"Why not?"

Dominique shrugged. "First there's the matter of getting past his guard dog, otherwise known as his wife, Patricia, and second, there's the chance that Leland will do what he's done for the past five years . . . nothing."

Jake remained silent. Dominique understood why. What could he say to a statement like this?

"Jake? You there?" Dominique asked when the silence continued.

"Yeah, I'm here."

"Oh, I thought we got disconnected."

"You know I want to see you."

Memories of last night warmed Dominique all over, and she refused to think about the fact that she'd done what she said she'd never do again. "Me, too," she whispered. "But you know I can't leave."

"I could come over there." When Dominique hesitated, Jake added, "He doesn't have to know."

"I know, Jake. But I made a rule to never have men over here when Justin is home."

Jake's voice dropped even deeper. "Rules are made to be broken."

Dominique figured that Jake was right. She nodded and told him, "Come on."

On the drive over to her house, Jake pondered the concerns about Justin that Dominique had shared and wondered how he'd feel if it were his child. Jake had no experience in the daddy department. The familiar feelings of hurt mixed with longing rose unbidden. Flashes of life with his father: the football tosses, movie watching, men-only hunting trips with all of the brothers. The worst day of his life—when his mother broke the news that Jake Sr. had died—and the second worst day, his father's funeral.

Then there was Robin and the discussions they'd had as newlyweds. She'd wanted to start a family right away, but Jake's fears had blocked those desires. How could he bring a child into this world, only to leave him or her during its formative years? This is what Jake believed—that even if he had a child, he wouldn't live to see it grown. His father hadn't. His favorite uncle hadn't. His oldest brother, Harold, was nearing fifty and experiencing the same heart problems that had taken out both of those men. At forty-five, the next son, Mike, had experienced a heart scare two years ago. That both of these men were sixty to seventy pounds overweight made little difference to Jake. For the McDonalds, matters of the heart took on a whole different meaning and even though Jake and his twin, Johnny, were the health fanatics, the legacy of heart disease and the havoc it could wreak in a young man's life were never far from Jake's thoughts. A couple weeks before the aneurysm, Robin had started bugging him again. "Come on," she'd whined. "You'll make a great father." Jake had agreed to think about it, had begun entertaining the possibility. And then, once again, death had come knocking.

I wish you were my dad.

Jake closed his eyes against the memory, while wondering for the umpteenth time if he should tell Dominique what her son had uttered that day he gave him a ride home after tutoring him. "I'm built like my father," Jake had told him, when Justin had questioned him about his size. And that's when Justin had uttered the six words that had imprinted themselves on his mind.

She needs to know, Jake thought as he pulled into

the driveway of Dominique's well-landscaped home. *But not tonight.* This visit wasn't about having a discussion. Once Jake got behind Dominique's closed door once again, he didn't intend for there to be a whole lot of talking.

23

Dominique yawned, glad she'd made it through the magazine's weekly pitch session. Besides the double-shot espresso, the only thing that had kept her awake was Emily's exciting feature idea for the magazine's summer issue, which would be focused on shedding those winter pounds in anticipation of a long, hot summer. Dominique had heard of JaJuan "Night" Simmons and his popular LA gym known for its trend-setting workouts and party atmosphere. While the senior writer's outline mentioned these components, the focus of her article would be on one particular program, called J.E.W.E.L.S. Geared toward overweight women, this program combined proper exercise with a sensible diet and was championed by Night's wife D'Andra, who was not only a dietician and nutritionist but was also the poster child for this regimen's potential success. The couple's story was the stuff of movies. With Night as her personal trainer, D'Andra had lost sixty pounds and gained a husband. Their first child, JaJuan Jr., had been born six months ago and once again D'Andra would be the example for losing pounds—these the post-baby kind. The magazine would track and document her progress for the next four months, and in the six-page photo spread of the gym and the family behind it would be before-and-after pictures of this modern working woman and proud new mom.

"Ooh, Miss Dom!" Reggie pranced into Dominique's office decked in a loud orange shirt with ruffles and puffed sleeves. Ensconced in light-colored snakeskin pants, he had a booty that most women would envy. "I think I'm in love!"

"With Quinn?" Dominique asked dryly. "Boy, you go through men like I do pantyhose."

"Not Quinn," Reggie answered, placing a pile of photos on her desk. "With *him*."

Dominique laughed as she took the pictures that Reggie had gathered of Night Simmons. "He is easy on the eyes," she admitted. "But he's also a husband and new father. I don't think you're his type"

"Hmph. That's just because he ain't had this type before."

"You'd better stop playing, or else I'll be forced to replace you on this upcoming shoot."

"I'll behave, I promise," Reggie said with an exaggerated batting of the eyes. "But if he finds me irresistible, don't get mad at me. Who wouldn't choose this," he ran his hands over narrow hips, "over that Jell-O-Pudding sistah who just had his kid?"

Dominique's eyes narrowed. "Careful, Reggie. You're about to get on my bad side. I was once that Jell-O-Pudding who'd just had a child."

"Sorry, boss, but you know I'm just wishful thinking. I already got the 411 on him from one of his instructors." Reggie sighed. "He's totally faithful."

Dominique laughed at Reggie's emoting. "Well, thank God for that."

The two settled in, with Dominique planning out the rest of the week and Reggie making notes to ensure that his boss's wishes were followed. Before either knew it, lunch time had arrived. Reggie returned to his desk and just as Dominique finished writing the editor's note for the spring "get in shape" edition, her cell phone rang. She smiled and answered.

"What are you doing?" Jake asked without preamble.

"Just finished up a project and thinking about lunch. What about you?"

"Meet me at my house in fifteen minutes."

Dominique scowled slightly. "Why?"

"Because it's lunchtime, you're hungry, and I'm cooking. Now stop asking questions and get over here."

Dominique shivered even though her office thermostat was set on seventy-five degrees. She was surprised at her body's reaction, given the fact that Jake had kept her up most of the night, leaving just before dawn. They'd made love twice but her body reacted as if it was love-starved and it had been eons since she'd experienced a man's touch. Dominique looked at the day's itinerary, noting that no other meeting was scheduled until three o'clock. She reached for her purse and headed toward the door as she answered, "I'm on my way."

After making a quick stop at the bathroom, Dominique left the floors of *Capricious* magazine. Traffic was light, so she reached Jake's house in ten

minutes. His truck was parked in the drive and
Dominique pulled her car up behind it. Feeling delicious and decadent, she placed her four-inch heels
on the pavement and within seconds was knocking
on Jake's door.

"Damn, you look good." That was Jake's greeting
before he folded Dominique in his arms and seared
her with a long, wet kiss. Dominique's bare nana
screamed its agreement, the panties she'd shed in
the bathroom now occupying a corner of her purse.
Jake looked good, too, she decided, dressed in a
tight navy tee and simple black warm-ups. His size-
fourteen feet were encased in leather Jordans, and
the woodsy scent that loosely clung to his body was
about to drive a girlfriend wild. Dominique eased
her hand into his waistband and pulled at his top.

"Whoa, wait a minute, baby. When I told you I'd
fixed you a meal, I meant food."

"Oh."

Jake grabbed Dominique's hand and led her
toward the kitchen. That his chest puffed out a bit
more at her obvious sexual hunger was an under-
statement. *I'm the man* was written all over his face.
They passed Jake's dining room en route to the
kitchen. Indeed, there was a table setting for two,
complete with water glasses already filled. They
reached the kitchen and Jake grabbed a towel before
opening the oven, pulling out two perfectly baked
pieces of farm-fresh salmon.

"The plates are in the far left cabinet," he said
over his shoulder. "Salad bowls are there as well."

A few minutes later, he and Dominique were
seated at the dining-room table enjoying a simple

yet satisfying lunch of salmon, salad, and corn on
the cob. Large chunks of French bread dripping in
non-hydrogenated margarine rounded out the
meal. Dominique learned that Jake's two hours of
free time had come courtesy of a teachers' meeting
in which his participation was not required. He
showed real interest as she shared her enthusiasm
about the upcoming article on fitness, having attended the opening of Night Simmons's gym, which
was called Body By Night. The unexpected midday
reprieve was so enjoyable that Dominique totally
forgot about her first assumption—an hour filled
with hot, lusty sex. Once finished, she followed Jake
into the kitchen, placing her dishes in the dishwasher next to his.

"That was delicious, Jake," she said after washing
her hands at the kitchen sink and preparing to walk
out the door. "And this was a nice change of pace in
my day. Thanks for inviting me." She gave him a
quick peck on the lips and headed toward the
dining room and the front door.

As she passed the dining room table, Jake grabbed
her from behind. "Not so fast," he whispered, his
breath hot and heavy against her right earlobe.
"There's still dessert."

Dominique melted against his broad chest as his
fingers sought and found their destination underneath her dress. She stood in four-inch heels, legs
spread, body dripping with desire, Jake's fingers
feeling every drop. Without a word, he guided her
to the table, his hand on her back silently instruct-
ing her to strike an easy-access pose. She did, turning around and raising her wrinkle-free skirt. After

hearing the snap of a fastener and the unzipping of steel, she felt her heated dessert at the entry of her sweetness. She braced herself for the familiar assault, moaned again as he eased into her, inch by thick, delicious inch. He rode her low and slow, side to side, and then teased her by pulling out to the tip before sinking back in to the hilt. He palmed her ample buttocks like a work of art—kneading and stroking, slapping as one would a horse to giddyup. Dominique ground back against him, oblivious of everything except Jake's hands on her engorged nipples and his sausage in her bun. Their climaxes came simultaneously, the scream spilling from Dominique's throat before she could catch it, Jake's growl of pleasure the harmony to her orgasmic melody.

Jake leaned over and squeezed Dominique's body with a tenderness unlike she had ever felt. He pulled out, and wordlessly guided her to the bathroom where they both freshened up. Without a sound, he watched as Dominique reapplied her makeup, then led them both back into the living room.

"Thanks for lunch," Jake whispered as they reached the living room.

"It was yummy," Dominique replied. "The best meal I've ever had."

"I agree," Jake said, "that salmon was delicious." He laughed, successfully avoiding Dominique's swat at his face. "You were the best tasting dish on the menu," he admitted, taking Dominique's hand and walking to the door. "And just so you know . . . I'll be coming back for seconds . . ." He kissed her neck.

"And thirds . . ." He rubbed his hand over her butt, and squeezed. "And—"

"Jake, I have to go!" Dominique hurriedly finished and rushed out the door.

"Ha! You'd better run," Jake said to her fleeing back. "Because you're like an all-you-can-eat buffet and you make me want to throw down all day long!"

24

"Okay, team, listen up. For this week's game, we're going to a spread offense and a three-four defense: three linemen, four defensive backs, and four linebackers." The boys' eyes were glued to the board as Jake drew *x*'s and *o*'s to mark out each position. "We're going to interchange this with the nickel defense we used last week. Aiden, you'll switch with Matt and play right corner. Matt, you'll be working with Shawn and the running backs. Kareem, you and the backups will work with him as well. Justin, you'll stay at tight end and work with the backs, too. I want the defense to come with me. We're doing special drills today."

For the next ninety minutes the boys ripped up and down the field, repeating plays over and over again until they unfolded as if by second nature. October had brought with it cooler temps, but you couldn't tell it by the stained, sweaty practice gear and smudged faces. Spirits were high as practice ended and the boys filed off the grass.

Jake sauntered into his office, using the towel

around his neck to wipe sweat from his face. He reached into the mini fridge, pulled out an ice-cold bottle of water, and took a long swig. He plopped into his roomy office chair, glad that the practice had gone well but equally glad that the day was over. Between last night's marathon sex romp with Dominique and the loving that continued at lunch today, the brothah was tired, but satisfied.

Shawn bounced into his boss's office and also pulled out a cold bottle of water. "Wow, Big Mac, what got into you?"

Jake placed the bottle on the table, and turned on his computer. "What do you mean?"

"I don't know, but something about you was different at practice today. You seemed more fired up, happier. Did you finally take the fourth-grade teacher up on her offer?"

"Man, when are you going to quit it with the talk about that chick? She's a good person who's never offered me anything, not that I'd accept if she would. As for my good mood," Jake shrugged, "I guess it was just the relaxing weekend I had and the fact that the team is just where I wanted them to be—4 and 0." Jake clicked on a few keys and soon the hum of the printer filled the space.

After conversation about the day's practice had ended, Shawn stood. "Guess I'll head home and get in the clown suit."

"Clown suit?"

"Well, some people call it a tuxedo."

"What's the special occasion?"

"In-laws' golden anniversary and a big shindig at a lah-di-dah restaurant in Beverly Hills. I swear that even after ten years, I sometimes still feel like an outsider in Taylor's family."

Jake nodded, but couldn't relate. Robin's father had died when she was young, another thing they had in common, but her mother had treated him like a son. Though less frequently, they still kept in touch. Jake made a mental note to give his former mother-in-law a call, then grabbed the stack of papers from the printer and headed to the classroom where he tutored math.

"Hey, Justin. You're early."

Justin shrugged, his head buried in a textbook.

"Well, let's get started." Jake placed a couple pieces of paper on Justin's desk. "I worked up these problems for you guys to solve, sort of a pre-test to the one you'll take next week."

Justin closed the book he was viewing but instead of picking up the papers, he looked at Jake. "Coach, can I ask you something?"

Jake pulled the teacher's chair from behind the desk, pushed it closer to Justin and sat. "Sure."

"How old were you when you started liking girls?"

The question was unexpected and Jake checked his watch, buying some time to gather his thoughts. Always a big guy, Jake had been accosted by a just-moved-in seventeen-year-old neighbor who thought he was older. He'd lost his virginity at the ripe old age of thirteen, a fact he wisely decided to keep to himself. "About your age," he finally said.

Justin eyed him for a moment, and then busied himself by working on the formulas Jake had given him.

Now Jake was surprised again. Instead of this one simple question, he'd expected an interrogation.

When that didn't seem likely, Jake pushed the issue. "Why do you ask?"

Justin shrugged.

"No reason?"

After a long pause, Justin added, "Mama's mad at me 'cause I like girls. She don't understand. . . ."

"She's mad because you like a girl here at school, in one of your classes?"

Justin's signature crooked smile appeared briefly before disappearing behind scrunched eyebrows. "She don't know about Ashley. But she's still mad that I like girls."

"If she doesn't know about this friend you have here at school, why is she angry?"

Justin slouched down in the desk seat and mumbled, "Moms are a trip."

Jake hid his smile. "Talk to me, son."

Justin looked up at Jake, his expression unreadable but his thought clear: *I wish . . .*

"So what did you do, beat up a girl and take her lunch money?"

"Ha! No, Coach!"

"Push her down on the playground and look under her dress?"

Justin laughed. "No!"

Jake laughed as well, easing the tension of the moment. "Of course you don't have to tell me, but I am curious."

Justin squirmed in his chair, picked up his pencil, and tapped on the desk. When he answered his voice was barely above a whisper. "I looked at some pictures."

Jake leaned back in his chair. "Some pictures, huh?"

Justin nodded. "My aunt caught me and my cousin looking at naked women and told Mama. I'm in all kinds of trouble, Coach Mac, and I don't understand why looking at those pictures was so bad."

"What kind of pictures were they?"

Again, Justin's voice was low, soft. "Nasty ones."

"Why were they nasty?"

"'Cause Mama said so. The girls were naked, and Mama said I was looking at filth and being disrespectful to women. But all we was doing was looking at them!" Justin's head was bowed but he sneaked peeks at the man he idolized to gauge his reaction. "Was I wrong, Coach?"

Jake toyed with the papers on his desk, thinking through his answer. On one hand, he didn't want to counter what Dominique had told her son but on the other, he didn't want the young man thinking it wrong to do something that in Jake's mind was a male rite of passage. What red-blooded young man hadn't looked at a girly mag at least once in his lifetime?

"Look here, Justin. I understand why your mom is upset. To her, you're still a little boy, her baby."

"I'm almost twelve," Justin sulkily replied. "That's almost a teenager!"

"True, but you're not a teenager yet. And your mom probably thinks eleven is a little too young to look at the type of pictures your cousin showed you."

Justin's shoulders slouched. The last thing he wanted to do was disappoint his coach. "So you're mad at me, too?" After asking this question, Justin looked Jake straight in the eye.

"Not at all," Jake responded, shaking his head. "I was once your age, and did my share of looking." Jake noticed how Justin sat a little straighter, his eyes sparkling at this admission. "There's nothing wrong with being curious, especially as you adjust to the changes happening to your body. But you'll have plenty of time for girls, Justin. Right now I think your focus should be on school and football, especially how you're going to get past Carter Woodson this Friday."

"Aw, c'mon now, Coach. Carter's a chump. I'ma run right through him."

Jake laughed. "Is that right?"

Justin nodded.

"We'll see," Jake said, turning the pages of the book in front of him. "But before you do that, let's see if you can run past these mathematical equations."

Later that evening, Dominique was pleased to see that instead of sulking and staying in his room, Justin was back to his chatty self.

"Did you have a good time at school today?" she asked, hoping to root out the cause for Justin's changed mood.

"Uh-huh."

"What was so good about it?"

"I made a forty-yard touchdown at practice today. Coach Mac showed us this new play and I got it right the first time!"

"That sounds great, baby. Is that why you're in such a good mood?"

"Yeah, that and the fact that me and Coach talked."

Dominique's parental antennae immediately went up. She didn't even bother correcting the poor grammar that was her pet peeve. "Oh," she nonchalantly responded. "What about?"

"Man stuff, Mama," Justin answered as he stood and grabbed an apple from the bowl of fruit centered on the dining room table. "You wouldn't understand."

"What do you mean, 'man stuff,'" Dominique probed. "Was it about those nasty pictures you viewed?"

"They weren't nasty."

"Is that what he told you?"

"What he said is between me and Coach Mac!" Justin raced toward the stairs.

"Justin! Get back here."

Justin ignored his mother. "I wish he was my dad," he mumbled under his breath. But not low enough. Dominique heard.

"Wait a minute, boy. What did you say?"

"Nothing!" Justin said, as he continued up the stairs and slammed the door to his room.

Dominique resisted the urge to follow after Justin and force him to talk. She needed the time alone as much as he did; time to calm down and gather her thoughts. *He wishes Jake was his father?* This declaration had thrown her for a loop. Her mind reeled as she tidied up the kitchen and once done, she went upstairs as well. In the privacy of her master domain, she reached for her phone.

"Jake, it's me," Dominique said once her phone call had been answered. "When it comes to Justin and how I raise him, I think you're crossing the line."

"What?" Jake responded, incredulity wrapped around all three consonants and the vowel.

"You heard me," Dominique retorted, her tone low and unyielding. "I want to know what you discussed with my son, and I want to know now."

25

Dominique eased her car into what looked like the last spot in the parking lot, not at all happy at the distance between her and a seat in the bleachers for today's game. It still amazed her that so many people showed up to support a grade-school team. But here they were five games into the season and the parking lot was packed. The article on Jake McDonald that had appeared in the sports section of last week's *LA Times* had further increased the team's popularity.

Today, Dominique blended in a bit more with the crowd. Her CJ Jeans fit her thick thighs and juicy derriere to perfection and the light gold mohair sweater not only gave a nod to the team's colors but also highlighted the golden tones in her skin. Her short, springy locs shined from the leave in conditioner she'd sprayed on just before leaving the house and the subtle scent of her favorite cologne, along with gold hoop earrings, bangles, and a chunky necklace were the perfect accessories. But anyone thinking Dominique was anything less than a fashion statement had to look no further than her four-inch Jimmy Choo shoes for the truth— Dominique dominated full-figure fashion . . . even at her son's sixth grade football game.

Dominique had just sat down on a bleacher near the top of the stands when her phone beeped.

It was Reggie who'd begged out of accompanying her to the game because of a hot date with Quinn, his new man. **Do you need me at work on Monday, Miss Dom?**

Dominique quickly typed in her response. **Don't I need you most Mondays?**

Yes, but Quinn surprised me with a trip to Las Vegas, and tickets to see Celine Dion's Sunday night show. Girl, after an evening with that voice I'll be no good the next day. Maybe come in by the afternoon? Plz, Miss Dom!!!

Dominique laughed out loud, shaking her head as she remembered how distraught Reggie had been just a little over a month ago, when his former lover decided he wanted to move back to Italy without him. And now he was head over heels in love with Quinn, who Dominique had to admit looked like Boris Kodjoe with hair. In other words, fine forever. Reggie changed men like she changed shoes and almost as easily. She typed back a reply that she'd see him Monday afternoon just as a cheer went up from the enthusiastic crowd. The Middleton Hurricanes had taken the field.

A little under two hours later, parents and supporters were hugging each other in the stands. The Hurricanes remained undefeated, beating their opponents in a nail-biting game won by a field goal with two minutes remaining. Dominique was just as excited as the rest of the onlookers, not only because her son's team had won, but also because she'd actually been able to follow the game. Six short weeks ago, she wouldn't have been able to tell a touchdown from a touchback but, thanks to Jake's patient tutoring, could now spout football jargon with the best of them. She turned toward the field to look for Justin and encountered two dark chocolate-brown eyes staring at her. She still had a bone or two to pick with Jake McDonald, but Dominique's heart skipped a beat as she nodded in acknowledgement and he motioned for her to join him on the field.

"Great game, Coach," she said, once she'd worked her way through the throng of people surrounding him. The warm words were paired with a cold stare.

"Glad you enjoyed," Jake responded, ignoring her demeanor while lazily running his eyes along Dominique's ample frame. "I see you're getting into the groove, wearing the colors and what not."

Noting the listening ears around them, Dominique smiled as she straightened the purple and gold scarf loosely tied around her neck. "What else would you expect from the proud mother of your star tight end?"

Both Jake and Dominique burst out laughing, remembering when she'd first talked about her son and his position at *right* end. Their camaraderie was interrupted, however, when a television reporter wrangled her way into the mix.

"Can we get a quick interview, Coach?"

"Sure, Madison," Jake said, with a wink to the reporter and a nod to the cameraman. The reporter stepped between Jake and Dominique and began firing appropriately honed questions at the man who led one of only two undefeated teams in the league.

Dominique took in the attractive blonde, from her skintight jeans to her low-cut top exposing large boobs on a slender frame, and backed away. She tried not to feel the quick stab of jealousy that shot through her heart, tried not to analyze why Jake smiling at the reporter had affected her the way it had. She'd never given much thought to the type of woman Jake liked, or if he were dating anyone but her. They'd never had the conversation about exclusivity and why would they? Dominique wasn't even ready to acknowledge that they were in a relationship, especially now. She'd referred to their being together as "scratching an itch." But was that really all she wanted and if so, when would this itch go away?

"Mom!" Justin ran up to her, followed by another football player and a haggard-looking mom. "Travis's mom is taking us out for pizza. Can I go?"

A young, brunette woman, who looked little over the age of a kid herself, came up behind the two boys. "Hi," she said, reaching a hand out to Dominique. "I'm Kathy, Travis's mom."

"Hi, I'm Dominique."

"Nice to meet you. Wow, now I see where Justin got his build! I mean . . . height," Kathy added after belatedly realizing how her comment may have sounded.

Dominique laughed. "He got his height and build from me. His father was average size." *Average at everything*, Dominique thought but didn't voice.

"Well, he's a star for sure, already got a fan club."

"Really?"

"Yes," Kathy answered. She leaned in and continued. "Especially that cute cheerleader over there. I think her name is Ashley."

Dominique followed Kathy's pointing finger. "Oh, really?"

"Yes," Kathy said, with a laugh. "But you didn't hear that from me."

Dominique waved at Justin as he and a group of boys followed Kathy out of the stadium. She looked back to see Jake and the blonde still deep in conversation. She watched as the woman touched him with familiarity, and he laughed at something she said. Dominique whirled around, totally forgetting that she was upset with Jake and shouldn't care who he talked to. Instead, she barely resisted stomping out of the stadium. If not for the fact that her Jimmy Choos were reminding her that they weren't made for foot stomping, cement pounding, and jumping up and down at each spectacular Hurricane play, she may not have been successful. She wrapped her scarf tighter around her neck against the unexpected October chill, joined the masses exiting the stadium on the way to their cars, and convinced herself that what Jake did and who he did it with was none of her business.

She'd just pulled into her driveway when the phone rang. A sound as smooth and sweet as fresh maple syrup poured into her ear. "Hey, baby."

Dominique knew her body had no business growing warm with two simple words. But it did. "Hey," she responded.

"Why'd you run off?"

"You were busy working, which I totally understand. I didn't want to intrude. Plus, the reporter

looked like she definitely wanted you all to herself."
Dominique hoped that she didn't sound jealous . . .
but she knew that she did.

"You should have waited. Madison is an old
friend."

"I see," Dominique said, not at all happy that she
could detect a smile in Jake's voice.

"Ha! No, you don't. Madison used to be married
to one of the Raiders. That's how I know her. The interview was quick, only a couple minutes. But then
I got sidetracked by a group representing a summer
training camp. They had all kinds of questions about
me, my career . . . and a couple about your son. He's
making an impression in this league."

At the mention of Justin, Dominique remembered why she shouldn't be feeling all warm and
fuzzy where Jake was concerned. "Speaking of
Justin," she continued with less warmth in her voice,
"Jake, I'm still very concerned that you're sharing
confidences with my son and then keeping them
from me."

"Dominique, like I said the other night, I planned
to tell you what Justin said about wanting me to be
his father."

"And exactly when were you planning on telling
me that?"

"What does it matter? I obviously didn't tell you
soon enough. And for that, again, I apologize."

"This is exactly why I didn't want to start this."

"Baby, there are some things in life that we simply
can't control. Besides, I'd think Justin having positive male role models in his life would be considered a good thing."

"Positive role models are good; keeping secrets isn't."

"Fair enough."

"Really? So you're ready to share with me what you discussed with my child?"

Jake laughed. "Woman, I already told you. What we discussed was man-to-man, not to mention that he specifically asked me not to tell you about it."

"I could care less what my son asked you. He's eleven years old, Jake. *Eleven.* Kids that age should have no secrets from their mama!"

"Calm down, baby. It's not that serious, really."

"If you'd just tell me what y'all talked about, there would be no need to calm down. As it is, I have my theories. It was about the pictures, right?"

Jake sighed. "As I said before, Dominique, if you want to know what your son talked to me about, you'll have to ask him. I will not break a confidence."

"Even though you know it's the right thing to do?"

"We obviously disagree with what is right in this instance. I will tell you this, Dominique. There is nothing he shared that you need to be worried about. Your son is a normal, growing boy, trying to navigate the journey to becoming a man."

"I need to be a part of that journey," Dominique huffed.

"And you are."

"Oh, really? I can't tell."

Jake ignored Dominique's comment and continued, "Some things about growing up can't be understood unless you've actually been there, walked in those shoes. I've been there." Jake's voice became softer as if emotions from past memories threatened to overtake him. "I've been a young man without a father. Thing about me, though, is that I had older brothers to help school me. Justin's by himself."

"No, he isn't. He has an uncle, and cousins."

"That he obviously didn't feel comfortable with exposing his feelings to. Trust me, baby. The last thing I'd ever want to do is steer any young man in the wrong direction. Especially Justin."

Used to getting her way, Dominique couldn't see past her anger at not being able to control Jake and hear the truth in his words. "Why especially Justin?" she countered. "Why are you so interested in my son?"

"Because he reminds me of myself at his age," Jake said. "When I see that unsure, lonely look in his eyes . . . it's like I'm looking in a mirror. Here's what I will say . . . the changes occurring in and to Justin's body are perfectly normal occurrences. He isn't some creature from outer space just because he's curious about the opposite sex. Sometimes these subjects are better handled man-to-man, baby. That's why he sought me out and shared what was on his mind."

Dominique fumed in silence, begrudgingly admitting that much of what Jake said was probably true. She thought back to an article she'd read on single parenting. In it, a father was quoted as saying that "while a female can nurture and love her son, it takes a male to turn a boy into a man." Dominique had balked at this ideology, knowing that no one knew her son better than she, or loved him more. But that was before last Sunday and the naked pics, before she'd entertained ideas of him masturbating and growing pubic hair. Now, she wondered . . . was she properly equipped to turn her spunky boy into a responsible man?

Jake spoke into the silence. "Why don't you come over?"

"I can't. Justin went for pizza with some of his friends and Tessa's off today. I need to be home when he gets there." And she also needed to pout some more, but Dominique withheld this information.

"Then I could come over there."

"Jake, you know how I feel about that. I've already broken rules with you as it is, and Justin is already too attached to you . . . as it is. I don't want to give him the wrong idea about us, or send you the wrong signal."

"And what signal would that be? That what we have here could be more than a sexual fling, could actually grow into some kind of relationship?"

"You know I don't think that's a good idea, and you also know why."

"What I know," Jake purred, his voice dropping lower and bringing a shiver to Dominique's spine, "is that there is a certain woman I want to kiss right now, in several places . . ."

Dominique almost acquiesced, but there was a trait called stubbornness between her and her desire to spend the afternoon wrapped in Jake's strong, muscled arms. He was standing his ground and she didn't like it. Since recovering from her last relationship and the betrayal that accompanied it, being in control was her territory. Jake was strong, a man's man, and while she knew that she'd be less impressed with a weakling, she wasn't sure how much she liked his being able to stand up against her.

After reaching her house, Dominique hit her garage door remote and eased her car forward. "I think I'll stay home and get some rest," she said, as she pushed the remote and exited her vehicle. "I plan to be in the office early in the morning."

"Okay," Jake said, disappointment dripping from the word, and added, "But instead of the fact that I'm a man of my word, I wish it were your body you were holding against me."

26

Monday morning, and Dominique was in a major mood. She tried to blame it on the fact that her subject for the summer issue, D'Andra Simmons, had had to cancel their interview because her son had gotten sick. But truth be told, Dominique was experiencing withdrawal of the Big Mac kind. Until yesterday, it hadn't dawned on her that Jake was becoming a part of her routine, his loving as expected as having breakfast in the morning. Since meeting him, this was the first weekend she'd spent alone and not having him by her side bothered her more than she cared to admit. Plus, she still hadn't broached the "Jake as a father" comment with her son and wasn't necessarily looking forward to the conversation.

"What is it, Reggie?" she barked into the phone.

"Ooh, excuse me, Miss Dom, but girlfriend . . . who's got your panties all in a bunch?"

Dominique sighed. "Get in here."

Reggie pranced into her office in his usual flamboyant fashion. Today he wore a turquoise shirt, black velvet pants, and—inspired by Miss Jay from

America's Next Top Model—his size-twelve feet were
enduring three-inch, custom-made heels. His hair
was freshly permed and extended beyond his shoulders, a nod to his respect for Beverly Hills's flamboyant hairdresser, Elgin Charles. His lashes were long
and his makeup flawless. In short, Reggie De-
Vaughn Williams looked amazing.

"So talk to me, Miss Dom," he said, once he'd
plopped his hard, round derrière into the seat
facing Dominique. "What's going on, girl?"

"I'm having a bit of an issue with Justin's football
coach," Dominique replied.

"That fine, strapping, corn- and beef-fed, weight-
lifting brothah?" Reggie uncrossed his legs, shifted,
and recrossed them. "I can think of a few *issues* I'd
like to have with that man."

Dominique laughed in spite of her bad mood.
That's why she kept Reggie around and put up with
his antics. Not only was he a top-notch administra-
tive assistant, but he was always good for putting a
smile on her face—a job she'd be the first to admit
wasn't always easy.

"Okay, here's what happened," she began, before
giving Reggie the skinny on how Jake refused to di-
vulge what had been discussed in the conversation
between him and her son. "Am I being too sensitive,
Reggie? Or, as his mother, don't you think I have a
right to know what my son talked to him about?"

Reggie took a sip from his ever-present latte.
"Well, Miss Dom, there's two ways to look at this sce-
nario. On one hand, your boy is showing character
by not wanting to break a confidence. But on the
other hand . . ." Reggie arched his eyebrow and
placed a manicured set of fingers in the air.

"On the other hand, what?"

"Let me ask you this. How often does Justin see his father?"

Dominique's eyes narrowed as she leaned back and matched Reggie's question with one of her own. "Why would you ask that?"

"Don't take it personally," Reggie said, his hands raised against her ire. "I know you're a great mom but . . ."

"But what?"

"But I know what it's like to grow up without a dad. Even with all the love I got from Mama, Grandma, and all my aunties, I sometimes wished there'd been a man around."

Dominique crossed her arms and sighed. "Justin wishes that, too."

Seeing how upsetting his comment had been, Reggie continued, "But then again, all kids are different—"

"Not Justin," Dominique interrupted. "He's like you in that respect. He wishes Jake was his father."

"He told you that?"

"He told Jake who, by the way, didn't bother sharing this not-so-little tidbit of information with me."

"Then how did you find out?"

"The other night when Justin became upset with me. He mumbled it under his breath."

"Oh, Miss Dom, a kid will say anything when he's angry."

"He meant it."

"Well . . . maybe the child will get what he's wishing for; I know for a fact that you're really feeling this dude."

"And how do you know that?"

"Girl, please. It's written all over your face. I can tell whenever you've been with him because you come in here beaming like Venus on a clear night."

"I won't deny that I'm very fond of him, Reggie. Jake is definitely someone with whom I could fall in love. But I'm just not willing to take the chance on things not working out and Justin being hurt again. I remember the days and weeks after Kevin left. Justin was so sad. He cried himself to sleep that first night, and then begged me to call Kevin and ask him to come back. I finally decided to tell him the truth, that Kevin had stolen from Mommy. He didn't want to believe me and when he finally did, I felt bad for telling him. Kevin had betrayed me, but to Justin, it was as if he was the one who'd been wronged. And to a degree, he had. In stealing from me, Kevin betrayed the trust that Justin had placed in him as a father figure. In Justin's young eyes, no man who cared about him would do that to his mom." Dominique was silent for a while, remembering that difficult period in her and her son's life. "It was awful," she concluded. "It was months before Justin was back to his old self. I swore that I'd never, ever, put him through anything like that again. And I meant it."

"I can understand you wanting to protect your child," Reggie said. "But try not to be over-protective. Don't deny his relationship with Jake based on what might happen. Life's too short for that, Miss Dom. Besides, there are worse role models for Justin than a strapping football coach who has a thing for his mother and whose mother has a thing right back. Trust me, I know."

Dominique spent the next hour finding more out

about her assistant than she'd ever known: that his grandmother had whipped him for being a "sissy"; that he'd held fashion shows for his aunts and dressed in their clothes; and that a twenty-something neighbor's son had introduced Reggie to sex when he was just ten years old. Time flew, and before either of them realized, it was time for the weekly editorial and pitch meeting.

For Dominique, a business luncheon followed and an afternoon of editing, reading and researching went by in a blur. But as she left the office and headed for a dinner engagement with a well-known, plus-size model, one thought remained and kept playing itself over and over in her head. It was Reggie's not-so-innocuous question: *How often does Justin get to see his father?* And then, his telling comment: *There are worse role models for Justin . . . trust me, I know.*

27

Jake eyed the caller ID and thought twice about taking the call. He picked up begrudgingly, knowing that he was in for a grilling. "Yo, bro."

"Hey, Jake," Harold replied. "What's going on with you, man?"

"Who says anything is going on?"

"Ha! Do you really want me to answer that question?"

"Yes, humor me."

"I've known you all your life, Jake, and when your phone calls get sporadic that means that something is going on. Besides, you didn't participate in this week's football blog. It's not often that you put a C-spot on the line in the betting pool and then don't show up on the chat for some trash talk when your team wins."

"I told y'all that the Chiefs were coming back," Jake replied, knowing that he'd bet on a team that in a lot of fans' minds was still a big question mark. "The new quarterback is on point, and their line is solid."

"Yeah, yeah, who asked you?" Harold said, still smarting from his loss. "Just be ready to give me back my money when Vick takes the field next week."

"Vick is washed up," Jake responded. "So get ready to give me some more of your cash."

"Don't start counting my dollars yet, bro. But what I really want to know is why you were MIA tonight. Your girl got you so sprung that you can't hang out with the fellas?"

My girl. Jake all but snorted at Dominique's fitting that definition. Because, without exception, Dominique Clark was the most stubborn, opinionated, strong-willed woman that he'd ever met. Which is what so exasperated him, and turned him on. She was also the warmest, smartest, most titillating woman he'd ever known. Which is what further exasperated him, and turned him on. She hadn't stayed after the game on Saturday and hadn't called, and when he'd finally given in to his desires and phoned her on Sunday, she'd informed him that she'd be spending the day in LA, with her family. Jake had thought about contacting one of his old hookups, had even toyed with the idea of calling the reporter who'd given him her cell number. But in his mind, none of the substitutes could replace the original. He wanted Dominique. He needed to sex her a few more times, get her totally out of his system. And then he needed to move on to someone who was more his speed, someone who in his mind wasn't trying to take the pants off of him and wear them.

"Did you hear what I said, Jake?"

"Oh, sorry, man. I got distracted."

"I asked what you were betting on next week's game."

"Another hundred, might as well not stop while I'm on a roll." Jake looked at the clock. "I need to run, Harold, and make a phone call."

"To Dominique?"

"No, the Raiders. The front office called me today. I need to see what's up. And thanks for calling, Harold. I love you like a brother."

"I am your brother, fool."

Jake laughed.

Harold joined in. "Okay, bro. Do your thing. But I've got dibs if they're calling you about some premium suite tickets. You know me and my wife are overdue for a trip to the West Coast. We can come over and hang out with you and this chick that's got you twisted."

"Man, you're trippin'."

"No. You are. And don't think I haven't noticed that you have yet to bring her around the family. I'd say that it's time for all of us to meet, get to know each other."

"Whatever, man. I'll call you later in the week."

"Okay, later."

Jake hung up from talking with his brother and called Damien Jones, one of his best friends and a former Oakland Raider teammate. "Yo, dog, what up?" he said, when Damien's deep bass voice echoed through the receiver.

"Big Mac!" Damien replied. "I'm just a squirrel in your world, man. Nothing to it but to do it, know what I'm saying?"

Jake nodded, with a big smile on his face. He and Damien had shared some amazing times together, both on and off the field. They each had enough on the other to set up a big-time blackmail, but when it came to the antics of their ballplayer days, their lips were sealed. "Yeah, I know."

"So what's up, Big Mac? You coming to the ceremony this Sunday or what?"

"That's why I called, to find out what was going on."

"They want us to be a part of the halftime celebration."

"Oh, yeah?"

"Yeah, man, honoring some of us *former* stars. They've got that stuff twisted for real, dog, because my star is still lighting up Oaktown."

Jake laughed, and got up to grab a cool bottle of water from the fridge.

Damien continued, "I guess when it comes to that *former* nonsense they're looking at your name on the list."

"Okay, my man has jokes. I was the heartbeat of the defensive line, as you, our opponents, and the record books will attest."

"I can't even lie about that, dog," Damien readily agreed. "You held it down! So that's what's up this weekend; a big shindig on Saturday night, followed by a presentation at halftime. Sounds like it's going to be pretty cool and they gave us eight guest passes each, along with a badge for total access. My boys are crazy excited about going and Alison is, too, although she's trying to act all nonchalant and whatnot."

"Alison has been trying to act like that since she saw you in the college cafeteria. I'm convinced that her not paying you any attention is how she became your wife."

"Ha! You're probably right about that. You know I

always relished a challenge." Damien paused, and took a swig from his bottle of beer. "So who are you dating now, dog? Grab her and a few of your friends, maybe some of your students, and let's get down in Oaktown next weekend."

"I'll think about it," Jake responded.

"Don't even think about being a no-show," Damien countered. "Otherwise I'll spill some of those secrets that would best be left unsaid."

"Let's not start on who's got the most dirt to dish. Remember the blond twins who were double-jointed?"

"Aw, man!" Damien exclaimed. "Don't remind me and please . . . don't ever let Alison hear that story!"

"All right then, don't play."

"It'll be good to see you, man."

"Me, too, dog. I'll see you at the game."

28

"Hey, baby, it's me." Jake leaned back in his office chair. He'd shaken off the discomfort that Dominique's lack of calling had brought about and even though she hadn't returned his phone calls in three days, decided to be the bigger person. "You must be busy."

"Why would you think that?"

Jake heard paper rustling in the background and imagined Dominique poring over an article with those cute reading glasses she sometimes wore perched on her nose. "Because you've left me hanging like a red-headed stepchild, that's why," he easily countered. Truth be told, his bruised ego was smarting over the fact that Dominique could spend so many days without him. "I haven't heard from you. I miss you."

"It's a crazy time," Dominique said. "Our offices pretty much shut down during the holidays so the next few weeks are crucial to getting our spring and summer issues into press."

"So that's it? You haven't called me or returned your calls only because you're busy?"

"Exactly." It sounded like Dominique knew she was busted, but figured that being busy was her story and she was sticking to it. "Why did you call, Jake?"

"Well, aside from the fact that the only way we'd talk is if I called you, I wanted to know what you and Justin were doing this weekend."

"The usual. After the game, I'll be at work and he'll visit his cousin in LA."

"Michael?" *Aw, hell.* Belatedly, Jake realized that knowing Michael's name was a dead giveaway to at least part of what Justin had shared with him.

"So that *is* what you two talked about. Justin told you about him and his cousin gawking at naked girls."

"Please, Dominique. Let's not go there. Justin has mentioned his cousin on several occasions. He's talked about how good a quarterback he is, and how he, too, has dreams of going pro." This was a true statement, but it was also true that Jake was aware of Michael's role in Justin's maturation. He decided that there were worse crimes than lying by omission. "Justin's doing much better in math," he continued, making no bones about changing the subject. "But then, I'm sure you're aware of the A he got on his last test."

"He was very proud of that grade," Dominique conceded. "I'm sure that came in no small part to your tutoring efforts. And even though it's obvious that you're changing the subject . . . thank you for taking time with him."

"It is my pleasure to tutor those kids. And you're

welcome." Feeling that he'd once again sidestepped one of the bones of contention between them, Jake got down to the business of his call. "I asked what Justin was doing this weekend because I've been invited to a special tribute for next Sunday's Raiders game in Oakland. I'd like to take Justin with me. And I'd like—"

"An overnight trip?" Dominique interrupted. She sounded suspicious.

"We'd leave on Saturday morning and return after the game on Sunday night. It would mean a late night for the boys, but I figure one night's lack of sleep won't kill them."

"Boys? Who else is going? You know what, it doesn't even matter. I've already made plans for Justin. He can't go."

"Trust me, Dominique. Justin would rather come on this trip, no matter what other plans you've made."

"Listen, I have another call coming. Thanks for the invite, Jake, but I'm going to have to pass on this one."

Several hours later, Dominique pulled into her garage and closed the door. She sat there for a few moments, trying to still the discomforting feelings roiling inside her. She'd been on edge ever since Jake's phone call. Actually, Dominique realized, she'd been edgy for about a week now, the time that had passed since she and Jake last made love. Throughout the day, she'd gone back and forth with her decision not to let Justin go to Oakland. On one hand, she knew that Justin loved the Raiders. And to attend the game with Jake, a former Raiders star? For her son, it would be like a dream come true. But on the other hand, Dominique knew that a shared experience such as this one would only deepen Justin's feelings for Jake, make it even easier for Justin to imagine him in a fatherly role. And it would only deepen the pain if things didn't work out, and Jake stopped being a part of their lives.

Dominique reached for the phone, but just as quickly changed her mind. Since her conversation with Reggie, she'd left two messages for Justin's father to call his son. But so far, Leland hadn't responded. *And that's if he even received the messages.* Dominique wouldn't for a moment put it past Leland's wife to delete the messages and not tell him about them. Since last year, when Patricia had considered a message Dominique left on his cell phone inappropriate, Dominique only had contact through their home number. Dominique had felt that calling Leland to wish him "Happy Father's Day," and to remind him that the son living under his roof was not his first-born, had been totally appropriate. Flying to Dallas and whipping his inattentive ass would have been inappropriate. But then again, maybe not. *Maybe I haven't been aggressive enough when it comes to Leland being involved in Justin's life.*

As Dominique left the office and headed home, the conversation with Jake was still on her mind, as was her questioning whether the decision to not let Justin go to Oakland had been the right one. And then came one final thought as she pulled into the garage:

Was it possible that Justin knew about the trip, and would therefore know she had forbidden it? *No.*

There's no way Jake would tell these kids about the trip before talking to the parents. Dominique sighed as she reached for the door handle. *At least I won't have to deal with an upset son,* she thought.

As soon as she stepped from the garage into the kitchen, she knew she'd thought wrong.

29

First of all, the house was deathly quiet, something highly unusual at seven PM. She normally came in to the sounds of the TV blasting with a movie or video game and/or Tessa playing some of the pop, hip-hop or reggaeton music she loved.

Dominique placed her purse and briefcase on the island in the kitchen and reached for the mail that sat there. "Tessa? Justin? I'm home!"

Tessa rounded the corner. "Hey, Dominique," she said, her greeting subdued. "I was in the study, organizing your library."

Dominique rifled through the mail. "Where's Justin?"

Tessa was only partly successful at stifling a sigh. "In his room."

Dominique looked at Tessa, eyes narrowing. "What's wrong?"

"He's really upset."

"About what?" Dominique asked, although she well knew the answer.

"About not going with his coach on that trip to

Oakland. He's been in his room all evening, not even coming out for dinner. I tried to get him to eat, but he's locked the door."

"Thanks, Tessa. I appreciate it. You can go home now. I'll take it from here."

After seeing Tessa out and locking the door, Dominique mounted the stairs. She hesitated a brief moment at Justin's door, and then knocked softly. "Hey, baby."

No answer.

"Justin?"

Silence.

Dominique tried the door. "Justin, open the door."

"I don't want to. Go away!"

Dominique's eyes widened as she looked at the mahogany wood that separated her from her heartbeat. *Did my eleven-year-old angel just tell the person who paid mortgage on this door to go away from it?* Dominique understood Justin being upset, but she was still Mama and this was still her house.

"Justin, open this door. Don't make me ask again!" Losing her patience, Dominique rapped on the door. "Justin!"

Seconds later, the door opened. Without looking at or speaking to his mother, Justin skulked back to his bed and plopped down on it.

Dominique took a deep breath and stepped inside the room. "Justin," she began calmly, "what's wrong?"

Justin grabbed a pillow from his bed, hugged it to his chest, and kept sulking.

Dominique walked over to where Justin was and sat. She reached down, took off her heels, and moved farther onto the bed. "Something happen at school today?" Instead of going from what she knew, Dominique figured she'd start dealing with this from her son's point of view.

"Coach picked four boys to go to a Raiders game. He didn't pick me." A solitary tear rolled down Justin's face, which otherwise was fixed in a fierce scowl.

Dominique's heart broke.

She knew she had to tell the truth. She couldn't have her son feeling like he was unwanted. But where to begin? "Baby, how did you hear about the trip? Did Jake tell you?"

Justin shook his head. "No, Travis did. He wasn't supposed to say anything but he thought I was going, so he told me."

Oh, Lord. What have I done? "Justin, there's something I need to tell you."

Justin's eyes rose to meet hers—sad, searching.

"I know about the trip to Oakland. Jake called and told me about it."

"Did he tell you why he didn't pick me? I scored two touchdowns last weekend. Mom, I work harder than everybody!"

Dominique reached out and placed her hand on Justin's leg. She was thankful when he didn't flinch or pull away. "It wasn't Jake, baby. He asked me if you could travel to Oakland."

A smile broke through the storm that was Justin's countenance. "Yes!" he exclaimed, rising to his knees. "So I get to go see the Raiders?"

"I told Jake that you couldn't go."

"Why, Mom?" Justin jumped off of the bed. "Why did you say I can't go?"

"I just didn't think it was a good idea. Oakland is so far, and you wouldn't get back until late. I didn't know who all would be going . . ." As she rambled on, the excuses sounded lame to Dominique's own ears.

"But it's the Raiders, Mom. My favorite team!"

"I know, baby. We'll go another time."

"I don't want to go another time! I want to go now!"

"I'm sorry, Justin." Dominique stood and reached for her son.

"No, you're not!" he yelled, running to the other side of the room. "It's your fault. You said I can't go! You're mad at Coach and taking it out on me!"

"Baby, that's not true."

"It is, too!"

"Why would you think I'm mad at him?"

"Because he hasn't been over here again. Probably because he don't like you no more."

Dominique pondered where this statement had come from but chose to keep the focus on the issue at hand. "Let me call Jake, see what I can do."

Dominique left Justin's room and walked to the master suite at the end of the hall. She went straight to the phone and dialed Jake's number. That it went to voicemail wasn't a total surprise. Even if he were home and available, she hadn't been the friendliest person lately. She pressed the pound key to bypass the message. "Jake, it's Dominique. I'm sorry about the interruption earlier, but it was an important phone call. Listen, I'm calling about the Oakland trip. Maybe I spoke too soon about Justin not going. Can you give me a call when you get this message, and tell me more about the trip? He's pretty upset, as you can imagine. So I hope to hear from you soon."

Dominique pressed the end button and walked to her closet where she made quick work of shedding her clothes. From there she entered her bathroom, turned on the water full blast, and stepped into the shower. She took her time soaping her body, inhaling the citrusy scent. She casually rubbed the loofah sponge over her body, paying keen attention to her elbows, knees, and feet. By the time she left the shower fifteen minutes later, she felt a little more relaxed.

She walked over to the phone and was glad to see a missed call from Jake and her voicemail indicator lit. She sat on her bed and pushed the button.

Jake's voice came through the speaker, strong and matter-of-fact. "Dominique, it's Jake. Got your message. You were the first person I called about this trip. Unfortunately I only had eight passes and all of the spaces have been filled. I can't believe that you'd let a beef with me get in the way of something for Justin." There was a short pause before he continued, and Dominique thought she detected a sigh. "Between me and you, there might be another opportunity. At the end of the season, I'm hoping to take the entire team on a bus trip to one of the final games. It won't be quite the same as this one, with the boys in the suite, but it will still be a good time. But I don't know if the trip will get approved, so don't tell Justin."

The call ended with that last sentence. No "Goodbye," "Call me later," or huskily delivered terms of endearment. Since Justin had sought Jake's counsel, she'd been subconsciously—and sometimes not so subconsciously—pushing Jake away, putting the

brakes on the relationship (which she wouldn't call
a relationship), and throwing up one defense after
another. It looked like Jake had gotten the message.
Now, unfortunately, Dominique realized that the
distance she'd created was not at all what she wanted.

30

As had often been the case, for the rest of the
week work was Dominique's saving grace. Throughout the day, she was too busy to focus on Justin's un-
happiness. But that only left the other twelve to
fourteen hours in the day. Even though he'd perked
up a bit after Dominique promised him a chance to
see his favorite team play—without divulging that
this would be with his classmates—he still spent a lot
of time in his room. After the incident with Michael,
Dominique had had parental controls installed on
Justin's computer and hoped that there was no way
he could work his way around them. From the
couple times she'd checked, she knew he erased his
cookies. There were other ways to delve into the
computer's history, but so far she hadn't gone to
those measures. But he'd been so unhappy and so
uncharacteristically quiet that Dominique would
have almost allowed him a peek at a boob. Almost.
But not quite.

Now it was Friday afternoon, and the craze of the
week had subsided to a steadier pulse. It had been

an intense five days, so much of the staff had kicked off early meetings for drinks at the nearby P. F. Changs. Dominique had declined the invitation, choosing instead to finish the edit she was working on before heading home. She was well aware of the fact that her Saturday mornings had become more exciting than her Friday nights and that her anticipation of tomorrow's game had little to do with the boys on the field but a lot to do with their coach. It would be the first time she'd seen Jake in a week. She hadn't talked to him in three days, since she'd passed on his offer to take Justin to the football game. *God only knows how this will turn out.*

"Miss Dom." Reggie's voice coming through the intercom roused Dominique from her musings.

"Yes, Reggie."

"What time is the game tomorrow?"

A big smile spread across Dominique's face. "You're coming with me?"

"I sure am! Making up for your giving me last Monday morning off. Plus I'm guessing you could use the support."

Dominique had shared with Reggie what was going on with Justin, without totally revealing her part in his heartache. Telling him everything would reveal that their conversation had played a part in her decision to keep Justin home. She figured that one person feeling bad was enough. Especially now, when he was coming through as the friend that he was. "Reggie, you're a sweetheart. The game starts at noon but let's go to your favorite place for their champagne brunch." Dominique had already decided that tomorrow she'd work from home.

"Sounds like a plan, but who's the designated driver?"

"We'll use the company town car."

The next day, Dominique and Reggie walked the short distance from their chauffeured car to the stadium bleachers. They were both feeling all warm and fuzzy after several mimosas accompanied their breakfast fare and Reggie, relishing a rare Saturday off, had added a couple shots of Patron Silver to the mix.

"Where's that fine coach?" Reggie asked, tossing a bright pink cashmere scarf over his shoulder and hitting the tight-lipped man behind him in the face. "What do we do?"

Dominique finished the team's oft-stated chant. "We tear it up!"

"Tear it up, baby!" Reggie exclaimed, giving Dominique a high five. "Ooh, there he is," he whispered a moment later, when Jake and the coaches came off the bench. "Girl . . . that man is Grade A prime beef, USDA approved!"

"You're so bad," Dominique said, swatting Reggie playfully on the arm. She looked up in time to see Jake's frown before he turned away from her. But there was no chance to ponder the scowl and its meaning. Several raucous spectators began to chant: *Through hail, snow, sleet, rain . . . we are the Hurricanes!* It was time to play ball!

The Hurricanes took the field, and even though the game was a rout, with the Hurricanes winning 21–0, it was still a welcome diversion. Reggie's ongoing commentary about everything from the cheerleaders' less-than-creative chants to the referees he thought over-the-hill, and his commenting on the spectators' wardrobes as if they were in a fashion show, kept Dominique laughing, thinking about the game and not about the conversation she'd have to have when it was over. Especially with her son, who'd delivered a lackluster performance at best. It was the first game where he hadn't made a touchdown, and he'd fumbled the ball twice. She had drilled the lesson of excellence and doing one's best in her son's head since he was a toddler. Being unhappy with what life had handed him was no reason to—no pun intended—drop the ball.

"Come on, Reggie," Dominique said, once the game ended. "Time to enter the fray and try and talk to the coach."

"Miss Dom," Reggie yelled into Dominique's ear, "Quinn has been blowing up my phone. I'll wait for you in the car."

"Okay," Dominique replied, noting that her voice faltered a bit. "I'll only be a minute."

Dominique and her four-inch heels made their way down the steps and onto the field. As usual, Jake was surrounded by his adoring public, and the reporter who'd interviewed him a week ago was front and center. Moving with purpose and determination, Dominique eased her way into the tight circle.

"Jake, can I speak with you?" she asked, once she'd reached his side.

"I'm kinda busy right now, Dominique," he responded.

"I know, but I want to talk to you about Justin. He played so poorly today."

As he turned to look at her dead in the eye, Jake's chocolate orbs were like lasers straight into Dominique's heart. "He's upset, Dominique. And I think you know why." Jake turned to shake the hands of a few parents who'd gathered around him, and then before Dominique could try and reclaim the conversation, Madison, the reporter whose ex-husband had played with Jake in the NFL, was pushing up on him. Dominique watched Jake step away from the crowd so that his answers would be picked up by her microphone, noted how being the gentleman that he was, he took Madison's elbow and gently guided her over the rough spots in the field. The look of admiration in the woman's eyes as she looked up at Jake wasn't lost on Dominique, who wondered if she'd ever looked at Jake with the true admiration that until recently she'd always felt. Or had she felt it, she wondered. Had she given Jake his due, or terribly underestimated his worth?

31

Until now, Dominique hadn't realized this awful truth: weekends sucked. Even though she was pretty much caught up, she buried herself in work on Saturday and, after Anita picked up Justin, accepted a dinner invitation from a casual friend, a colleague who worked at another magazine, just to not be sitting at home alone and lonely on Saturday night.

By Sunday, she'd run out of busywork. She called Anita and found out that Faith and Aaron had taken the boys to Knotts Berry Farm and not only that, were planning to bring Justin home after their outing. This took away the one time-consuming task Dominique had to look forward to . . . driving to Inglewood to pick up her son. After doing several activities that were totally unlike her, including reading the *LA Times* online and watching a movie on Lifetime, Dominique was ready to climb the walls. It was three o'clock, and a rumbling stomach reminded her that she'd only had a bagel, an apple, and a glass of juice all day. Dominique went downstairs and looked in the fridge. Nothing there to spark her interest. She browsed through the half dozen takeout menus in one of the kitchen drawers. None of the cultures represented—from Italian to Chinese, Indian to Mexican—sounded good. *Maybe it's because I've been eating out all week,* Dominique decided. *Maybe I'll go to the store and get the makings for a nice, big, healthy salad.* The sound of Justin's voice immediately popped into her head. "Coach says there should always be something green, yellow, and orange on your plate." When it came to her son's nutrition, Dominique had tried to do better, and Tessa was a big help. Still, she'd be the first person to admit that there was still a considerable distance between herself and Suzy Homemaker.

Fifteen minutes later, Dominique pulled into the Whole Foods parking lot. She got a cart and entered the store, heading for the organic produce aisle. After placing salad fixings in her basket, she browsed the lane, picking up veggies she'd never heard of and fresh herbs which, to her knowledge, she'd never tried. After deciding on a bleu cheese dressing that would probably not meet with the approval of Justin's coach, Dominique was on her way to get croutons and a few more items when she heard her name.

"Dominique?"

She turned and saw a woman that looked vaguely familiar. "Hello."

"I'm Kathy, Travis's mom. We met a couple weeks ago when your son came over for pizza."

"Of course," Dominique replied, smiling as she wheeled her cart back to where Kathy was standing. "How are you doing?"

"Great," Kathy said. "Especially since I have the

house all to myself. Travis and his dad are in Oakland, and my parents picked up Sarah for a day at the beach. It's been so long since I've had 'me' time that I hardly know what to do!"

"So Travis went to Oakland for the Raiders game? You didn't have any qualms about letting your son take the trip?"

"Why would I, especially since his dad was invited as well?"

"Oh, your husband accompanied your son on the trip."

"Yes. Coach had eight passes to the game and all the special events, so he invited four students and one parent of each." Kathy's expression turned quizzical. "But then again, I'm sure you know this since Justin is in Oakland."

Dominique's newly found comfort zone was immediately replaced by the slightly queasy feeling that she'd endured all week. "Uh, no. Justin is at Knotts Berry Farm with my sister and her family."

"Wow. Knotts Berry is a great amusement park but I'm surprised that Justin turned down a chance to cheer for the silver and black! I even wanted to go, but with Ian being a football fanatic that decision was never up for discussion."

"Who's Ian?"

"Oh, my husband, the guy who's always yelling 'Tear it up' at the top of his lungs."

"Ah, yes. I've heard him."

"Trust me . . . *everybody's* heard him. Anyway, he's there along with three other parents and a local reporter who's doing a documentary on Coach. When it comes to men, he's one of the good ones. Isn't it incredible what he's doing for the boys?"

"Yes, it's . . . great." With each comment that Kathy so happily delivered, Dominique's spirits sank. Parents had been invited along on the trip? Was she to have been included in Jake's invite to Oakland? Dominique thought back to Jake's happy mood when he'd called her last Tuesday, asking what she and Justin would be doing the following weekend. Both of them—she *and* Justin. Suddenly, Dominique's voracious appetite escaped her. All week she'd had a niggling feeling that turning down Jake's invitation had been a huge mistake. Now . . . she was sure of it.

"I've messed up." Dominique was back at home, in the kitchen, the salad fixings that she'd purchased sitting untouched on the island. As soon as she'd gotten in the house, she'd phoned her sister, Faith.

"What? Nikki, we're in the arcade and I can barely hear you."

"I said I messed up!" Dominique yelled. "Big time!"

Faith heard the panic in Dominique's voice, a rare occurrence. "Wait a minute."

Dominique heard Faith mumble something, presumably to Aaron. Moments later, the din of the arcade receded as Faith obviously had stepped outside.

"Okay, Nikki. What's wrong?"

"Faith, I've totally misjudged Jake and I stopped Justin from going on a field trip."

"He told us."

"He did? What did he say?"

"That he was supposed to go to a Raiders game but you wouldn't let him. He was quiet last night, didn't play much with Michael at all. But he's doing better now. A couple turns on the roller coasters loosened him up."

Dominique felt herself get teary. If there was one thing she didn't like it was the thought of her son being unhappy. "This is all my fault," she said softly.

"Why didn't you let him go, Nikki?"

Dominique told Faith about Jake's conversation with Justin, of which he refused to share the details, the subsequent strain on their relationship, and Justin's comment about being Jake's son. "He called me at work, in the middle of a busy day. I told him no on the trip before giving him a chance to fully explain it. Was I wrong, Faith? I know I was wrong about the trip, and feel so badly that I deprived Justin of what I now know was an awesome opportunity. But as a mother, don't I have the right to protect my son's feelings, and to know what he and Jake talked about?"

"Tell me this, Nikki. Do you trust Jake?"

Dominique pondered the question. From the first time she'd met him, Dominique had sensed a man of good character, one who was truthful with his words and sincere in his actions. Any boy would be lucky to have him as a father. "Yes, Faith," she finally answered. "In my heart, I trust Jake."

"With that in mind, and because you asked me, I'm going to give you my truthful opinion. I think that, yes, there are some things best shared between males, that boys feel more comfortable talking about with another man. I'm sure there are secrets between Aaron and Michael that I'll never know."

"But Aaron is his father!"

"And for Justin, Jake is a father figure, someone he looks up to and respects. You may not want to hear it, Nikki, but I think you overreacted regarding whatever Justin shared with his coach. And I think that the fact that Jake wouldn't break your son's confidence, despite what I'm sure were some very persuasive arguments . . . well . . . that should speak for itself."

"What about Justin wanting Jake to be his father? You remember how upset he was when Kevin walked out?"

"Got kicked to the curb as I remember, and rightly so. Kevin was an asshole and from what you've shared about Jake, there is simply no comparison. I understand your being cautious and wanting to spare Justin's feelings but from the sounds of it, he's already quite attached to his coach. Teachers come and go from our children's lives and often leave life-long impressions that serve them well. Remember Mrs. Ricci and how I cried because I couldn't spend the summer in Maine with her and her family?"

Dominique laughed. "I remember."

"There was a part of me that probably wished she was my mom, at least for a hot minute, especially once I saw how their summer cottage sat right on the beach!" Faith smiled, then continued, her voice softer, "Perhaps looking at Jake as Justin's teacher instead of your man will change your perspective, so that you can view this as a positive experience for both of them."

"You're right, sister," Dominique replied, her own voice filled with guilt and regret. "I've been both father and mother for so long and I admit . . . it bothers me to not be in control. But Jake doesn't deserve the way I've treated him lately."

"Well, darlin', what are you going to do?"

"I've got to talk to him," Dominique said as she looked out the window onto a picture-perfect day and wishing her life resembled it. "He may not forgive me, or want to see me again after our conversation. But I've got to apologize. I owe him that."

32

Dominique yawned as she looked at her watch. It was 11:30 and she had a full, busy day tomorrow. Earlier, Aaron and Faith had dropped off Justin and after staying for only half an hour or so, had continued home to Inglewood. She'd offered to order in a pizza, but Justin had said that he wasn't hungry, that he just wanted to go to his room. So she'd gained a little info about his weekend (as exciting as pulling teeth) and then allowed him to retire to his room at eight-thirty. Her hopes that he'd gotten over being angry with her were dashed, and tomorrow she planned to have a heart-to-heart and apologize. By the time she'd left the house at ten-thirty, Justin was sound asleep. She'd set the alarm and, breaking yet another one of her rules, had risked leaving her baby home alone for the must-have meeting that night with Jake McDonald.

A car turned the corner and the headlights shone into her rearview mirror. Dominique's heartbeat quickened as she recognized Jake's SUV made visible by the streetlights. He slowed, turned into his driveway, and shut off the motor. Knowing he'd seen her car and therefore hadn't pulled into the garage, Dominique hurriedly reached for the door handle, got out of the car, and met Jake just as he was opening his car door.

"What are you doing here?" he asked as he walked to the back and retrieved his carryon.

"I need to talk to you." Jake walked to his front door and Dominique followed him. "I want to apologize for undermining your and Justin's relationship, and for becoming angry and distant because you wouldn't tell me what at the time I thought I needed to know."

They reached the front door. Jake inserted the key but turned to face Dominique before opening the door. "Couldn't you have called to tell me this?"

Dominique looked Jake squarely in the eye. "No. I wanted to tell you in person."

"Okay, you just did."

"But I want to explain."

"It's late, Dominique."

"This won't take long."

Jake looked at Dominique a long moment. He unlocked and opened the front door, then stepped back to allow Dominique to enter in front of him. He closed and locked the door, and then, after setting his carryon by the steps leading to the home's second floor, joined Dominique in the living room. She was standing in the middle of the floor, waiting to have Jake's full attention.

Jake also remained standing. He looked at Dominique and when she didn't begin talking immediately crossed his massive arms across his chest and raised an eyebrow. "Well?"

Dominique swallowed and tried to not be nervous. But she felt out of her element. She was used to being in charge, her word being law, and not being questioned. In this moment, she realized that even in relationships things mostly went her way. Justin's father, Leland, abhorred arguing and would often give in to Dominique just to shut her up. Kevin, her last partner, was more than happy to let her run things. It wasn't until later that she found out that he did so just so that he could run away with her money. But here stood someone she'd rarely encountered in her life—a man who stood his ground. And looked pretty good while doing it, she also noted.

"Can we sit down?" Her voice was soft and tentative, sounding foreign to her own ears.

Jake simply cocked his head.

Dominique cleared her throat and lifted her chin. *You are not that quiet, insecure school girl who ran from trouble. So quit acting like it!* Dominique calmly walked over to a chair, and sat.

"I've never thought of myself as controlling; it simply seems I've often been put in the position where I've had to be. I've lived this way for so long that letting go of the reins is hard, no matter the issue. Justin looks up to you, idolizes you, and that frightens me. I know it shouldn't," she hurried on when Jake would have interrupted. "But it does. When my last relationship ended, Justin's heart also got broken. He and Kevin were very close." Dominique paused to gather her thoughts. Jake watched, waited. "And then there's the confidential discussion you had with

Justin, I overreacted, Jake, and I'm sorry that I did. It was wrong of me to demand that you tell me what he'd said and then get angry at you for not breaking his confidence. That right there should have told me what kind of man you are."

"And what kind of man is that, Dominique?" Jake's stance remained formidable, but his voice had softened.

She answered simply, "A good one."

The air crackled between them.

Neither one moved.

"How was the game?" Dominique asked, after a pause.

"It was all right. Raiders lost, though."

"That probably won't make a difference to Justin. He's furious with me."

"He's a kid. He'll live."

"When it comes to my son, I haven't been able to depend on the men in his life. Guess I'm a bit overprotective, but I've had to be strong. I'm all he has."

Jake uncrossed his arms. "I understand. But you might want to consider that there are other people out here who also have your son's best interests at heart. I'm one of those people."

"I know that now."

More air, more crackling.

"So . . . are we cool? Am I forgiven?" Dominique's eyes dropped to Jake's full lips, and she instantly remembered how well he could use them. She quickly scanned his chest, arms, and large hands that now rested lightly on solid hips.

Jake watched Dominique look him over. Something stirred inside him as he watched a myriad of emotions play across her face, even as she tried to keep her expression blank. He'd had women coming at him from all angles in Oakland; but Dominique was the woman who'd occupied his thoughts. But Jake didn't know if a woman like her was ready for a man like him. If she got this upset over something as small as a conversation between him and her son, who knew what would happen if something more serious came up. He'd dealt with competition all his life on the field, and it continued as the Hurricanes' coach. Did he want to be going head-to-head and toe-to-toe with the woman in his life?

"I miss you, Jake."

Damn, you're not making this easy. But it was late and Jake was tired. Now was not the time to be making any major decisions and it was only in this moment that Jake realized what a major decision it was. If he and Dominique got back together, he'd no longer be satisfied being her live sex toy. She'd have to be ready for a relationship.

"I appreciate you coming over, Dominique," Jake said, as he turned and walked to the door. "I'll think about what you said."

She didn't want to leave, but Dominique stood and headed towards the now open door. "You sure you want me to leave?" she said, stopping to stand so close to him that she could swear she felt heat emanating from his body.

"Go home to your son, Dominique. I know you don't like to leave him home alone."

Dominique couldn't resist at least a small touch. She laid her hand on his chest. "Good-bye, Jake."

Jake watched her lips form those words and his manhood twitched. "Drive safe, baby."

A slight smile scampered across Dominique's face as she walked to her car. He hadn't said he accepted her apology, but he had called her *baby*. *Maybe I haven't messed up this good thing. Maybe there's a chance . . .*

33

The next morning, Dominique prepared to face her accuser—Justin. She showered and dressed, and after checking her appointment calendar and noting that there were no scheduled meetings until one, she texted Reggie to let him know that she'd spend the morning working from home. When she walked downstairs, Tessa and Justin were sitting at the kitchen island eating oatmeal loaded with fruit.

"Good morning, Dominique," Tessa said, rising from her chair. "Can I fix you a bowl of oatmeal?"

"No, I'll just have orange juice. But I'll get it. I need a few moments with Justin, alone."

Tessa picked up her bowl and juice and left the kitchen. Dominique poured herself a glass of orange juice and joined Justin at the counter.

She eyed her son for a moment, noting how he was maturing seemingly overnight, right before her eyes. The chubby baby face that had caused countless women to pinch his cheeks was being replaced by prominent cheekbones and a strong jawline. *I see Leland in him,* she thought with a tinge of sadness.

She wished that her ex-husband would choose to play a bigger role in his child's life and wondered if her bossiness had been part of the reason for his continued absence. Then she remembered Leland's new wife and new family and knew that, at best, she was only part of the cause.

"Good morning, Justin."

"Morning, Mom," Justin mumbled.

"I'm very sorry about not letting you go on the football trip. I was wrong, Justin. I should have let you go."

"Then why didn't you?" Large, brown, questioning eyes bore into her.

"Because sometimes mommies make mistakes and this was one of those times. I love you so much, baby, and sometimes forget that you're not a little boy anymore, that I need to loosen up. I know you're angry, and I understand. But do you think you can forgive me? Maybe a little bit?"

Justin didn't respond, just kept eating his oatmeal.

"Hey, remember that time when I'd just brought a brand-new suit home from the cleaners? It was a red Armani, with big gold buttons and bold stripes on the shoulders and cuffs. You were five years old, remember that?"

A wisp of the familiar smirk of a smile scampered across Justin's mouth before he could stifle it. "Yeah."

"Yes, Justin. The word is 'yes.'"

"Yes, I remember it."

"And what happened?"

"I got into the cleaning stuff and spilled bleach all over it."

"Ruined my fifteen-hundred-dollar suit before I could even wear it!"

"I was a little kid. I didn't know that it cost so much."

"But you did know that you weren't supposed to be in the cabinet under the sink." Justin remained silent. "And what I didn't know is that you'd figured out how to pop the child lock. By the time I discovered where you were, my beautiful designer outfit looked like a polka-dotted clown suit!"

Justin smiled. A little.

"Your grandma thought you deserved a spanking, but I blamed myself for not having a better lock on the cabinet and putting you in danger. You told me that you were sorry and what did I say?"

Justin responded softly, "That you forgave me.'"

"That's right," Dominique answered, her voice becoming soft as well. "Because no one's perfect, Justin. We all make mistakes: children and parents." Dominique reached out and rubbed her son's shoulder. "Everything I do is with your best interest at heart, Justin. It's because I love you. Do you understand?"

Justin nodded.

"So you forgive me?"

He nodded again.

"I didn't hear you," Dominique said softly, a smile in her voice.

"Yes, Mommy. I forgive you."

"Thanks, baby. Do you think I could get a hug to go along with that? I haven't had one in a while."

Justin got out of his chair, and came over to where Dominique sat. She wrapped her arms around him and held him tight, breathing in his fresh-washed scent, and rubbing her cheek against his still-smooth skin. She cherished the moment, knowing that all too soon things would change: he'd become a teenager and a rowdy peer would replace her as his best friend. And then the thought occurred to her that maybe she'd already been replaced . . . by Jake McDonald.

After Justin left for school, Dominique called her sister. "Hey, Faith."

"Good morning, sister," Faith answered. "This is a pleasant surprise. Your Monday mornings are usually jam-packed."

"Yes, well, I'm thinking that maybe I need to rethink my priorities." She paused. "I talked to Jake."

"Oh, really?"

"Yes, and I apologized to Justin *again*. I reminded him about the time he ruined my expensive suit and I forgave him."

"You should have reminded him about those doggone porno pics and how you didn't ground him until he was eighteen."

"Girl, I didn't even want to go there."

"That was probably best. What happened this time?"

"He's removed the iceberg that existed between us."

"Good. What about Jake? Any melting going on there?"

Dominique knew by Faith's inflection that hers was a question with multiple meanings. "I don't know whether Jake is still angry with me or just done with me."

"What did he say when you apologized?"

"That he appreciated me coming over and would think about what I said."

"You saw him?"

"Yes."

"I assumed you guys talked on the phone."

"No, I went over to his house; didn't want to risk him not answering my call." Dominique paused, remembering the encounter. "He looked good, Faith. I wanted to stay with him."

"Why didn't you?"

"Because I refuse to beg. I told him that I missed him. And his response was basically, 'See you later, bye.'"

"Give him time, Nikki. And a little room. You bruised his ego, sister, and you know how men can be. You took away something that is probably very important to a man like Jake . . . your trust—"

"But I do trust him!

"Maybe, but you don't trust the situation. You're so busy worrying about what might happen in the future that you're sabotaging something that's developing right now." When Dominique didn't respond, Faith continued, "You're my big sis and I've always admired you—how you go after what you want, and how strong and confident you are."

"I wasn't always, Faith."

"Yes, but very few knew it. You faked it until you made it, and when the men in your life brought disappointment you stepped up to the plate and handled your business. But sometimes it's okay to let go of some of the control. Especially when it comes to Jake, you're going to have to take off your chief hat and brush off those feminine wiles that are currently gathering dust. He sounds like a good man and you deserve to be happy."

"I am happy. I have my work."

"Your work can't keep you warm at night."

Dominique smiled. "True."

"So just go with the flow, and let things unfold. And keep me posted."

"I will, Faith. Now, tell me, how are *you* doing?"

They talked for almost an hour, and afterwards, instead of reaching for her laptop, Dominique reached for the television remote and turned on the set. Wendy Williams was on *The View*, talking about her experiences in radio and television, including her stint on *Dancing with the Stars*. Unable to totally disconnect from work for more than a few moments, Dominique reached for her phone and sent a text to Emily, the senior writer, requesting that the magazine contact Wendy's agent for a possible cover and interview. Then she sat back and listened as the ladies of *The View* fired questions at Wendy, who answered them with humor and truthfulness. Dominique remembered that Reggie had brought up Wendy's name before. Her editorial staff were probably already on it. She punched the remote and turned the channel, flipping through game shows, more talk shows, news channels, and sports. After five minutes of seeing some of her one-hundred-plus channels for the first time, Dominique deduced that those who didn't have all day to spend watching TV weren't missing much. She turned off the tube and powered up her laptop, checking e-mails and the other goings-on at *Capricious*. All seemed to be in order and though she knew she should make a move towards the office, she still didn't feel ready to step into her editor-in-chief shoes.

Dominique got up to use the bathroom. On the way there, her home phone rang.

"Who could be calling me on my home phone?" she asked aloud. Everybody who knew Dominique knew that she was at work at this time on a Monday morning. She looked at the caller ID and her frown deepened. "Mama?"

"Hey, Nikki."

"I'm surprised that you called my home phone. I'm usually at work by now."

"I know, which is why I called your office first. They put me through to Reggie, who told me you were home. Are you all right?"

"I'm fine."

"Then why are you home? Did you decide to heed my advice, take a few days off and focus on you?"

"In a way. It's been hectic both at the office and at home. I'm going in this afternoon but decided to take the morning off."

"What's going on at the house? Justin seemed fine when he came over yesterday, although now that I think of it, he was quieter than usual."

"It's nothing for you to worry about." The last thing Dominique wanted to do was upset her mother, which is why she hadn't told her about Jake. Anita was always trying to get Dominique married. If she heard there was a potential mate in the vicinity, Dominique knew she'd get no rest.

She hadn't told her about the recent disagreements with Justin either. "Your grandson is growing up," she finally said into the silence. "I'm dealing with some of what I'm sure you experienced as I entered my teens."

"You weren't so bad," Anita answered, with a chuckle in her voice. "In fact, I was glad when you came out of your shell a little bit and proved that you weren't just another big girl with an attitude."

"But at times," Dominique said, her voice sounding like the young, vulnerable woman she once was, "that's exactly who I was."

Dominique didn't remember a time when she wasn't a big girl. Her earliest memories were from the age of four, when she'd help her grandmother make lemon icebox pies in the brightly colored Alabama kitchen where she spent a good deal of her childhood. Grandma Ella always encouraged her to eat her fill and complimented her when she cleaned her plate and asked for seconds. It was the world as Dominique knew it and, except for Anita and Faith, most of the people around her were big. It wasn't until the family relocated to California that she found out that being thick wasn't considered cute and she started having a hard time because of her size. She was ten years old.

At first, Dominique didn't know how to handle these taunts, and she tried to diffuse them by becoming everybody's friend. When that didn't work, she resorted to serving up fist sandwiches to those who opened their mouths with put-downs. That solution wasn't satisfactory either. Anita wasn't trying to have her daughter in the principal's office every other week, nor was she willing to take off work to attend counseling sessions. Then one day a teacher took note of Dominique's gift of writing and encouraged her. That and a school outing helped to build her esteem and boost her confidence. She worked on the student newspaper and yearbook through junior high and high school, and even had an article published in a regional magazine. Dominique never stood a chance of being voted Most Popular, but she had a place where she felt her power. When she hung out with the people putting pen to paper to create inspirations that people read . . . she belonged. She graduated high school, got a degree in journalism, and never looked back.

Her first boyfriend was a math and science whiz who was labeled a nerd because, well, because he was. William was a year younger than Dominique. He was a senior in high school when they met at a party. She was a freshman in college who figured that to lose her virginity she'd have to take the proverbial bull by the horns. They dated off and on for three years before Dominique decided she needed a little more excitement in her life than William provided. Enter Leland, Justin's father. Where William's personality was quiet and laid back, Leland brought a bit of swagger to the mix. She was a senior in college when they met. He was an engineer, with a car, a condo, and a wicked smile. Dominique had been immediately impressed and after experiencing a type of attraction that she'd never felt with William, she and Leland hooked up. Justin came six years later, almost a year to the day after they married. By that time, Dominique had all but forgotten the taunts that used to follow the chubby brown girl with the strange accent who had moved to a new neighborhood on the West Coast. She knew she had an eye for fashion and a gift of language. She'd hung her confidence on those pegs and kept it moving.

Dominique and Anita's conversation drifted from reminiscing about old times to the goings-on in her mother's neighborhood and at the church that Anita attended. After dodging her mother's offer to "set her up with a nice deacon," Dominique looked at her watch, realized it was time to get to the office, and ended the call.

On her way to *Capricious,* she continued to reflect over her life and at the fact that work had often been the balm that soothed and covered personal sorrows: low self-esteem issues brought on by weight, not being considered popular or pretty, and, Dominique realized in her later years, not having a father figure to set the example for how a man should treat her.

As she pulled into her reserved parking spot at *Capricious* magazine's offices Dominique had a thought: Maybe God was sending her someone to show her how it was done. Someone named Jake.

34

Jake left Middleton Prep's main building and headed for the football field. Preoccupied with what had been offered during this impromptu meeting with the principal, he didn't notice the admiring glances from female peers and moms in the parking lot waiting to pick up their kids. *A five year contract? At double the salary?* That's what he'd been offered to remain at Middleton as Athletic Director, along with other perks and incentives. The program responsible for the football team's undefeated record was obviously something the school wanted to see continue. As he neared his office on the side of the stadium, he pulled out his phone to call Johnny. It was time for a pow-wow. But just as he prepared to flip through the phone list for his twin brother's name, he heard voices coming from the locker room, which was next door to his office. He looked at his watch and reached for the door. School wasn't officially out for another ten minutes so whoever was in here was playing hooky.

Jake eased open the door and quietly stepped

inside the room made cool by cement walls. No one was in the main area; the voices were coming from the area where practice gear was kept in locked cages. He took a couple more steps and was just about to bust the class-skipping students when he recognized the voices.

"It sucked that they lost." Jake listened as Travis discussed what wasn't supposed to be shared with anyone who'd not been on the trip. "Especially to the Chiefs."

In spite of the situation, Jake smirked at the comment. The Kansas City Chiefs were long time Raider rivals, so of course the boys hated them.

"Yeah, but how was it being in the stadium? Who did you meet on the team? Man, I'm still so mad that I didn't get to go. I bet it was so cool."

Jake's heart clenched at the somberness in Justin's tone, and his anger at Dominique was rekindled. As far as he was concerned, anyone who knew Justin knew that he should have been on that trip, including his mother. *No,* especially *her.* A vision from the other night when Dominique sat in his living room flashed in his mind. A vision of vulnerable yet determined loveliness. *Are we cool. Am I forgiven?* Jake had yet to answer Dominique's question, but he intended to, and soon.

"The guys were cool," Jake heard Travis continue. "And they are huge, like Coach. We got to take pictures with them and everything."

"Man, I'm so jealous."

Jake rounded the corner to where Travis and Justin stood just as several other teammates entered the locker room. "You boys are a bit early for practice, don't you think?"

"We finished our quiz early, Coach," Travis explained. "Miss Banks excused us."

"Oh, really? Well, I'm going to speak with Miss Banks. Your story better check out or I might be looking at a couple of Saturday morning bench warmers."

Justin's eyes widened at the thought of not seeing action on game day. "She said we could leave, Coach, promise!"

Jake nodded, thankful for the change in Justin's demeanor, even though his disappointment had been replaced by fear. "All right, then. Let's get moving. Oh, and Travis?"

"Yes, Coach?"

"Make sure you see me once practice is over."

Travis's head dropped. Jake noticed the action and understood why: Travis knew that Jake had heard him talking about the trip to the Raiders' game and knew he was in trouble.

Ninety sweaty minutes later, the boys trudged off the field. Jake talked to Travis, and much to the boy's surprise, told him that while it was never okay to disobey rules, he understood why Travis had felt the need to confide in Justin, one of his best friends. As a relieved Travis raced away, Jake noticed Justin ambling toward him with a troubled look once again marring his handsome countenance.

"Hey buddy," Jake said as Justin approached. "You all right?"

Justin shrugged, continuing into the locker room. Jake followed him there.

"I heard you and Travis discussing yesterday's game."

Justin looked up, but said nothing.

"The defense didn't hold the line," Jake continued, pointedly referring to the game and not the trip. That's why Oakland lost."

"I didn't see the game. We were at Knott's Berry Farm."

"Did you have fun?"

"It was all right."

"Justin, you know that I wanted you to be there, right? In Oakland, at the game?"

"Yeah, and my stupid mother messed it up for me so I couldn't go!"

Jake came around the bench that separated them and clinched a towel in his fist. "Don't you ever refer to your mother as stupid, or use any other demeaning description, understood?"

Justin was surprised at Jake's reaction and stepped back a bit. "But she apologized this morning and admitted that she should have let me take the trip!"

"Justin, let me tell you something. Under the circumstances, your mother was doing the best she could. She loves you, and would do any and everything to protect you. That's all she was thinking about when she decided against your coming with us." When Justin continued to sulk in silence, Jake added, "Dominique is a good woman, Justin. And you might not understand it now but everything that she does . . . she does for you."

"That's what she said," Justin said as he continued to pout.

Jake smiled. "You remind me a lot of myself at your age and Dominique reminds me of my mother."

This statement got Justin's attention. "She does?" He listened while continuing to place his school clothes in his backpack.

"You know I grew up without a dad, right?"

Justin nodded, remembering the speech that Coach had delivered shortly after their first home game, when he'd told the players a bit about himself, and how his mother's firm guiding hand and his love of sports kept him out of trouble.

"After my father died, my mother had her hands full raising four boisterous boys. She had to be strong to handle us, and often made us do things that I would rather not have done—my homework, for instance, and cooking."

"But you're a good cook!"

"And that's because my mother forced me into the kitchen. I didn't like it at first, thought cooking was for girls. If Mama hadn't put her foot down, I may never have discovered how much I enjoy it."

Justin chewed on his bottom lip as he pondered Jake's words. He followed Jake out of the locker room and across the field toward the parking lot. "Do you like my mom?"

Jake was taken aback by the question. "Of course; I like all of my players' parents."

"Not like that," Justin countered, shifting his weight from one foot to the other. "I mean *like* her like her."

He thought about making light of the question, but upon taking in the vulnerable look in Justin's eyes, Jake decided on a more serious, yet still light approach. He stopped and turned to Justin. "Would you like me to *like her like her?*"

Justin shrugged, even as he dropped his head to hide a grin. "I dunno." Pause. "I guess so." He kicked a clod of dirt across the grassy field. "Do you think she's pretty?"

"Yes."

Justin squinted up at Jake. "I think she likes you."

Jake worked to keep his voice casual. "Why's that?"

"I heard her talk about you to Aunt Faith."

What did she say? You shouldn't be eavesdropping, is what he thought. And then, because he couldn't resist, asked, "What did she say?"

"That y'all went to dinner and stuff. And she said you look good, too!"

"You really shouldn't be listening to your mother's conversations," Jake admonished, even as the ray of brightness that burst forth in his heart competed with the sun shining overhead. "That isn't polite."

"I know," Justin admitted. "But I made you happy, huh?"

Jake placed a hand on Justin's shoulder as they reached the edge of the field. His answer was simple. "Yes."

35

Moments later, Justin caught up to and chatted with a few of the other boys as they reached the parking lot. Once there, they said their good-byes and walked to whoever waited to pick them up. Justin scanned the cars for Tessa's silver Mazda. His face contorted in surprise and confusion when he saw his mother's Mercedes instead.

"Mom," he said after racing to the car and jerking open the door, "what are you doing here?"

"Hello to you too, darlin'."

"Hi, Mom." Justin threw his gear in the backseat and climbed into the car. "What are you doing here?"

"Buckle your seatbelt," Dominique said as she started the car and navigated out of the parking lot. "I was able to leave work early today and thought it would be nice for you and I to hang out tonight . . . just the two of us."

"Where are we going to eat?"

"I'm fixing dinner."

Justin looked at Dominique with wide eyes. "You?"

"Ha! Boy, don't sound so incredulous. I've worked my way around the kitchen a time or two."

"Yeah, but . . ."

Dominique's brow arched. "But what?"

"Never mind." Justin looked out the window for a moment and then asked, "What are we having?"

"Taco salad."

"Yum, Mom. That sounds good!"

"It will be delicious, and you can help me make it if you'd like."

"Yeah, like Coach Mac!"

"The word is yes, Justin, not yeah."

"Yeah, okay. I mean, yes." Justin giggled and then continued without skipping a beat. "You know what Coach Mac did in practice today?"

"No, but I have a feeling you're going to tell me."

And for the next ten minutes, Justin did just that—rattling nonstop about plays and team members and his beloved coach. Dominique listened and laughed, glad to see that Mr. Sulky had left the building and the affable, chattering love of her life was back in town.

Later, Dominique breathed a sigh of satisfaction as she entered the master suite. She and Justin had spent the entire afternoon and evening together. Before going home, they'd stopped by the grocer and then by Justin's favorite ice-cream store, where he readily ignored his coach's healthy eating rhetoric for a quart of his favorite vanilla ice cream loaded with chunks of real candy bars. Using the salad fixings that had gone uneaten the day before, Dominique had impressed her son with the ground turkey–based taco salad she'd prepared. He hadn't minded at all that the seasonings were from a package and the sauce was from a jar. "It's good, Mom," he'd said simply after the first bite. Dominique's heart had bloomed with joy. After helping Justin with his homework, something that Tessa normally did, he and Dominique had danced with Michael Jackson on the Wii and laughed more than they had in years. And then, in the quiet of his bedroom with him all tucked in, she'd begun "the conversation."

"Honey, I want to talk with you about something." Justin turned to Dominique with questioning eyes. "It's about the comment you made the other day when you were angry. About wishing that Jake was your dad."

"I'm sorry, Mom. I—"

"It's okay, Justin. You don't have to apologize; especially if that is really how you feel."

Silence.

Dominique's voice was low, soft. "Is it?" Still no answer. "Do you think about how things might be if Jake were your father?"

Justin's nod was almost imperceptible. "Travis and his dad are always doing things: going fishing, golfing, stuff like that. And so do some of my other friends with dads in the house."

"You do those types of things with Michael and Uncle Aaron."

"Yeah, but it's not the same."

Dominique sighed softly. "I know." And then, "Your father called yesterday. How would you like to spend Thanksgiving in Dallas?"

Justin shrugged.

"You could spend time with your brother and sister, get to know them better?"

Justin snorted. "It doesn't even feel like they're my family. Leland Clark is more like a stranger on the street."

"Leland?" Dominique repeated. "Don't you mean *Dad*?" While she agreed with her son, she would not allow him to be disrespectful.

"Travis said he wasn't a dad, he was a sperm donor."

Dominique inwardly cringed as she answered, "Sounds like Travis has a lot to say."

"But he knows!"

"How?"

"Because Ian, the guy who comes to the games?"

"Yes, Kathy's husband."

"Uh huh. He's not Travis's biological father. But Ian adopted him when Travis was like one year old. So when Travis asked about his real dad, they say that Ian was his real dad and that the other man was just a sperm donor."

Dominique simply nodded her understanding. There was nothing she could add to the mouthful of wisdom her son had just spouted, courtesy of Travis and his clan. "Baby," she said, switching the subject after a beat. "I can understand why you admire Jake, and even why you want to be like him. But please try not to get too attached. Soon, you'll leave Middleton Prep and enter junior high. There will be other coaches, other teachers."

"Not like Coach Mac."

"Maybe not. But just remember that some relationships are not meant to last forever. I don't want you to get hurt."

"Like last time, with Kevin?"

Dominique nodded. "Like last time." This time it was Justin who nodded, seemingly with an understanding that belied his young years. "So will you promise to remember what Mommy is saying, and not expect too much from Coach Mac? Because the truth of the matter, Justin, is that no matter how we feel about it you already have a father and his name is Leland Clark. Not Jake. I want you to stay clear on that. Okay?"

"Okay," Justin whispered.

"I'll speak with Leland about your spending more time with him. Okay?"

Justin nodded.

Dominique leaned over and kissed Justin's forehead. "I love you, baby. And just for the record, I'm glad that Jake McDonald is your coach. He's a good man to look up to."

"So he can be like . . . my hero?"

Dominique smiled. "Yes, baby, he can be your hero." *And maybe mine, too.*

The phone rang, and Dominique started. Her first thought was Jake and she eagerly reached for the phone. She'd been thinking of him all day.

Looking at the caller ID, her spirits sank. "Hey, Reggie."

"Don't sound so down, Miss Dom. This call isn't work-related."

"That's okay. What's up?"

"That's what I'm calling to find out. Are you okay?"

"I'm fine, why?"

"You weren't yourself today. You came in at noon and then left at four. I don't mean to be nosy—no, wait, yes I do. But I'm concerned, too."

"I appreciate that, Reggie. I'm fine. Just decided to take advantage of a rare day not filled with meetings to spend more time with Justin."

"Aw, you put your mommy hat on."

Dominique smiled. "Yes, I did and I plan to do it more often. He's entering his formative years and I need to pay attention and step up my parenting game."

"Well, know I'm here to help pick up the slack. And while you're busy taking care of your son and the magazine, don't forget to take care of yourself."

"Thanks, Reggie. See you tomorrow."

Dominique hung up the phone and walked to her closet. Reggie's comment had once again placed Jake front and center in her mind. It was all she could do not to call him. But Faith had been right. When it came to dealing with Jake, she needed to check her controlling nature and let him take the lead. She'd just finished changing into a nightgown and was heading into the bathroom when her cell phone rang again.

That's probably Faith. She said she'd call me later. Dominique and her sister had always been close but Faith's marriage and Dominique's career had made in-depth visits and phone calls less and less frequent. Dominique was glad that they were communicating more, and made a mental note to schedule more time with Faith and her family.

Jake! Dominique took a deep breath before answering the call. "Hello."

"I accept."

"Excuse me?"

"Your apology," Jake said, his voice low and sexy. "I accept it."

Dominique smiled, even as a squiggle of heat hit her nana and spread out in all directions. "Thanks, Jake. I'm glad. I've gotten your forgiveness, Justin is back to his chatty self, my life is almost back to . . ." Belatedly, Dominique realized what could be implied by what she was about to say.

"Normal? Is that what you were going to say?"

"Yes," Dominique answered, her voice low and soft.

"So are you saying that your life isn't normal without me in it?"

Dominique walked the short distance to her bed and sank down. In the seconds it took to do so, she decided to throw caution to the wind and acknowledge the feelings she had for Jake, to stop acting like all he was to her was a piece of meat. In the week she'd been without him, she'd realized that he was so much more.

"Like I said last night, I miss you, Jake. I didn't realize how much I'd grown accustomed to our regular chats and . . ."

"Regular sex?"

"Yes." Dominique squirmed, the thought of what she missed and how much she wanted it causing her heartbeat to increase and her mouth to go dry. She reached for the glass of water that sat on her night-stand.

"Baby?"

"I'm here. I was just taking a drink."

"Have I driven my baby to drinking?"

"Ha! *Almost.* Only water, Mr. McDonald." She paused for a moment, trying to figure how best to put her feelings into words. "You know, Jake, I haven't always been the strong, confident woman you met. I didn't have an easy time of it when I was younger. I was always a big girl and when we moved from Alabama to Los Angeles, I became the country girl as well. Like all young females, I wanted to belong and when the clique on the block deemed me not good enough, that left a scar."

"What happened to change things?" he asked.

"My teachers," Dominique readily replied. "Thank God I was smart. They recognized that and were also aware of my challenges in adapting to a new environment. One teacher in particular, Mrs. Calvin, noticed that I had a flair for writing and that I liked clothes. She took the class on an outing to the Los Angeles County Museum of Art. There was an exhibit on fashion in the 1800s, when buxom women with curvy, full figures were all the rage. I think I stood a little taller after that visit, which came not too long after I'd read a magazine article about Nell Carter and Jennifer Holliday. I saw beautiful, successful women who were my size and larger. I think that's when the seed for *Capricious* was planted, subconsciously anyway."

"And then you became a force to be reckoned with."

"Not right away," Dominique replied. "I dealt with

my share of fad diets and squeezing myself into various contraptions trying to look thin. And then I met Leland, who was the first person besides my family who made me feel beautiful just like I was."

"Is that why you married him?"

"I loved Leland, but I think we were too young to get married. It wasn't until after the 'I dos' that I realized how different we truly are. And then it seemed that the more successful I became, the more resentful he felt. My professional life is where my confidence flourished and when Leland didn't think I needed him anymore . . . he found someone who did."

"That still doesn't excuse him abandoning his child."

"You're right, it doesn't. He's remarried with two children by his present wife. She discourages his continued involvement with Justin. He was only three years old when Leland left, but he still misses his father. Especially after my last relationship ended."

"With the asshole who stole from you, right?"

"Despite his ulterior motives where I was concerned, I believe Kevin genuinely cared for Justin. He spent a lot of time with him: playing ball, video games, stuff like that. Justin was crazy about him and was affected by our breakup. That's when I vowed to never again put him in that position . . . to get attached to someone only for them to leave."

"Is that what you think will always happen, Nick? That a man will always leave you?"

"That's the way it's been so far."

"That's because you were with senseless jerks!"

Dominique warmed at the vehemence she heard

in Jake's voice. It had been a long time since she'd felt like a man was truly on her side. "I talked to Justin about his comment on your being his father."

"And?"

"And I reminded him that he already has a dad."

"Sounds like you need to remind the dad that he has a son."

"Point well taken. I'm working on that. In the meantime, we've decided that you can be Justin's hero."

"Is that so?" Jake said, his voice dropping low, dripping with sexuality.

"Yes," Dominique replied. "I told him that you were a good man to look up to."

"You told him correctly, baby. There are men out here who are loving, loyal, and stand by their word."

Dominique stretched out, running her hand back and forth across her smooth, silk comforter. "Do you know anybody like that?"

"Yes," Jake answered, his voice barely a whisper. "Do you?"

36

Dominique reached her office and as soon as she'd settled behind the desk, she called Reggie. "Are you at the coffee shop?" she asked, once he'd answered.

"You know I am."

"Glad I caught you. Can you add a double shot of espresso to my latte?"

"Whoa, Miss Dom. Sounds like somebody had a late night."

"It's not what you think."

"Whatever you say." Reggie sang in a voice that suggested things were exactly as he imagined. "Two shots and a latte coming up!"

Dominique rubbed her eyes and tried to shake the cobwebs out of her head. She and Jake had talked until two in the morning, and she'd enjoyed every minute of it. He'd opened up to her about the intimate details of his life: his father, marriage to Robin, and how her death had affected him, and how his own sense of mortality was never far from his thoughts. Later, Dominique would realize that it was in the wee hours of this very morning, as he exposed his fears and vulnerability, that she fell in love with him.

Twenty minutes later, Reggie switched into Dominique's office. Today he wore tight-fighting cream-colored slacks, a beige sweater, and three-inch heels. She looked up as he approached her desk and thought that no man should look prettier than a woman.

"Here you go, Miss Dom."

"Thanks, Reggie. Check your Outlook; I've sent you a list of things that need to be done today—and oh, don't forget to call the Body By Night gym and remind Night and D'Andra that their shoot is scheduled for next week."

"Ooh, I see Miss Dom doesn't kiss and tell."

Dominique knew exactly what Reggie was talking about. "Okay, so I was up late last night. But," she hurried on as Reggie's eyes sparkled and he fairly preened before her, "all we did was talk. On the phone. It was nice actually," Dominique continued, after taking a sip of her extrastrong brew. "Jake is a good listener."

"Child, I can think of better attributes on him than his ear!"

"Ha! Reggie, you have a one-track mind."

Reggie picked up his coffee and headed for the door. He stopped just inside the office, his hand on the knob. "Is there anything wrong with that?"

Dominique laughed and moments later was buried in work. The day passed quickly and as she handled one issue after another she realized what a blessing the previous day had been. *How can I do it?* she wondered, as she browsed through potential topics for the *Capricious* issue that was due to hit the newsstands in five months. *How can I stay on top of everything here, and still carve out time for a personal life?*

That question was put on hold as Dominique prepared for her luncheon meeting with François Deux. He had always gotten on her nerves but she felt his timing right now was particularly annoying. In the past two years, she'd only had to deal with his bitchiness in person three times. And now he was requesting another meeting after seeing her just a few weeks ago? *What can he possibly want now?*

Fifteen minutes into their lunch, she found out.

"Dominique, the point of this meeting is quite simple. *Capricious* has to take everything to the next level."

Dominique prided herself on being able to maintain a straight, interested face when all she wanted to do was barf. She was normally a sucker for an accent, and François's whiny voice and puckered pronunciations of *o*'s and *oo*'s reminded her of Dr. Oz on *Oprah,* when he'd puckered his mouth and said it resembled an anus. François was an asshole all right.

"François," she began, in the calm voice she would use to tell Justin his boo-boo would heal, "I am well aware that there is a competitor on the horizon. If you'll remember, this was mentioned at our last meeting. I am confident in what we have here: solid writers, great features, interesting subjects, and a loyal reader base. The numbers for *Capricious* are higher than they've ever been. Last year, our circulation increased 10 percent. We're not yet in the league of *Glamour* and *Cosmopolitan,* but considering how long we've been out here, we're strongly holding our own.

We're getting A-list interviews, our advertisers are solid. Everyone in the industry knows we're one to watch." Dominique paused, and took another calming breath. "To help me be on the same page with you, can you be more specific about this next level?"

"Are you questioning my belief that this magazine can become *much* more than it is now, that we are nowhere near where we should be?"

"Of course not. I—"

"Need I remind you that as editor-in-chief of *Capricious* magazine, it is your sole responsibility to oversee not only its success with the readers but the satisfaction of investors and of the board?" He pressed thin lips together and raised an eyebrow as he pierced Dominique with a questioning look. She remained silent. "If you don't think you can do that, well, I know several people who can."

By the time the luncheon was over, Dominique thought that the other restaurant patrons may be able to see smoke coming out of her ears. She was livid. But she knew what François's anger was about and new competition had nothing to do with it. Ever since the board and investors had chosen her name suggestion, *Capricious,* over his, *Grand,* he'd been upset. Dominique had thought at the time, *Are you serious?* Who'd ever know that a magazine called *Grand* was a fashion rag catering to the plus-size community? She wasn't the one who'd called the idea stupid. That had been one of the other investors, a former model turned tycoon named Mirabelle. But Dominique had agreed with her. All these years later and François was obviously still smarting. As far as she was concerned, he needed to pull up his big boy britches and leave her the hell alone. She'd poured blood, sweat, and tears into this company. This was her baby and she wasn't going anywhere!

Thirty minutes after leaving the restaurant, the frown hadn't left Dominique's face. She wheeled into her parking lot and strode purposely to the elevator. "Get me the sales figures for the last twelve months," she barked at Reggie as soon as she reached the executive offices. "And the last six issues of the magazine." She stormed past him and slammed her office door.

Dominique reached her desk and put her head in her hands. Just when she decides to loosen her professional reins and focus more on her personal life, here comes this asshole, trying to back her into a corner. Dominique knew that she was good at what she did. But she also knew that the magazine industry and the fashion world could be cutthroat. She'd have to dot every *i* and cross every *t* to make sure every argument that she may need in the coming weeks and months was sound.

Reggie gave a soft knock and then entered. He bore a look of concern as he placed the items Dominique had requested on her desk. "Want to talk about it?" he asked.

Dominique sighed. "Sit down." She gave him the short version of what had transpired at the luncheon.

"That bastard," Reggie said, a scowl accompanying this declaration. "You work your butt off for this company. *Capricious* can stand toe-to-toe with any magazine out there. And Doo-doo Deux knows that!"

"It doesn't matter," Dominique answered, shaking her head. "He's out for blood, and I'm going to make sure that it's not mine that gets splattered across the pages. Do I have any meetings this afternoon?"

Reggie shook his head. "But you do have that premiere tonight."

"Oh, shoot. I forgot all about that. Reggie, would you like my tickets? I'm really not feeling the red carpet right now."

Reggie clapped his hands together in glee. "Girl, you know I would! Oh my gosh, but it starts at 6:30. That only gives me five hours to plan what I'm going to wear. Ooh, Quinn is going to be over the moon." Reggie jumped up, walked over, and gave Dominique a big hug. "Don't let them see you sweat, Miss Dom. You've got this."

"Thanks, Reggie. Have fun tonight." Reggie started toward the door, busy texting away as he walked. "Oh, and unless it's an emergency, hold my calls for the remainder of the afternoon."

For the next two hours, Dominique buried herself in more facts and figures. She buzzed Reggie several times, having him bring in various reports on the competition, trends in the industry, and the like. For the most part, she felt satisfied with the information she'd have to present in any forthcoming meetings on her performance. But there were a couple of potentially problematic areas. Dominique sighed. *This is going to be a long night.*

Dominique reached for the phone. "Tessa, it's me. Can you stay a few extra hours? I'm going to be working late."

"No problem, Dominique."

"Thank you." Before she'd replaced the office phone on its receiver, her cell phone rang. "Hello?"

"Hey, baby. It's me."

"Hey, Jake."

Jake immediately sensed tension in Dominique's voice. "Whoa. What's wrong?"

Dominique gave him a brief rundown of her day.

"Then what I've planned is right on time."

"What's that?" Dominique asked, her voice wary.

"I'll tell you tonight . . . at dinner."

"Ooh, baby, that sounds great. But I have to work late. I just called Tessa so she could stay with Justin."

There was a pause before Jake replied, "Okay." And then he added, "Last night you said you were going to start focusing more on yourself and your family."

"That was before today's luncheon!"

"So now the workaholic is back, with no thoughts to what happens outside of the office?"

"That's not fair, Jake. My career may be at stake here," Dominique said, continuing when Jake didn't respond. "This situation is temporary. There is another meeting with the investors soon and Solveig Ericksson, a good friend of mine who is a supporter and also on the board, will be there. She knows exactly what François is up to and, believe me, neither one of us is planning for his shenanigans to succeed."

"All right, then. I'll talk to you later."

"Okay." Dominique replied, though she didn't think things were okay at all.

37

Three hours later and Dominique was still at her desk. She felt a little better having talked with Solveig in Stockholm to come up with a loose game plan on how to proceed in the coming months. But now she felt even more pressure for the upcoming issues to be flawless. She spent the next thirty minutes talking to the photographer who was scheduled to do the Body By Night shoot the following day, then continued checking the layouts for the upcoming issue.

Her phone rang. Dominique looked at her watch. It was 7:00 PM. *Who's calling the office line at this hour?*

"Dominique Clark."

"Miss Clark, it's Peter." Peter was one of the building's evening security guards.

"Oh hi, Peter."

"You have a visitor."

Dominique's brow rose. "I do?"

"Yes. His name is Jake McDonald. He says that you know him."

Dominique smiled as she relaxed. "Yes, Peter. I do. Please send him up."

"Okay, ma'am."

Dominique walked to the main reception area and unlocked the outer door. Seconds later the elevator dinged, indicating a stop on their floor. Jake walked out, looking like six feet five inches of sexy and smelling the same. She caught a hint of his woodsy cologne as he hugged her, followed by the smell of something delicious.

"Um, what's that smell?"

Jake broke their embrace. "I figured you might be hungry. Hope you like Greek."

"Sounds delicious. Let's go to the dining room."

Jake and Dominique engaged in small talk while enjoying moussaka, lamb skewers, lemon potatoes, and tapenade. She was glad for the company.

"Thanks, baby," Dominique said as she finished the last of her tea. "This was such a thoughtful thing to do, and much better than the Chinese takeout I'd planned to order."

"I'm glad you enjoyed it."

Dominique rested her chin on her hand and peered at him. "You really are special, you know that?"

"That's what I've been trying to tell you, woman!"

They laughed.

Jake leaned forward, kissed Dominique on the lips. "And there's more."

"Oh?" Dominique's nipples hardened of their own accord. At the thought of his "more," her vaginal walls contracted and images of their last time together wafted before her eyes.

"Yes." The look of pure desire in her eyes caused

Jake's dick to twitch and begin to harden. He was thinking about that, too, but later, when he could give her body the type of treatment it deserved. He reached into his pocket and pulled out an envelope. "These."

Curiosity replaced disappointment as Dominique reached for the envelope. "What's this?" She reached inside the unsealed envelope and removed the contents. Her eyes widened. "Tickets to the Raiders' game?"

"I always have access to Raiders tickets. Just haven't taken advantage of it much in the past few years. But with Justin so disappointed over not being able to go last week, I thought that we could take in Sunday's game . . . just the three of us."

"Oh." Dominique's smile faded. "This Sunday."

"Yes, but you don't have to worry about a thing. A friend of mine is flying up to the game in his private plane. He invited us to join him. We'll leave Saturday evening and return Sunday, right after the game. Justin's going to be so excited . . . I can't wait to tell him!" When he saw that Dominique didn't share his enthusiasm, his smile faded. "What is it, Nick?"

"Jake, I'd love to go, but with this new development and my job potentially being on the line . . . I just can't. But Justin can," she hurried on, placing the tickets back in the envelope and sliding it over near Jake's hand. "You two can go, have a great time, and then fill me in on the details when you come back."

"This trip wasn't going to just be about me and Justin, baby. It was going to be about us, and where this attraction we have for each other is going." He waited for Dominique to respond. She didn't. "But I see how it is." Jake placed the envelope back in his pocket and stood. "Your work comes first."

"That's not fair!" Dominique came around the table and placed her arms around Jake's waist. "I care for you, Jake," she whispered into his chest. "And I want to keep seeing you." She tilted her head back to see his expression. His expression was unreadable, but he finally placed his arms around her shoulders and hugged her to him. "You feel good." Dominique tilted her head once again, and placed her lips along Jake's strong jaw line. "Maybe I can see you later?" No response. "Jake?" she whispered, lifting her head to place her lips against his.

The warmth of her breath was Jake's undoing. He opened his mouth, forced his tongue into hers and crushed her ample breasts against his hard chest. Dominique moaned, and he slanted his mouth over hers to deepen the kiss, running his hands over the silky fabric of her dress, wanting her out of it, wanting to be inside of her. Dominique felt his arousal and ran her hand along the hardened shaft. The throbbing at her core grew more prominent, the wetness between her thighs evidence of her raw desire.

Jake broke the kiss. "Dominique, stop." He took her arms from around him, his breath coming in quick, short spurts. "I want you, baby, but not like this. Not here, like a wham, bam, thank you, ma'am."

"Tessa is watching Justin. Can I come over when I'm done here?" In a flash, Dominique was transported back nineteen years ago, when she was in college and TLC was all the rage. It was all she could do not to scream their hook: "I ain't 2 proud 2 beg."

Fortunately, she didn't have to. Jake stepped up to

her, and placed a kiss on her forehead. "All right.
I'll see you then." They left the dining room and
walked in silence to the elevator. "I enjoyed the
baklava," Jake said, just before the elevator doors
closed. "But I have a taste for something sweeter. . . ."

38

Dominique stood over the table working with the order of interviews and pictures for an upcoming issue. She was satisfied with the Kirstie Alley interview and the accompanying photos. She studied the pictures carefully and felt the one of Kirstie relaxing in her Southern California home should be the centerfold. She went back and forth on what should precede this article and which advertisements should frame it. She liked the idea of the plus-size fashion spread from an up-and-coming designer dedicated to making fabulous clothes for big girls. *Move over, Lane Bryant. Get out of the way, Ashley!* Dominique loved the form-flattering separates the young Asian designer (who was all of a size 2) had created. She especially loved that he didn't try to hide full figures, but rather accentuated them. "Yes. This should definitely follow the lead article." She typed notes on her iPad and looked at the next set of pages. But there it was again. Thoughts of Jake, and the night that awaited her. His parting words had plagued her for the last two hours. It was a miracle that more work had gotten done. But covering her back by focusing on the magazine's future direction had put her behind in her regular duties and, as it was, she saw herself working through the weekend.

"Come on, Dominique," she told herself. "Keep it together." But Jake's words kept floating back into her mind. *I figured you might be hungry.* Dominique redoubled her efforts to concentrate on the model shots, and what sequence would best highlight the designer's talents. *I want you, baby. But not like this.*

Dominique shut her eyes, trying in vain to block out the message of her heart—the message that told her to leave now and go to her beloved. She looked at her watch. Only 9:00, barely an hour since Jake had left the office. "This photo spread is fabulous," she said aloud, in an attempt to infuse enthusiasm into what she least felt like doing right now. She moved around a grouping of four pictures and placed next to it an ad for Bulgari watches. *I have a taste for something sweeter . . . you.*

Dominique almost moaned aloud at the thought, and as it were, she felt a shiver run down her spine. Adding to her lack of concentration was her text message indicator going off on her desk. She thought she'd be home by now, and knew Tessa was probably wondering if she should prepare to spend the night.

But the message wasn't from Tessa.

It was from Jake.

My tongue. Your pussy.

That was it. Stick a fork in it because Dominique was done. She didn't even bother with her usual routine—stacking the mock-up pages to the left of the table and tidying up her desk. She didn't even stop to text back an answer. She simply walked over to her desk, turned off her computer, grabbed her briefcase and purse, and was gone.

Jake turned off the shower spigots. He stepped from the oversized stall, reached for a towel, and wrapped it around his waist. He tried not to feel down, but at almost ten PM, he felt that he had to face the facts. Dominique was not coming over. Work came first.

He eyed himself in the mirror a moment before deciding to go downstairs and grab a beer. He'd brought home the video from the previous Saturday's game and figured there were a few tricks for his team he could pull from his sleeve if he continued watching it. The opponent's quarterback was good, but even the best player had his weakness. Jake had spotted one of them—his inability to run well from side to side. Jake determined that there were probably more where that came from.

There was something else on his mind—an offer that had come to him last week. A school in Texas was waving big bucks in his face to come and direct their athletic department. Middleton Prep's offer notwithstanding, when it came to being involved in elementary through high school football, Texas was the state where you wanted to be. The Lone Stars took their pigskin seriously and when it came to salary, they'd basically said he could name his price. Part of his hesitation to even considering the offer had been his love for Middleton Prep and the Hurricanes in general, and his growing feelings for Justin and Dominique in particular. *But maybe I should consider putting my work first for a change.* Jake reached into the fridge, grabbed a beer, unscrewed the top, and leaned against the counter as he took a long, refreshing drink. Many of his family lived near where he'd be working. His twin, Johnny, lived in Baton Rouge; Mike lived in Atlanta; and Harold lived in Birmingham, not too far from where they'd all grown up and where his mother, Bernadette, still lived. He'd been on the West Coast for over twenty years. *Maybe it's time for me to move closer to home.*

The ringing doorbell pierced his thoughts. Jake knew it could only be one person. He strode purposefully to the front door.

"Sorry I'm late," Dominique murmured.

Jake's eyes narrowed as she leaned provocatively against the jamb. He saw her eyes move from his face to his groin and back again. "Get in here." Jake pulled her inside the door and into his arms, closing the door with his foot. He seared her mouth with his, thrusting his tongue into her warmth, taking her breath away.

"Wow, that's some greeting," she said when they came up for air.

A confident, predatory look came across Jake's face. "There's more where that came from. Would you like something to drink? Water, a glass of wine?"

"A glass of wine sounds nice." Dominique followed Jake into the kitchen.

He reached into the cabinet and pulled out a wineglass, and then into the fridge for a cold bottle of chardonnay. "Did you finish up with everything?"

he asked, taking a corkscrew and making quick work of opening the bottle.

"We're never done," Dominique answered. "But I was able to cross a couple more things off my to-do list."

"Let's take our drinks to the bedroom." Jake spoke with authority, and without waiting for an answer began walking toward the stairs. As he mounted them, Dominique took in his strong calves, thick thighs, and again, that ass. Her legs faltered for a moment, as she imagined how Jake would use those long, strong legs—all three of them—in just a few minutes. She took a deep breath, and tried to get ahold of herself. But all she could think of was Jake getting ahold of her.

They entered Jake's master bedroom. With one hand, he took another swig of his beer. With the other, he dropped the towel.

"Take off your clothes."

His eyes were dark, filled with desire. His stance was strong, with legs apart, his burgeoning soldier standing at full attention, ready to gain entry.

Dominique took another sip of wine and then placed it on the table beside her. With her eyes locked on Jake's, she reached for the large buttons that decorated the front of her silk, floral-print dress. She'd meant to take her time, but found herself fumbling to hurriedly rid herself of the fabric. She watched Jake's eyes darken even further, if that were possible, as she stood in her custom-made lace see-through bra and hip-hugging panties—in hot, bright pink. It looked as if one good breath and her girls would spill out of their confines. The panties clung possessively to her generous hips, caressing a stomach that made no apologies for its folds and jiggles. She reached behind her and undid the bra clasp.

Later, she would swear Jake reached her before the lacy number hit the floor. He walked them back to the bed and directed Dominique down on it. All conversation ceased. His focus was singular. He went straight for Dominique's dark, hardened nipple and hungrily sucked it into his mouth. With his other hand, he worked her other areola into a hardened peak, before brushing his hand over her stomach, and then farther down, using his hand to silently demand that she spread her legs.

Dominique gladly complied.

When she did, he took his finger and ran it back and forth over the thin, wispy fabric covering her heat. He felt her wetness through the material and smiled at the effect that he had on her. It made him harden even more, and he released Dominique's peak so that he could slide off the bed. With one determined move, he gripped the sides of her panties with both hands and yanked them down her legs. All elegance was over. All pretense was gone. He bent his head and kissed her nether lips, once and again. He parted her folds with his tongue. Dominique moaned as he stroked her, even as she placed her hands on his head and silently demanded more.

He complied.

Deeper, wetter, more forcefully, he kissed, licked, nibbled, loved her.

"Jake!" Dominique's voice came out in a harsh whisper.

Jake's laughter was a low rumbling from his chest. But he knew how she felt. He felt it, too. He had to get inside of her before he exploded. Their thoughts were on a singular goal—becoming one. The previous night's conversation had revealed that both had been tested, and neither had had another partner since beginning to see each other. Neither of them thought about the condoms that rested in Jake's top nightstand drawer. There were way more important things to think about right now.

For Jake, it was the feel of Dominique's luscious body as he covered it with his own. How her generous orbs cushioned his hard chest and how their hips fit together as if sculpted by the same artist. She lifted her leg and he felt the wetness of her heat, poised the thick, hard evidence of his desire at its entrance and then slowly, oh . . . so . . . slowly . . . slid inside her.

For Dominique, it was the feel of Jake's big, strong body covering hers, making her feel all girly inside. The way he moved his manhood against her sex, making her wetter still, poking promises of things to come. She spread her legs farther apart, feeling powerful and wanton all at the same time. It was the feel of the girth she'd dreamed up, longed for, filling her full, inch by excruciating inch. *Ahhhh . . .*

He sank in to her core, until their bodies touched in the most intimate of ways. For a moment, he just lay there, basking in a place that felt like home. He felt Dominique's walls clamping and contracting against him. He pulled out, and in again . . . slowly . . . just like before.

It was driving her mad. Dominique lifted herself

off the bed, trying to force Jake into the frenzied dance her body craved.

Jake laughed. "You want this, baby?"

Dominique raked long, manicured nails down the length of his back.

Jake broke out in goose bumps, but he refused to be hurried. Plus, Dominique hadn't answered his question. He pulled all of the way out. He'd give her what she wanted, everything she wanted . . . but in his time.

"Jake!" Dominique panted. She opened her eyes to see where he had gone, just in time to see him ease down her body until his tongue had found her paradise once more. His tongue worked better than any fencer's sword ever could. Dominique almost blacked out from the pleasure. He spread her wide and proceeded to act as if he hadn't eaten a meal in days. Just when Dominique thought she could take no more, Jake climbed back on top of her, sank himself inside to the hilt, and used those strong legs and wide hips just the way Dominique thought he could.

She'd been a part of conversations where women asked the question if bigger was better. Dominique could answer that in one word: abso-effing-lutely!

39

Shawn walked into Jake's office and saw a brooding man, staring at the playbook. But Shawn knew Jake wasn't seeing a thing.

"What's on your mind, Coach? And don't tell me work because I know it's not the Panthers."

Jake had tried to keep his mind on this Saturday's opponents. They were the biggest challenge to the Hurricanes' undefeated record. His lack of concentration had nothing to do with the two hours' sleep he'd had, but more about the comment Dominique made as she slipped into her dress and scurried home. "We're going to have to be weekend lovers, baby, so I can stay awake at work!" The casual comment bothered him, had him asking questions. Could he have a serious relationship with a career woman? And was it right for him to expect someone to deny a part of themselves to be with him?

Jake put down the book he was holding. "Taylor works in PR, right?"

Shawn sat across from Jake and nodded. "Yep,

she's had her own company now for the past five years."

"And her being a career woman never gets in the way of the relationship? You never feel that you come in second to the career, the kids, everything else going on?"

"Ha! Of course, I do. But you forgot the dog." Jake fixed Shawn with a quizzical expression. "I come after the job, the career, the kids, and good old Rupert, the Great Dane."

Shawn laughed. Jake kept scowling.

"Look, man, I'm teasing. I know where Taylor's heart is, with me. Our marriage is all about compromise and communication. It's not always easy to strike a balance but both of us are committed to working at it. There are times when my job takes precedence and Taylor pulls back on her work to pick up the slack. At other times, it's vice versa. If I know she's up against a crazy deadline or dealing with a high-maintenance client, then that's when you don't see me joining you guys for beers. But anything worth having is worth making sacrifices for. Before Taylor and I married we decided that divorce was not an option. So we know we have to do whatever it takes to make it work."

"It looks like so far so good."

"Eight years, two kids, and counting. And I love her more today than the day we married."

Jake got through practice and was especially pleased with the progress of his offensive line. That was in no small part due to Shawn and his role as offensive coordinator. The boys loved his quiet yet intense focus, and the way he made them feel that they could do anything. In this attribute, both Shawn and Jake were the same. Around them, the boys felt invincible.

Jake watched as Justin approached him. "How'd I do, Coach?"

"As I said in practice, Justin, all of you did very well. But the Panthers aren't going to give it to you. You're going to have to take it; keep your head in the game for sixty ticks."

"Right, Coach." Justin began to walk out of the locker room.

"Your mama talk to you?" Jake asked.

Justin stopped and turned. "What about?"

"Nothing in particular," Jake said nonchalantly. "I talked to her yesterday and thought she may have discussed your latest test results. You're killing those math scores, son."

Justin's lopsided grin filled his face. "Thanks, Coach."

With the locker room once again empty, Jake walked back into his office and sent a text to Dominique.

Why haven't you told Justin about the Raiders trip?

Jake placed his clipboard, whistle, playbook, and other items into his duffle bag as he awaited her response. He stopped when his text message indicator beeped, and picked up the phone.

I figured I'd wait until Saturday, after the game. Otherwise, he'll drive me nuts.

Jake laughed out loud as he typed in his response. What about his mother? Any chance of her driving me nuts this weekend?

Her smiley face and LOL weren't quite the answer he was looking for. But then again she hadn't said no.

Jake finished clearing his desk and headed out of his office. He was in need of a good meal and a warm bed, and in that order. He went to one of his favorite Italian eateries near his home and was enjoying a beer while waiting for his order when his phone rang.

"What's up, big bro?"

Harold McDonald was Jake's oldest brother by seven years. Jake looked up to this military man, who'd joined the Navy right out of high school, as a second father. Though Harold was out of the house before Jake reached junior high, he'd always made time to keep in contact with his younger brother, even corresponding regularly while on the ship. He'd retired five years ago and settled near their mother and childhood home with his wife, Mary. Their four children, two boys and two girls, were all grown and living in various parts of the country. After having the first child when barely out of their teens, Harold and Mary were now living their dream of being home alone.

"Hey there, Jake. How goes it, brother?"

"Fine, man, I can't complain."

"Even though I took your money and won't give it back?"

"Yeah, whatever, man. Rub it in." Jake laughed at how Harold still gloated over his team's victory. "I called the house last week, and your cell. Where have y'all been?"

"Sorry about that, man. My wife has me gallivanting all over the place. I'd totally forgotten that our oldest gifted us with a cruise to the Bahamas. We just got back yesterday, and after her one-hour conversation about trying to run our baby daughter's life, I think we're going to get another trip gifted real soon."

"Ha! At least something good came from her meddling. Women can be a handful sometimes."

"Sounds like you're talking from experience, Jake."

Jake didn't respond. There's no way Harold would know what he was going through. Mary had been a stay-at-home mom throughout their marriage—content to rule the roost with an iron fist clad in a velvet glove.

"That LA filly giving you the blues?"

Jake laughed. Harold had been extremely close to their grandfather, Thomas, the only McDonald man who'd made it into his eighties, at least that Jake knew of. Harold's speech was often peppered with Thomas-inspired descriptions mined straight from Alabama. Calling a woman a "fine filly" was one of them. "I'm holding my own, Harold," he finally answered good-naturedly.

"Just checking," Harold replied. "You're the only one of us not married, so you know we won't rest until you're as miserable as the rest of us."

Jake smiled, realizing that a little of Mary was rubbing off on the eldest Mac. Harold was hiding his nosy concern behind a joking façade but truth be told, Jake knew where Harold was coming from. The McDonald men had always been the marrying kind.

"How's everything else?" Jake said. "You feeling all right?"

"Getting check-ups every two months, like clock-work. The doctor wants me to lose about forty, fifty pounds. I need to get back on the treadmill and lay off the red meat."

"Then make that happen, brother! We all want you to hang around."

Both men were silent, remembering last year and the scare Harold had given the family when he'd gone into cardiac arrest at a church picnic. Fortunately one of the members was a nurse who knew CPR. She revived him and got him to the hospital with no major damage. Harold had become the first McDonald to have his heart tested and live to tell the story.

Harold broke the silence. "The wife and I are thinking about hosting Thanksgiving dinner this year. There's a bed and breakfast not far from our house and those of you who don't bunk down here or at Mama's can use those rooms. So put that on your calendar. And invite that woman who's got you holding your own."

40

Dominique forced herself out from under the covers. It had been a crazy week and between her increased workload and her workouts with Jake, staying in bed all day sounded like a wonderful, if impossible, option. She peeked at the clock and was dismayed to see that it was 9:45. The game started at noon, giving her a little over two hours to get dressed, swing by the offices, and get to the stadium. It had taken everything she had not to cancel and go straight to work, but the look in Justin's eyes as he talked about the plays they'd planned for their opponents, the Panthers, made being a no-show not an option. She'd decided to watch as much of the game as she could and then, after the Hurricanes had clinched the victory, she'd slip out of the stands and head over to *Capricious*.

An hour and a half later, Dominique walked into the Hurricanes' stands as if she owned them. She wore form-flattering chocolate-colored velvet pants, a multicolored striped turtleneck and a deep purple cashmere poncho. Her gold-colored suede and leather ankle boots took the ensemble to another level and Dominique's flawless hair and makeup looked runway-ready. Dominique had learned a long time ago that no matter how one felt, as long as they looked good, it would be a better day.

Joining the throngs of people in the stand, Dominique looked up into the full bleachers, waving at a few of the parents she'd gotten to know since becoming an avid Hurricanes supporter. A movement caught the corner of her eye and she turned to see Travis's mother, Kathy, waving her up to where she sat, with space next to her. Dominique mounted the stairs, opened her purple and gold Hurricanes bleacher seat and placed it beneath her before sitting down.

"Hey, girl," she said, giving Kathy a hug. She leaned over and waved at Kathy's husband, Ian, who was decked out in a loud purple sweatshirt and a gold and purple knit cap. He held a large, home-made sign that read: WE TEAR IT UP! His eyes were as sparkly as those of the boys on the field. Dominique noted that while Ian was not his biological father, somehow Travis resembled him. They both had light brown hair, hazel eyes, and similar builds. She guessed it was love rubbing off.

"Well, here we go," Kathy said, holding up her cherry cola for a toast. "To 6 and 0."

Dominique clinked her water bottle against Kathy's styrofoam cup. "To 6 and 0."

The game started and soon the whole crowd was enveloped in the electricity coming from the field. The Panthers were matching the Hurricanes, touchdown for touchdown, and Dominique noticed that

Justin seemed to be having another off day. He'd dropped one pass and fumbled another. Meanwhile, everything the Panthers touched was turning to gold.

The longer the game continued the more quiet the crowd became. The Hurricane players seemed out of sorts while their opponents were squarely in control. The fans watched in disbelief as the Panthers made one great play after another and when the scoreboard showed 28–14 in the fourth quarter with four minutes left, you could have heard a pin drop on the Hurricanes' side in the stadium.

In the last two minutes, Justin caught a slant pass seven yards out and ran fifteen more yards to score his only touchdown of the game. But it wasn't enough. The Hurricanes experienced their first loss of the season. The final score: 28–21.

Dominique hugged Kathy and Ian before the dejected parents went down to the field to wait on what was sure to be equally crestfallen children. Dominique sat back in her seat, giving the crowd a chance to clear. She watched her son, who was sitting on the bench with his head hung low. Her heart clenched at seeing him so miserable. But on the other hand, she felt it was a good experience. When it came to the game of life, losing came with the territory. And in the end she felt it wasn't who fell down, but who was able to get back up again. She looked at her watch and even though she'd vowed to be in the office by two, she knew where her priorities lay and right now . . . they lay with her son.

Jake stayed out on the field to handle the myriad of reporters that gathered around him. Meanwhile, after congratulating the other players, the Hurricanes trudged to the locker room. Dominique checked e-mails and sent instructions via texting while she waited for Justin to come back out. After forty-five minutes of watching other players file out and join their parents, she was out of patience and called her son on his cell phone. When it went to voice mail, she called Jake.

"Hey, baby."

"How's he doing?" Dominique asked.

"The first loss is always the hardest," Jake replied.

"Listen, I want to give him a hug, let him know I'm there for him. But it's getting late and . . ."

"And you've got to get to work."

"I was hoping to get there within the hour." Dominique noted that Jake's comment was stated as fact, without judgment. But she felt that when it came to *Capricious* and the current situation, there wasn't much she could do. It was what it was.

"We'll be out shortly," Jake said, and then hung up the phone.

Moments later she looked up from texting to see Jake and Justin exiting the locker room. She walked over to where her son was, resisting the urge to pull him into her arms. He was getting older and becoming less accepting of her PDAs. So she waited until they met her at the fence.

"I'm sorry, son," she said when they'd reached her. "You played a good game."

"I did not," he countered. "I messed up. It's my fault we lost."

Dominique glanced at Jake, who motioned her to silence with his eyes. He put his hands on Justin's shoulders. "Look at me, Justin."

Justin reluctantly looked up.

"I thought we'd been through this already. No one person wins a game, and no one person loses it. There were a lot of things that went wrong today. We'll shake it off, review the tape, and work like hell next week to make sure that what happened today never happens again. All right?"

Justin nodded.

Jake glanced at Dominique. "Let's head to my car. I'll drive you over to wherever you're parked." She fell into step beside Jake and her son. The area surrounding the field was almost empty, and the heels of Dominique's boots beat a steady rhythm across the asphalt. Jake winked at Dominique before turning to Justin. "What do you say we do something to take your mind off the game and what happened today."

"Like what?" Justin asked, as if he knew of absolutely nothing that could make him forget one of the worst days of his life.

"Like flying to Oakland so that we can watch the Raiders play tomorrow."

Justin stopped in his tracks. "Coach! Are you serious?"

"I wouldn't tease about something like this."

Justin let out a whoop, his eyes shining with excitement. In a moment, the excruciating pain of his first grade-school football loss seemed all but forgotten. He turned to his mother. "Can I go, Mom? Please say yes."

Jake knew this next move was a bit risky but then again, he felt, nothing ventured, nothing gained. "Your mom can come too, if she wants."

"Yes!" Justin said, pumping a fist in the air. Then,

without warning, he threw himself into Jake's arms, hugging him tightly. "Thanks, Coach," he whispered, his voice choked with emotion. Then he looked at Dominique. "Mommy, can we go?"

A war was waging inside Dominique's head. On one side was logic—saying that it would be ridiculous for her to shuck off the day's responsibilities and hop a plane to watch twenty-two grown men fight over a pointed ball. On the other side was love—saying that sometimes one had to do the ridiculous to experience the sublime.

They reached Jake's truck and she allowed Justin to sit up front with him while she sat in the back. "We're going—right, Mom?" Justin repeated, before Jake could start the engine.

"Buckle your seatbelt, Justin." After she'd buckled her own and Jake had started across the parking lot to her car, she continued. "I'd love to go, Justin. But Mommy has a lot of work to do. You can go. And I want you to have lots of fun and remember everything so that you can tell me all about it."

"But you're always working, Mommy," Justin replied, his voice reverting to the whine he perfected when he was three years old. "Why can't you come with us?" He turned to Jake. "Don't you want her to come with us, Coach Mac?"

"Yes," Jake said, looking intently at Dominique in his rearview mirror. "I very much want her to come."

41

"We will, we will *rock you!*"

Jake, Dominique, and Justin sang along with the boisterous Raider Nation assembled at the Oakland Coliseum. They'd forgone Jake's friend's offer to join them in an executive suite and sat outside, along with the masses, soaking up bright sun and a brisk, late October breeze. For one day, Jake had also abandoned his rhetoric of eating healthy and when the hawker came by selling popcorn, peanuts, and hot dogs, he brought food for the three of them.

In a nod to Justin's football heroes, both she and Jake wore black sweaters with jeans. Dominique's jewelry was all silver, and Jake wore a leather Raiders jacket. Fans who noticed him shouted their hellos or gave him pats on the back. Justin's eyes sparkled as he took it all in, dressed in Raiders regalia from head to toe: knitted cap, jacket, T-shirt, and socks.

"This is awesome!" Justin cried, after the crowd had helped to successfully stop the Denver Broncos from making a first down. Justin joined in the chanting, waving the oversized foam Raiders hand that

Jake had bought him. When the Raiders' star corner-back intercepted a pass and ran it back for a touchdown, Dominique thought that Justin would leap from the stands and run down the field with him.

After the game, Jake took Justin into the locker room to meet the team. Dominique waited in a lounge, glad for the chance to check her e-mails and send a few texts. She knew she'd have to work extra hard next week to make up for the time she'd missed this weekend but seeing the smile on Justin's face made it all worth it. And the smile Jake put on her face last night made it worth it, too.

It was a little after seven PM when the plane landed on its private strip in Van Nuys, California. Jake watched as Dominique shook a sleeping Justin awake and after once again thanking their hosts, the three of them piled into Jake's SUV. He left the parking lot and turned onto Van Nuys Boulevard heading for Sepulveda. He'd had a wonderful time with Dominique and Justin, and wasn't quite ready for the weekend to end. He reached for Dominique's hand, entwined his long, thick fingers with hers. "Thank you for coming, baby. I had a great time."

Dominique leaned over and gave him a kiss. "Me, too."

"I saw that!" Justin groggily mumbled from the back seat.

Dang, I thought he was asleep! "Saw what?" Dominique asked innocently, as she turned and looked at him.

"You kissing Coach. Ha! I *saw* it!"

"It was just a little thank-you kiss on the cheek," Jake replied. "Like the kind that Ashley gave you after last week's game."

Justin's eyes widened as he looked from Jake to Dominique. "Coach!"

Jake laughed. "Uh-huh, I saw *you*."

Dominique looked between the men, giving a surreptitious wink to Jake for successfully switching the focus away from their kissing. "Who's Ashley?"

Silence.

"Justin . . ." Dominique used the authoritative mommy voice that said he'd better answer, drawing out his name in an implied threat.

Justin made a face and looked out of the window. "One of my girlfriends."

"One of . . . !" Dominique looked from Justin to Jake and back to Justin again. "How many girlfriends do you have?"

"I don't know." Justin shrugged and then added matter-of-factly, "They all like me."

Dominique and Jake exchanged looks before Jake changed the subject. He and Justin started talking football but Dominique didn't really hear them. She was too focused on the past moment's revelations that, one, Justin had a girlfriend whom Jake knew about and she didn't and, two, her eleven-year-old son was obviously still very interested in the opposite sex. She knew that men and women were different but considering how boys were the last thing on her mind when she was eleven, she was finding it hard to wrap her mind around Justin's casual comment that *they all like me.*

"Dominique, did you hear me?"

Jake's question pulled Dominique from her reverie. "No, Jake. What did you say?"

"I asked if you wanted to stop off and grab a bite to eat before I dropped y'all off."

"I want a burger!" Justin yelled from the back, casting his vote for Jake's idea.

Dominique looked at her watch. If she got to the office within the next thirty minutes or so, she could put in a solid four hours of work. "I can't, Jake. It's getting late and I have to—"

"Never mind," Jake interrupted. "It's cool," he added.

Dominique took one look at his countenance and felt that it was anything but.

They reached Dominique and Justin's home. Jake pulled into the driveway but did not turn off the engine.

"Get your things, Justin," Dominique said. "And don't forget to thank Jake for what a wonderful time we had."

"Thanks, Coach," Justin said, after he'd followed Jake to the trunk and pulled a small carryon and duffle bag out of it.

"You're welcome, Justin. And remember, we're going to keep this little trip between us, right? Don't want the other players feeling bad that they didn't get to go."

"Right."

The two men exchanged a pound.

"Go on in, Justin. I'll be there in a minute." Dominique watched her son until he'd disappeared behind the front door. Then she turned to Jake. "Thanks again, Jake. I meant what I said earlier. I had a wonderful time with you this weekend, the best time I've had in years."

Jake's eyes raked over her, pausing on her lips before returning to meet her eyes. "When am I going to see you again?"

"When do you want to see me?" she asked playfully, even though Dominique knew what he was really asking. He was wondering if work was always going to continue to come between them, if he'd always feel that he was taking a backseat to her next deadline, photo shoot, or hoop that she had to jump through. The trouble was that Dominique didn't know the answer to that question. By the look in his eyes she also knew that she'd have to find one soon.

"Tonight." Jake's answer was serious, not playful at all.

"You're insatiable," Dominique said, hoping to stroke his ego since tonight she wouldn't be stroking anything else. "You've already kept me up the past three nights. Don't you need some sleep?"

"Like Diddy says, we can sleep when we're dead."

"Which won't be long if I don't get rest. I'll call you later, okay?"

Jake nodded and gave Dominique a hug before pulling out of her driveway. As he entered the boulevard, he tried to ignore the emptiness he felt, tried to justify why Dominique couldn't spend more time with him. He knew one thing: he wouldn't be happy just seeing her once or twice a week. His sexual appetite had been voracious since he got turned out at thirteen and with Dominique's hot body, it was even more so. But could she make room for a demanding man like him in her life?

Jake knew that part of the reason his brother's marriages were successful was that they all worked on them, just like Shawn and Taylor. *She just doesn't get it,* he thought with a tinge of sadness. *She doesn't understand that I don't want a part-time lover.* Jake sat up straighter with the realization of what he did want—a full-time wife.

42

Dominique worked at the office until almost midnight, editing until her eyes and brains simply refused their continued cooperation. She went home and fell asleep before her head hit the pillow. It seemed mere minutes went by before she was hearing the jazz instrumental from her alarm. With eyes closed, she swatted at the clock, hitting the snooze button twice before finally forcing herself from the bed at seven A.M. It was now eight o'clock, and Dominique was the first one in the building, latte with double espresso shot in hand. She'd need this one *and* the one Reggie would bring in at nine to make it through the day.

She put down her purse and briefcase and immediately opened up Outlook on her computer. After scanning the task and to-do bar, she clicked on her inbox. One e-mail was marked URGENT. It was from Solveig in Stockholm. Dominique clicked on the link and quickly read the three succinct sentences: Call Mirabelle as soon as you get this. She's on your side. Wants to talk to you ASAP.

Looking at her watch, Dominique calculated that in Paris it was five o'clock in the afternoon. Dominique reached for the phone and within minutes heard Mirabelle's lilting accent in her ear.

"*Chérie,* you are calling from work!"

"Yes, Mirabelle. Solveig said to call you as soon as possible."

"But it is early there, no?"

"Eight o'clock," Dominique said with a yawn.

"I hate to see you working so hard, but you are doing the right thing." Mirabelle's voice lowered, and took on a conspiratorial tone. "François is crazy; he is obsessing with replacing you."

Dominique rubbed her forehead, suddenly feeling even more tired than she was a few seconds ago. She'd worked too hard the last five years to be dealing with this crap. She'd already paid her dues and felt that now all she should be seeing were the rewards of her labor. Instead, she saw a fight brewing. "What has he done now?"

"Flown over a candidate for an interview with some of the investors, an editor from an Italian fashion magazine."

Dominique sat up straight. "Who?"

"A puppet whose strings he can pull." Mirabelle told Dominique the editor's name. "You intimidate him, Dominique. In your presence he feels like a fool. This bimbo arrived last night and I believe that her and François shared more than dinner, if you know what I mean."

"But I thought he was gay?"

"He's whatever to whomever . . . and I hear he likes whips and chains."

"Please!" Dominique interrupted. "Spare me the details, Mirabelle."

Mirabelle's tinkling laughter poured through the receiver. "Anyway, she is here, and he doesn't know that I know it. Her visit is very hush-hush but Mirabelle makes it her business to know everything."

"That man has had it out for me from the beginning. I'm sick of feeling his daggers in my back."

"That's why I'm calling—to warn you. But also to tell you don't worry. That I have—how do you Americans say—a trick up my sleeve?"

"I appreciate that, Mirabelle. But François has some of the other investors in his back pocket. They really listen to him."

"Don't worry, *chérie*. When the time comes, they'll listen to *me*. Take down this name. He's a dear friend of mine who lives in Los Angeles and he's ready to come on board with enough money to shut up François and his gang." Mirabelle chuckled again, clearly enjoying the messiness. "Are you ready?"

"Yes."

"Okay, his name is . . ."

The rest of the day went by in a whirlwind as Dominique worked to keep her attention on the matters at hand. But Mirabelle's phone call had affected her more than she'd let on and now, for the first time since being hired into the best job of her life, she felt the real possibility that she could lose it. She'd called and left a message with Mirabelle's friend but so far he hadn't called back. By five o'clock she'd had all of *Capricious* that she could handle and began clearing off her desk.

"You're going home, Miss Dom?" Reggie asked, as he walked into her office and placed several pieces of correspondence on her desk.

"Yes."

"Thank God!"

Dominique fixed Reggie with a questioning look.

"Girl, you can't let these people kill you. Don't those French fools know that the Emancipation Proclamation has been proclamated?"

"I believe the word is 'proclaimed,' Reggie, and yes, they know." Not wanting to upset him or have him fearful of losing his job, she chose not to share the earlier transatlantic conversation. "These extra hours are all about me. I'm working on a little project."

"If I were you, I'd be working on a big project—about six foot five and about three-hundred pounds to be exact."

Dominique smiled. "Good advice, Reggie. That's where I'm off to now. You've been putting in the hours, too. Why don't you knock off early, take Quinn out to dinner?"

"Girl, Quinn is getting on my nerves. I'm getting ready to drop him like he's hot."

"What happened? Oh, never mind." Dominique turned off her computer, placed the papers Reggie had brought her into her briefcase and stood. "Let's blow this popsicle stand," she said, letting Reggie go in front of her so that she could lock her door.

"You need to blow something else," Reggie murmured.

"What did you say?"

"Nothing, Miss Dom. You go on and have a good night now, you hear?"

Thirty minutes later Dominique was sitting in one of Jake's large leather recliners. He was standing behind her, massaging her neck and shoulders.

"What's got you so uptight?" he asked, kneading a particularly troublesome spot.

"Work." Dominique dropped her head as Jake worked his way down her spine.

"What happened?"

"Don't worry about it, baby. I can handle it."

Jake stopped massaging Dominique's neck. He came from behind her, pulled up the ottoman and sat directly in front of her. "I know you can handle it," he said, taking her hands in his. "But I do worry about it. I worry about you and the weight of the world that is putting those kinks in your shoulders. You're a strong woman. I get that. But what I'm trying to tell you is that I'm here for you, to support you and protect you. You don't have to handle everything alone." He paused, his stare unflinching. "I love you, Nick, and want to help make life easier."

Jake's unexpected declaration almost moved Dominique to tears, and his offer to help was her further undoing. It had been so long since she'd had anyone to depend on that she'd forgotten how it felt. "I don't know what to say," she finally uttered, a single tear running down her cheek.

"What happened, baby?"

Dominique told Jake about François Deux, the earlier phone call with Mirabelle, and how she actually feared for her job. "I'm Justin's sole provider," she finished. "And I've worked damned hard for this company. That's why I have to do whatever it takes to protect my investment and keep my job."

"No, baby," Jake countered. "You are not Justin's sole provider and you don't have to kiss anybody's ass to save your job. I've got more than enough for the three of us. If anything happens . . . I've got you."

43

It was Championship Saturday and the Hurricanes and Panthers were about to square off for winner take all. Their records were equal: 8 and 1. Because the Hurricanes' sole loss had been at the Panthers' paws, the Panthers had home-field advantage. The game was taking place at their Van Nuys stadium but at least half of it was bleeding purple and gold as the Hurricanes' supporters gathered en masse to cheer on their team. Dominique was sitting with Kathy, Ian, and other parents who'd become friendly over the past eight weeks. Reggie sat beside her and next to him was Alejandro, Reggie's drop-dead gorgeous new flavor of the month. The Hurricanes took the field and half of the crowd stood up and cheered, stomping their feet and chanting, "Tear it up! Tear it up!" The Panthers followed suit and the other half roared, "Panther pride! Panther pride!" The boys ran on the field and began warming up. The excitement in the air rivaled that of the Super Bowl.

"Okay, team," Jake said, once the boys had finished their exercises and huddled around him.

"This is it. This is where we leave it all on the field. We're good. But so are they. So what's going to make the difference in who wins this game?"

"Hurricane heart!" was the boisterous reply, spoken in unison by team and coaches alike.

"I want you to keep it one hundred on every play. We've got sixty ticks to get it done, gentlemen. And I want you to play every one of them like it's the fourth quarter with two minutes left and we're trailing by seven. Travis, I want you in Brad's face on every play. I want you on him so tough that he thinks you're his shadow. Understood?"

Travis nodded. He'd been watching tape on the Panthers' star quarterback all week.

"Justin, we want you to block for Duane like your life depended on it the whole first quarter. Lull them into complacency so that when we toss in the trick play, they won't know what hit 'em. You feel me?"

"Yeah, Coach," Justin said, nodding along with the rest of the players.

"Keep your eyes on the ball. Defense: beware of every opportunity to strip. Guard your man, tear up that line, and go after those interceptions. Offense: hold the line, run your routes with conviction. Hit your marks, and don't be intimidated by anyone or anything. You boys go out there and give it all you've got because believe me . . . we're going to give you all we've got."

Jake reached his hand into the circle. The players followed suit.

"Who are we?"

"Hurricanes!"

"What do we do?"

"Tear it up!"

"On three: one, two, three."

"Hurricanes!"

Jake clapped his hands together. "Let's go to work!"

Both teams took to the field with fervor. The stands buzzed with excitement. Dominique fiddled with her purple and gold cashmere scarf, more nervous than she'd ever thought she'd be for grade-school football. Ian was a one-man cheering section, yelling out encouragement every five seconds: "Atta boy," "good job," and, of course, "Tear it up!" At the end of the first quarter the score was tied—7 all. By the end of the second, the Panthers were up by 7. She wondered why Justin had spent so much time blocking. They'd only thrown him the ball twice. Watching them run into the locker room at halftime, she wanted to run in there after them and tell Jake to throw the ball to her son! She also wanted to give her baby boy a hug and tell him that everything would be all right. Imagining the look of mortification on his face if she did so made her laugh out loud.

The third quarter started with a bang. The Hurricanes' punt returner fielded a short kick and ran it back sixty-five yards for a touchdown. The score was tied. Seven plays later, the Panthers had the answer. The Hurricanes fumbled the ball at the Panthers' twenty-yard line. Their cornerback recovered and ran it in for seven. As the final seconds of the third quarter ticked down, everyone's eyes went to the scoreboard—Panthers: 21, Hurricanes: 14.

"Shake it off, gentlemen," Jake barked as the team gathered around him. "We're in this hunt— new quarter, new mindset. Hurricane heart, right?"

Various responses proved the team agreed.

"We're in a fight, a good one. But we've got this!" He turned to the offensive coordinator who'd help bring this team to the championship. "Shawn, call the play."

"All right," Shawn said, his green eyes glistening with excitement. "We're going to kick it into high gear. First down, we're going to run the Big Mac. Patrick, make sure Kareem has time to throw the ball. Justin, on second down we're running the Hurricane Switch."

Justin nodded, his heart pumping adrenaline like crazy, his hands clammy with nerves.

The boys took the field and ran the Big Mac. Patrick guarded his man but Kareem overthrew his receiver. Jake prowled the sidelines, a stoic, calming presence, while Shawn yelled orders and the line coaches waved their boys into position.

Second down. The boys took their places at the twenty-yard line. A subtle look passed from Kareem to Justin, who nodded slightly before crouching into position.

"One, seventy-seven, seventy-seven, hut, hut!"

The center's toss to Kareem was perfect. Justin went straight for his man, blocking him to the left and taking him out of the play. Kareem faked a handoff to the running back while Justin came across the field. Kareem threw a short, five-yard dump over the tall defensive end to the even taller Hurricane tight end. Justin caught the pass, did a head shake on his defender, and started down the field. Thirty yard line. The offensive line was picking off their men. Out of the corner of his eye Justin saw the Panther cornerback heading his way. He put his head down and picked up speed. The wide receiver blocked the corner. Forty yard line. There was just one person between Justin and the goal. Jake's words floated across his mind. *Don't be intimidated by anyone or anything.* Justin ran right at the defender. Or, rather, he ran right over him. He hit his opponent square in the chest with his shoulder and made quick work of the remaining forty yards. Touchdown!

For the next ten minutes, the ball went back and forth—a fumble here, a missed pass there. Tension was high on both sides, nerves were higher, especially when the Panthers hit a field goal making the score 24–21.

They hit the two-minute mark: Panthers' ball. The Panthers made quick work of eating up the yards and with one minute and thirty seconds remaining, the Hurricanes found themselves defending at the thirty-yard line. The Panthers' sideline called the third-down play. Brad dropped back to pass. The Hurricane cornerback intercepted and ran the ball back to the thirty-yard line. Twenty-nine seconds remaining. Shawn called the play from the sideline: Twister on the Ground. The center snapped the ball. Justin shook his defender and streaked to the middle of the field. Kareem threw the pass. Justin literally plucked the ball from the halfback's would-be intercepting hands. He had to jump up to do it, though, and when he came down, it was with a defender's arms wrapped around his legs . . . ten yards from the goal line. Ten seconds left. No time outs. No huddle.

"Hut, hut, hike!"

Kareem caught the ball and ran straight for the middle. He spun once, twice, and sidestepped a tackle, high-stepping over the goal line. Dominique whooped as she jumped to her feet; she, Kathy, Ian, and other parents formed a group hug. Even Reggie caught the joy, giving Alejandro a cool high five. The bench rushed the field, followed by the fans. Dominique made her way to the grass, holding back from the swarm that surrounded her man.

Jake answered a couple questions and then noted Dominique standing on the side. He waved her over. When she reached him, he pulled her into his arms and kissed her soundly on the lips.

Dominique pulled back, surprised. During the week, she and Jake had agreed to take things to another level but he'd said nothing about their going public. "Baby," she whispered into his ear, against the din of those around him, "the team and parents don't know that we're seeing each other."

Jake's eyes sparkled as he once again hugged her hard against her chest. He leaned and spoke into her ear. "They do now."

44

Monday morning and Dominique's mood was as bright and colorful as the orange, red, and yellow autumn leaves that had fallen in her front yard. Even François's e-mail demanding ridiculous, unnecessary reports couldn't dampen her mood. Her son was a football star, the Hurricanes were champions, and she was in love.

"Hold my calls," she directed Reggie as she picked up her latte from his desk. "For the next hour, I don't wish to be disturbed."

She entered her office, turned on her computer, flipped through her task list and began wading through more than a hundred e-mails. She tried to focus but try as she might, she couldn't keep her mind on work. A man named Jake, and memories from the weekend, kept getting in the way.

"Who are we?"
"Hurricanes!"
"What do we do?"

"Tear it up!"

The party had moved from the stadium to Ian and Kathy's home, flowing between their kitchen, great room, and landscaped backyard complete with tennis court and swimming pool. Pizza, chicken wings, chips, and Jake's mandatory salad crowded the counter. The boys, filled with the adrenaline of victory, were boisterous in their celebration.

At one point, Dominique slipped away from the crowd in search of the bathroom and, honestly, some peace and quiet. She was as jubilant as the rest of them but for the first time she realized the advantage of having only one child—the noise ratio was decidedly less. She admired the Longmires' home as she made her way down a short stairway into what looked to be the den. She noted a bathroom to the left of the steps and was making a beeline to it when she was accosted from behind.

Dominique gasped and immediately smelled Jake's cologne right before she felt a large hand place a firm grasp on her behind. "Jake!" she hissed. "Stop, someone will see us!"

"I don't care," Jake murmured, reaching around and tweaking a nipple. "I'm ready to continue the celebration in the privacy of my bedroom."

Dominique turned around, admiration shining in her eyes. "You did good today, Coach. I'm so proud of you."

Jake acknowledged the compliment by pulling Dominique into his arms and grinding himself into her. "Justin is going to spend the night with Travis so you and I can be together."

Dominique looked up, surprised. "How did this happen?"

"You think Ian and Kathy don't know what's up?"

"I love you, Jake McDonald."

Later that night, with no one to distract them, she showed him just how much.

Dominique's cell phone rang. She smiled as she looked at the caller ID. "Hey, little sis."

"Hey, big sis," Faith replied. "For a minute, I thought I was going to have to send a search party out."

"Didn't you get my text?"

"Girl, you know I'm not into that newfangled stuff. I called your cell phone and your home phone. Went to voicemail all weekend." Dominique could imagine her sister's raised brow. "Hum. Wonder where we were . . ."

"Ha! You know where I was, girl—with Jake." Dominique paused, her face breaking out into a smile. "I told him, Faith."

"Told him what?"

"That I loved him, and that I was ready to put aside my fears and officially enter a relationship. We went public this weekend."

Faith whooped. "I love it! When you make a decision you don't waste time!"

"It wasn't planned; at least not by me. I think we just got caught up in the excitement of the game."

"Yeah, Aaron and Michael told me all about it, much to my dismay."

"Ha! Justin was so proud that his cousin was there; thank them again for me, because it meant the world to my son. I wish you'd been there, too."

"Next time, sis. You know that family has to support one another. By the time Justin makes it to the

NFL, I'll need him to support me!" The sisters laughed. "I haven't heard you this happy in a long time, Nikki. It warms my heart. So . . . when are we going to meet the big fella?"

Aaron and Michael had met Jake after the game, but he would be the first man Dominique would officially introduce to the family since the disaster called Kevin. Yet she answered with no hesitation. "How about this Sunday?"

The next few hours passed quickly and soon Dominique was on her way to Sunset Boulevard and her luncheon appointment with Mirabelle's contact, the man who was supposed to be her saving grace, should she go toe-to-toe with François in a *Capricious* showdown.

Dominique walked confidently to the swanky eatery that had been all the rage since it made its debut last year on Los Angeles's Westside. She'd visited the establishment a few times: once for a friend's birthday, another time for a benefit, and again on a sorta kinda blind date. On those occasions she'd admired the establishment's maître d' from a distance. Not only was he efficient in this position but he was also very easy on the eyes. Who knew that now, more than six months later, their paths would cross professionally.

She stepped inside and announced herself to the gorgeous redhead who greeted her. A few moments later she was escorted upstairs to the small yet luxuriously appointed offices. Her savior sat behind the desk, looking like a Michelangelo masterpiece.

Upon her entrance, he rose and walked to her with arms outstretched.

"Dominique, it is my pleasure." He air-kissed each side of her face.

"Mr. Marquis, the pleasure is mine."

"Please, call me Xavier." He led her to a sitting area opposite the black ebony desk that anchored one side of the room. "For you Americans it's early for drinking but we French rarely dine without embellishment. May I offer you a glass of champagne?"

"One small one," Dominique answered, emphasizing small with her thumb and forefinger.

Xavier pushed the intercom button and after informing the waiter of his request returned his attention to Dominique. "Mirabelle says you have a bit of a . . . situation, no?"

"How much of it did she share with you?"

"All of it. But I'd very much like to hear your perspective."

For the next hour, between delicious bites of tapas-style soul food dishes that the establishment, Tosts, was known for, Dominique shared her point of view. Marquis asked a few intelligent, pointed questions but mostly he listened—intently.

As they finished up with bite-sized sweet-potato balls covered with finely chopped pecans, Dominique got right to the point. "Do you have any suggestions on how best to counter the François situation?"

Xavier Marquis sat back, his tapered, manicured fingers steepled beneath his mouth. His startling brown eyes were framed with long, curly lashes and stood out of an aristocratic-looking face with sharp, defined features, and a shock of thick, black hair.

He studied Dominique for several seconds before blessing her with a dazzling white smile.

"As Mirabelle told you, I have long had an interest in fashion. Several of my very good friends are in the industry."

Dominique nodded, having heard from Mirabelle that Marquis and Christian Louboutin were long-time buds.

"I've followed your magazine's progress from the beginning and from where I sit I see only one thing that's missing."

A slight frown marred Dominique's face. "What's that?"

"You," Xavier calmly replied.

Instead of responding, Dominique sat back and continued to listen.

"You have made your presence known behind the scenes, but look at you. You are the very embodiment of what *Capricious* stands for: big, beautiful, and bodacious. You've told celebrity stories and put their pictures on the cover. Now, it is your turn. You, in my humble opinion, should become the official face of *Capricious*."

45

"Mon dieu! It is brilliant, Dominique, brilliant!"

It was eleven o'clock at night in Paris but, as requested, Dominique had called Mirabelle from her car as soon as she'd left Tosts and Xavier Marquis.

"I told you that he was the answer. I am right, always, tell me."

"You are always right," Dominique said, laughing. "But really, Mirabelle, what would people think of me putting myself on the cover?"

"They'd think you're as smart as Oprah Winfrey," Mirabelle replied. "She puts herself on every cover and the public loves it!"

"The public has had twenty-five years to get to know Oprah," Dominique commented drily. "People don't know Dominique Clark. They could give a hoot."

"A hoot?"

"They couldn't care less," Dominique said, adjusting her answer for one whose first language was not English.

"Not yet," Mirabelle went on, nonplussed. "Not

until you share your story, bare your soul. Don't you
see, Dominique? You are one of them, a working
woman and single mother. You've battled low self-
esteem, weight issues, and worthless men."

"I see that you and Solveig have been talking and
I've been the topic of discussion," Dominique said
matter-of-factly but without anger. "Thanks for
painting such a flattering picture."

"It is why people will find you so relatable. Your
story plus a beautiful fashion spread will endear you
to the subscribers and Xavier will make sure you get
seen by people who'll help your star rise. When
people think of *Capricious* they'll think of you, and
then there will be no way those sanctimonious scal-
lywags will think to let you go."

By the end of the day, Dominique's mood had
lightened considerably. She didn't even mind that
because of the time she'd spent securing her future,
she had to put back on her editor-in-chief hat and
work after hours. She called Tessa, spoke with
Justin, had Reggie bring her a smoothie before leaving, and then settled in for three or four more
hours of work.

It was a little after eight when Dominique heard a
soft knock on the outer executive office doors. She
frowned, thinking it odd that Peter would come up
without calling. Shrugging, she walked to the door
and pressed the intercom. "Peter, is that you?"

No answer.

Dominique's heart skipped a beat. "Peter?" she
asked, a little louder.

"No."

What? Dominique hurriedly opened the door. "How did you get up here?" she asked, pulling Jake into her personal domain.

"I've got connections." He followed her inside. "I bribed Peter into bringing me up."

"Remind me to thank him. Whatever is in that bag smells delicious. You're always thinking of me, baby. How'd you know I was hungry?"

Jake put down the bag and wrapped Dominique in his arms. "Because I knew that I was."

He tilted up Dominique's chin, and looked deep into her eyes. "You're beautiful, you know that?"

"It never hurts to hear it from the lips of a handsome man."

Jake did what he'd dreamed of all day: lowered said lips to Dominique's and, using his tongue, eased open her mouth. Dominique pressed her girls against his chest. Jake moaned and walked them to the love seat he spied in the distance. He eased them down onto it and began his assault in earnest, reaching for the buttons on Dominique's sleek, silk blouse, pushing away the fabric and filling his palms with her 44 DDDs. He tweaked each nipple before slipping his hand inside the staunch cotton of her bra and immediately knew that the item's full-figure, full-support was in his way.

"Take it off," he demanded, sitting up and pulling Dominique to a sitting position as well.

"Baby, I'm at work," she protested, even as her fingers went to the back clasp of their own volition.

"We're getting ready to work all right." He watched with fascination as the bra fell and twin brown balloons swayed their greeting. He responded by taking a dark nipple into his mouth, swirling his tongue around it even as he ran his hand along Dominique's gelatinous backside. "You're still wearing too many clothes."

"Jake . . ."

"You can either take off the skirt or I'm getting ready to make a belt out of it."

The commanding tone he used turned Dominique all the way on. She stood and quickly shed her skirt, totally unaware of what a picture she painted standing there in her thigh high hose, four-inch heels, and high-cut white panties against her smooth, cocoa skin. Jake dropped to his knees and buried his nose in her treasure. Dominique's knees almost buckled. She grabbed his shoulders for support and hung on for the ride. Jake lapped her nectar through the soft cotton fabric, an act that made her hotter than if he had touched her bare skin. It was a moment before she realized that the mewling sounds she heard were her own. He placed his hand between her legs, directing her to spread them. She did, and he shifted the fabric to the side, running a finger along her folds, nodding in satisfaction as if the play he called had been properly executed.

"Let's see what kind of work you do," he said, standing abruptly.

"Huh, uh, what?" Dominique asked weakly, her mind in a lust-induced haze.

"Come over here," he commanded, guiding her toward her desk. Dominique followed dumbly, as if this was her first time in the office. "Uh-huh, this looks interesting," he said as he carefully stacked the pictures and articles and placed them to the side. "Sit down. Oh, wait, you won't be needing these."

He pulled the panties over her full, rounded hips, down her thick thighs, and over calves that knew how to fill out a pair of boots.

Dominique sighed as she sat on the desk.

"Lay back."

She did.

Jake sat in Dominique's red leather-covered executive chair as if he owned it. Once again, he spread her wide and this time, there was no doubt left to his mission. He licked and sucked and nibbled until Dominique was in a frenzy, begging for him to get inside her. She didn't have to wait long—Jake was hard as a rock. He shed his pants and boxers, placed Dominique's legs over his shoulders and proceeded to "tear it up." Nine thick, throbbing inches of intense heat seared Dominique like iron. Her cat was as hot as molten lava. The dance was hard and intense and then slow and purposeful. Jake hit her spot, and Dominique hit a high note, her body shaking with the intensity of her release. Jake followed shortly after, hissing as he basked in his own ecstasy. Afterwards he leaned over, kissed Dominique lazily, lovingly, and then pulled her to him. He sat down in her chair, pulled her into his lap. An average-size man Dominique would have crushed, but with Jake she actually felt petite. There were no words. None were needed. She snuggled into his hard chest, relished the feel of his massive arms wrapped around her, and did something she'd never done in five years at *Capricious*. Dominique fell fast asleep at her desk.

46

"You did what?" Faith shooed Alexis out of her bedroom and closed the door.

Dominique giggled, glad to be able to finally share what had happened three days ago. Faith had been dealing with her daughter, who'd been home sick with the flu. This was the first chance she'd had for a heart-to-heart. "We made love in my office. Girl, it was so good, that man knocked me out!"

"What do you mean?"

"I fell asleep."

"Dang, girl. It was like that?"

"It was even better the second time."

"Ooh, sister, this is TMI!" And then in the next breath, "Don't tell me y'all did it again."

"Jake left the building at a little after four. I didn't even bother; just took a shower, curled up on the couch, and caught forty winks." Dominique paused, reminded of how thankful she was for an assistant like Tessa and the wardrobe she kept at the office so she could be like the Boy Scouts—always prepared. "He's amazing," she finished, her voice wistful.

"I'm so happy for you, sister," Faith answered, her voice also soft. And then she turned playful. "Except now when I meet him, I'll be looking at your man in a whole different way!"

"How do you think I feel? Sitting in my office chair will never be the same!"

That Sunday, Dominique took Jake to Anita's house to meet her immediate family. Almost two weeks later the roles were reversed as Dominique left Justin behind to spend Thanksgiving with his dad while she and Jake landed in Birmingham. Dominique was nervous, but there was no need. From the time Jake's mother, Miss Bernie, enveloped her in a big bear hug and said she was family, Dominique felt just that way.

Jake followed his mother into the kitchen where Dominique met the wives of Jake's brothers and a few of the kids. From there, Jake took her into the den, where the brothers were watching football.

"Big Mac!" one of the men shouted, getting up at the same time. He looked like an older, heavier version of Jake, sans hair.

"Harold," Jake said after hugging his brother. "This is Dominique."

"This is what I'm talking 'bout," Harold said, as he hugged Dominique. "Throw away those chicken legs and bring in a woman with some meat on her bones!"

Dominique met Jake's other brothers—Johnny

and Mike—and their wives, and shortly after that names became a blur. Amid turkey with all the trimmings Dominique met no less than thirty people, all Jake's kin. By the time they enjoyed desserts of pecan, sweet potato, and pumpkin pie (and a tangy lemon pound cake if pie wasn't your thing) her head was spinning, partly from the whir of activities and partly from the two glasses of homemade muscatel wine that Miss Bernie insisted she drink. In just one day of being around them, Dominique totally understood where Jake got his strength, his warmth, and sense of family. Where she'd grown up in a single-parent home—made that way because her father walked out—Jake had grown up surrounded by people with stable marriages. After dessert, the men retired to the game room for a rousing game of pool and darts, while the women gathered in the kitchen.

"Miss Bernie, you put your foot in this food today," Dominique said, spooning leftover greens from the pot to a storage container. "I don't think I can eat another bite."

"And look at her," Susie said, cocking her head toward Miss Bernie but talking to Lillian, Mike's wife. Susie was married to Harold and, at fifty-seven, was ten years Harold's senior. They'd met when he was seventeen and she was twenty-seven and to everyone's surprise, had married a short time later. "Talking like hers was the only hands working in the kitchen."

"We all helped," Lillian said, cosigning on Susie's statement. "But Miss Bernie was the orchestrator, though. If one person is going to get the credit for today's meal, it would be her."

"Thank you, Lilly," Miss Bernie said, her hand on an ample hip, the other grasping a wooden spoon being pointed at Susie. "It's good to know somebody in you all's generation has some manners."

"Our generation?" Lillian looked at Susie with feigned indignation. "I'm in the generation *after* you."

"Ha! Girl, you know you're flying toward fifty. Don't start none, won't be none."

The women laughed.

"On the real tip, though, Dominique, I was so glad to see you walk through the door." Susie wiped her hands on a dishcloth and paused to take a drink of sweet tea. "I've only met a couple women Jake has dated since Robin passed and they were snooty, skinny heifahs who couldn't see the floor in front of them for their nose in the air. You're real people. I like that."

"Yeah, and she won't blow away in an Alabama breeze," Miss Bernie added. "I like that, too."

After the women finished cleaning the kitchen and putting away the food, they joined the men in Miss Bernie's lived-in den/game room. Soon the photo albums came out and Dominique was regaled with colorful stories of Jake's childhood. It quickly became evident that Jake adored his brothers, and that Harold had assumed the father role with ease.

"I might not have been able to hunt," Mike said to Jake after Jake told Dominique that Mike couldn't shoot the side of a barn. "But back then, you couldn't drive. Harold, tell her about the driving lessons."

"Oh, man," Harold said, clutching his heart. "That boy like to gave me my first heart attack." He turned to Dominique and continued. "See, I'd spent a year saving up to buy me a brand-spanking-new Chevy Camaro. Let me tell you, baby girl, that ride was tight! Black on black with a wide white racing stripe down the middle, dice swinging from the mirror, fur on the seat, and Cameo blasting from the speakers. You couldn't tell a brothah that he wasn't cool! I'd had it for about a month, and Jake had bugged me every single day about driving it. You were what, Jake, twelve, thirteen?"

"About to turn thirteen," Jake said, smiling at the memory.

"Well, one day we were out at our grandparents' farm and I guess I was feeling generous because after about an hour of his begging, I told Jake to get behind the wheel. There was this long stretch of dirt road right next to the house so I figured not much can happen, right? Man, I'd barely showed him how to work the gas and brakes when the next thing I knew, brothah man had started the engine, thrown that puppy into drive, and before I could grab the wheel we were off the dirt road, racing across Grandma's field—"

"And headed straight for Mama's prized vegetable garden," Miss Bernie finished with a gleam in her eye.

"Seems like I blinked and there were tomatoes on the windshield, cornstalks whipping past my head . . ." Harold couldn't finish the sentence for laughing.

"Grandma came running out to the back porch with a broom in her hand," Mike continued, amid his own peals of laughter. "In the meantime, Harold finally got the car stopped. Jake knew he was in trouble and just took out running down the road."

"With Grandma on my heels waving that broom," Jake finished. "By the time Mama got through whipping me I'd rather have had that broom upside my head."

The whole room burst into laughter, and then they were on to Jake's twin, Johnny, and his shenanigans with stealing the chicken's eggs.

Later that night, after a round of leisurely lovemaking back at the hotel, Dominique cuddled up next to her gigantic teddy bear. "I really love your family," she whispered, rubbing her hand over his muscular shoulders and down his back.

"They love you, too," Jake replied. "Especially Mama. She's never acted so comfortable with any of the women I've brought around as she did with you."

Not even your late wife? Dominique thought but did not voice. She'd won Miss Bernie's approval, something that the wives had privately told her was no small feat. "If Miss Bernie likes you, that's saying something," John's wife Cynthia had told her when they'd both ended up in the kitchen alone. And then she'd added something that had given Dominique serious pause. "I'm glad Jake finally found you so he can get married again. He's not much for the single life."

Dominique turned her back to Jake so she could spoon up against him. She loved the fill of being in his embrace, his weighty arm slung around her waist, his thick thighs pressed against hers. "I love you, Jake," she whispered, thinking he was asleep.

But he wasn't, as she found out when he answered, "I love you, too."

47

Dominique returned from the Thanksgiving vacation refreshed, and very thankful. Meeting Jake's family had not only solidified their relationship, but it had bolstered her belief that relaxing her rule on not dating anyone seriously and giving Jake a real chance had been the right thing to do. He'd proven to be the missing puzzle piece from her life, someone with whom to share and confide. Jake had turned out to not only be a good listener, but a man whose opinion and advice were solid and helpful. He'd helped her feel better about her position at *Capricious,* encouraged her to embrace her power, and more importantly reminded her that she'd been looking for a job when she got that one. This is the reason she wasn't overly frazzled today when she was set to meet with the board and a number of investors. Jake's encouragement, plus the trick that Mirabelle pulled from her sleeve, gave her the assurance that all would be well.

An hour after arriving to work, Dominique stepped into the fashionably appointed conference room.

She'd dressed to impress and did so in her designer chocolate-brown power suit paired with an ivory shell and heels and gold jewelry. Her locs were shiny and freshly done, her makeup applied to perfection, and the scent of her favorite perfume clung to her body like a second skin. She walked to the table with authority, greeting those who were gathered around it. Neither François nor the magazine's newest investor had arrived.

"*Mon ami,*" Mirabelle purred as she stood to hug Dominique, giving air kisses to each side of her face. "You look marvelous!"

"Thank you," Dominique replied. "So do you. And have you lost more weight? Girl, you know you don't need to do that."

"Well," Mirabelle said, her voice lowering to an almost-whisper, "I've been getting quite the workout lately."

"What's his name?" Dominique replied without hesitation. She knew that Mirabelle wouldn't be caught dead in a gym unless it was to pick up her boy toy or for a fashion photo shoot.

Mirabelle's answer was interrupted when François entered, a look of superiority on his face. The Italian magazine editor was right behind him, her look smug even as her eyes nervously darted around the room. Everyone took the time to speak to each other and make pleasantries before the meeting was called to order.

"As you know," François began, once it was his turn to speak, "a competitor magazine will be releasing sometime this year, which is why I've asked Daniela Amato, the editor in chief of *La Prima*, Italy's leading fashion magazine, to join us. I'll detail why momentarily but secondly, I'm very pleased to hear that a *very* influential member of French society has a strong interest in becoming part of our family. He has royal ties," François gushed, his accent becoming even more pronounced as he widened his eyes and placed a hand on his chest. "And he is well-known among the A-listers of the Hollywood community. We are very excited about his potentially joining the magazine's board as a major investor. I've spoken with him *personally* about many things including changes I believe will help breathe new life into this publication." He cast a look in Dominique's direction, and then looked at his watch. "His name is—"

The door to the conference room opened.

"Xavier Marquis," François dramatically announced, his face beaming as he stood and walked over to greet Xavier. "I was just telling the room about you, sir. Please come in and have a seat."

Xavier strode into the room with a command reserved for those with rich, blue bloodlines and old wealth. He sat, greeted those around the table, and then sat back as François continued. For the next thirty minutes, those around the table provided their newest member with a snapshot of their responsibilities and how they felt the magazine was currently positioned in the publishing world. Dominique's presentation was strong. She purposely kept the focus squarely on *Capricious* instead of herself, spouting off facts and figures from memory and sharing her well-researched thoughts on what she felt was the right path for *Capricious* to follow from here on out. "The average woman in America is still a size 12," she finished, glad to see that she had everyone's undivided attention. Even François looked on with what appeared to be sincere interest. "Most women are not A-list celebrities and do not come from great wealth. Which is why I believe that while continuing to woo the big names for covers and lead stories, an emphasized focus on the average American woman— the working girl, single mother, married stay-at-home mom juggling four kids and the like—will help us keep the readers we now have and increase awareness of our brand into the breadbasket of America, and beyond."

"I disagree," François countered. "The woman washing clothes or changing diapers does not want to read about someone else's equally dull life. She wants fantasy, an escape from the mundane. Yes, she appreciates seeing a woman on the page who looks like her but she doesn't *care* about her." He smiled warmly at Daniela. "Ms. Amato has brought to my attention a bright idea, one that would take *Capricious* in the direction of, say, a glossy, upscale, *classy* version of the celebrity-driven tabloid magazine: beautiful big people, lots of gossip, and our continued commitment to fashion, nutrition, and exercise. I would add that in light of today's economic climate we scale back the number of pages in the magazine and reduce the price by one dollar. We'd sell more when people pay less and believe that the latest scoop on their favorite TV star awaits them between our pages." When François finished, his face was flushed red with excitement. He turned to Xavier, his eyes filled with anticipation of the praise that he expected. "What do you think, Mr. Marquis?"

Xavier made eye contact with several of those around the table. Then he turned to François. "I appreciate your enthusiasm, François. But I think that not only does Dominique Clark have her finger on the pulse of what today's woman desires to read, I believe that she is the very embodiment of *Capricious*. The idea I find intriguing and which brought me to the decision to put my influence and money behind this publication has at its heart the woman who not only helps tell these women's stories, but lives it. Ladies, gentlemen, when the next issue of *Capricious* goes into planning, my strong suggestion is that Dominique Clark come out from behind the scenes and leap onto the very pages of the magazine she helped make a household name."

Later that evening, Dominique recounted the events as she and Jake shared dinner in his dining room. Justin was at home doing his homework, under Tessa's watchful eye. While he knew that Jake and Dominique were very good friends, she'd purposely stopped short of using the word "dating" to describe their relationship. Justin didn't know that Dominique had met Jake's family. When asked, she'd told him she was going away on business. Initially Jake had balked at the deception, but Dominique explained that she didn't want to get Justin's hopes up until she was more sure of the relationship's potential for longevity. Fortunately, Leland had called, and Justin spent the holiday with his dad and half-siblings. He came back too excited about their time on the Gulf of Mexico to ask too many questions about her trip.

"So, in the boardroom old boy had to back that thing up and recognize, huh?" Jake said, scooping up a succulent bite of baked halibut.

"He was pitiful," Dominique replied, picking at the steamed vegetables on her plate. "As soon as he realized the winds had changed, he was running up behind me like a Pekingese in heat."

"What'd you do?"

"Well, I didn't bitch-slap him across the room the way I wanted."

"Ha!"

"I was gracious. But François Deux has torn his coat with me. I'll never forget this."

"Who's this French guy who came to your defense in such a hurry."

Dominique's hand stopped midway to her water glass. "What does that mean?"

"Are you sure a stake in the magazine is all he wants?"

Dominique smirked before taking a drink of water. "Jealousy doesn't look cute on you, baby, but I appreciate it. For the record, Xavier is married to a gorgeous sistah. I don't think he's going anywhere anytime soon."

"Well, for the *record*," Jake said, mimicking her statement, "you'd better not be thinking of going anywhere anytime soon either."

Dominique leaned over and kissed Jake full on the lips. "Baby, the only place I'm going is home to my son."

A half hour later, Dominique climbed into her car and headed home. She smiled when she saw Justin's face on her Caller ID. "Hey, baby."

"Mama, when are you coming home?"

"Right now, Justin. Why?"

"'Cause, I want to see you."

"What about?"

"Nothing." He paused. "I haven't seen you all day."

Dominique's heart clenched. "Aw, does my baby miss me?"

"I'm not a baby," he sulked. But he didn't say that she was wrong.

"I miss you too, baby. I'll be home in five minutes to beat you in a game of tennis."

"Girl, please. I'm gonna kick your butt! Bye!"

Dominique laughed as Justin hurried off the phone before she could correct him. Even as it seemed he grew an inch each time she blinked, there were still times like these when the little boy came through. "It goes fast," Faith had reminded her just last week, as they reminisced about Michael's rowdy thirteenth birthday party. Faith was right, Dominique decided. *I'm going to savor these moments for as long as I can.* As she opened the door and entered her house to the sound of Justin's laughter, she thought of her life: a fabulous job, a fine, strong man, and a son who made her heart swell. Dominique's life hadn't been this good in a long, long time but right now, it was perfect. She wouldn't change a thing.

48

Dominique sighed with contentment as she looked at the Christmas lights decorating the neighborhood. This was her favorite time of year: lighter schedule, cooler temperatures, and her favorite holiday right around the corner. This second Saturday in December was the first she'd taken off since going to Oakland for the Raiders' game. The last time before that had been at least four months. Relaxing felt good, and Dominique surmised that she would do it more often. She listened as Justin and Michael chatted in the backseat, going back and forth about who knew more about which team would win the Super Bowl. Jake was on the phone talking to Miss Bernie. In six short weeks, Dominique had gone from viewing Jake as a lover of convenience to thinking that he could quite possibly be her soul mate. They talked every day, often more than once, and saw each other often. Usually he'd come to the office or she'd visit his place, but occasionally, like today, they included Justin in their outing. She didn't know whether he'd accepted that she and

Jake were just friends, or whether he knew the deal and chose to remain silent. Jake had finally convinced her that the holiday season would be the perfect time to talk with him about their relationship, and ease him into the idea of their becoming a family.

Family. Dominique marveled that she was even entertaining the idea of the white picket fence. She'd thought those planks had been cut and burned a long time ago. Leland and Kevin had left a bad taste in her mouth, but Jake had turned sour to sweet and encouraged her to love again. She listened as he laughed at something Miss Bernie said, and wondered how she'd ever thought twice about having this man in her life.

"Mama said hello," Jake said, after the call had ended, "and that she's expecting to see you down there for Christmas."

"What did you tell her?"

Jake reached over and grabbed her hand. "I said we'd call her later. But she's not going to take no for an answer so . . . I know your mom is expecting us for dinner as well so we're going to have to figure out how to be in two places at once."

A few moments later, Jake pulled up to the outdoor ice skating rink. Though not visible from where they'd parked, Dominique still gazed towards the well landscaped walkway as if she were going to her doom.

"Come on, girl," Jake said, laughing at her expression.

"I still can't believe you talked me into doing this." Images of herself splayed across the ice looking like a beached whale kept dancing before her.

"I told you, it's easy. You'll do fine."

"If I fall, Jake, you'd better catch me. I mean it!"

Jake paid the entrance fee and soon they were sitting on benches lacing up their skates. Michael and Justin were old pros at this sport and were off in a flash. Jake skated out on the ice a ways before returning, spinning, and coming to a flawless stop directly in front of her.

"Show-off," Dominique pouted.

"Come on, baby," Jake said, laughing. "I've got you."

After a bit more coaxing, Dominique found herself skating. Okay, more like walking, gliding, and holding on to Jake's hips and being pulled across the rink. Fearless kids, teens, and adults whizzed around them. Jake guided them to the side where Dominique could grab on to the railing.

"Okay, baby, listen. I want you to put your arms around me and then mimic my feet. You told me you used to roller skate, right?"

"But that was years ago, Jake."

"Use that same rhythm, the same back and forth with the blade as you did with the roller. Just groove with my body," his voice lowered, "the way you did last night." Dominique felt her face grow warm. Jake kissed her on the nose. "Come on, now. Wrap your arms around me." She did, and Jake slowly began moving. "That's it. Now just let your body move with mine. Don't be afraid. I won't let you fall."

They took one complete turn around the rink with Dominique's triple D's pressed into Jake's back. During the second turn, she relaxed enough to release her grip a little, and even wave at Justin and Michael as they raced past them. By the third time around, she'd gained enough confidence to take his hand and skate side by side.

"I'm doing it!" Dominique exclaimed with excitement, as she navigated a turn looking only half as clumsy as she had before. "This is fun!"

They went around a couple more times. Jake joked with the boys and Dominique could tell that he wanted to let loose and put his skating skills to work. "Help me over to the snack bar," she said as they neared it.

"Are you sure?"

"Yes, baby. I'll grab some hot chocolate while you men do your thing."

She took a seat and after buying her a large hot chocolate topped with real marshmallows, Jake zoomed off in search of Justin and Michael. Moments later she laughed as she watched Jake roar past them and then witnessed the boys' vain attempt to catch up to his long, powerful strides. Soon other skaters joined them and before long, there was a large group zipping around the outer side of the rink, leaving the inner ice for the less brave. Jake said something to Justin and his peal of laughter bounced off of the ice and into her heart. It thrilled her to see him so happy. A few more bricks from the wall around her heart tumbled down and suddenly visions of future outings with the three of them, and with her and Jake's families, began dancing in her head.

"Stop it, Dominique," she warned herself. It had only been official for a few short weeks and the last thing she wanted to do was be a typical female and start prematurely imagining herself with his last

name. In spite of herself, however, she decided that
"Dominique McDonald" sounded pretty darn good.

Dominique took a sip of chocolate and reached
into her pocket for her cell phone. *Oh, darn it.* She'd
forgotten that, at Jake's insistence, she'd left it in the
car. He knew her penchant for working, even when
she was supposed to be taking a break. When she'd
protested, he'd countered, "Nothing is going to
happen in the next hour that you can't handle when
we get back to the car."

A little over an hour later, the group headed back
to Jake's SUV. On the way, Michael boasted that
he'd beaten Jake in a race while Justin insisted that
Jake had let him win. Sensing a fight coming on,
Dominique shifted the boys' attention by asking
where they wanted to eat. This brought on another
debate: Michael wanted pizza; Justin, tacos.

"I'll settle it," Jake said, in a commanding voice
that brooked no argument. "We're not going to
Italy or Mexico. We're going Chinese."

Michael and Justin immediately joined forces to
voice their objection, and soon Jake had joined the
fray. Dominique laughed as they reached the car
and Jake popped the lock so that they all could
climb inside.

"What about barbeque?" Dominique said, once
they'd all gotten in the car.

"Yeah!" was the chorus from the backseat.

"Yes," Dominique countered.

"And salad," Jake added, as he buckled his seatbelt. He put the keys in the ignition and was about
to start the car when he noticed his message light
blinking. He reached for his cell phone, looked at
it, and frowned.

Dominique was immediately concerned. "What is it?"

"I don't know, but something's up, several missed calls from Mama and my brothers." Jake touched the screen and put the phone to his ear. "Hey, man." Dominique held her breath as she watched Jake's expression. Later, she'd swear that she witnessed the blood drain from his face. "How is he?" Jake started the car, quickly backing up and heading for the boulevard. "Tell him to hang on, bro. I'll be there just as soon as I can."

Jake threw down the phone and gripped the wheel with both hands. Three pairs of bewildered eyes stared at him.

"What's wrong?" Dominique asked, a sense of dread hitting her stomach and spreading in all directions.

"It's Harold," Jake said. His voice grew hoarse as he continued. "He's had another heart attack. This was a big one. They don't know if he'll make it."

49

Dominique sat in the middle of her king-size bed, willing the phone to ring. She'd barely slept and had hardly eaten since dropping off Jake at the airport the night before. Knowing that time was of the essence, Jake had called the same friend with whom they'd flown to the Raiders' game and chartered his private jet to get to Alabama as soon as possible. Dominique had asked if he wanted her to go with him, but that would have meant more time lost as she got Justin and Michael situated. "Just let me get to him, baby," Jake had said, his voice strained with fear. "I'll call you as soon as I can."

That had been more than twelve hours ago. Several times, Dominique had reached for the phone. A couple times she'd even tapped his name on her Android screen. But figuring he'd call at his first opportunity, she'd stopped short of tapping his number and instead had texted that she was thinking of him, and praying.

Knowing that trying to sleep was futile, Dominique climbed out of bed, wrapped her robe around her, and padded barefoot downstairs. Today would be her day to handle the boys all alone. After so many weekends of Justin staying in Inglewood, Faith had left Alexis with Anita so that she and Aaron could spend a much-needed weekend alone. They'd gone to a spa in Palm Desert and Tessa had left a message saying her sister in Tucson had had her baby three weeks early and she'd be gone for several days. So even if Jake had wanted her to go, it would have been difficult.

Dominique put on a pot of coffee and then started browsing her fridge and pantry, seeing if there was anything she could put together as breakfast for the boys. She thanked God for Tessa as she noted eggs, turkey bacon, and frozen French toast. Sure that the boys had stayed up half the night, she decided against starting to cook until she heard them up and about. In the meantime, she poured herself a cup of coffee, sat at the counter, and reflected over how her life had changed since Jake had walked into it.

She was just about to pour her second cup of joe when the phone rang. "Jake, how is he?"

"Still with us," Jake replied, his voice raspy with weariness and emotion.

"Thank God," Dominique whispered, clutching the phone.

"Thank God is right. If the hospital hadn't had the records from his previous heart problems, they wouldn't have been able to react so quickly. They wheeled him straight into surgery. He was there for five hours. They just wheeled him down to ICU. It's still touch and go."

At this moment, there was no place Dominique

would rather be than in Alabama with her arms wrapped around Jake's waist. "Baby, how are you? You sound exhausted."

"It don't matter how I am," he responded, in a harsh voice.

Dominique wisely chose not to respond to this stress-induced comment. "Tessa's sister had her baby, but I can take the boys over to Mama's and catch a plane this evening . . . if you want me to."

Jake's emotions were clearly roiling. "It's crazy down here, baby," he said at last. "Stay up there and handle your business. I'll keep you posted."

"You've been here for me, Jake," Dominique countered. "Now, I want to be there for you."

"I gotta go. I'll call you later." The click of being disconnected was his good-bye.

Throughout the rest of the day and into the evening, Dominique warred with her thoughts. This side of Jake—subdued, curt, vulnerable—wasn't one she'd seen before. She tried to rationalize his behavior, put herself in his shoes. Should something happen to Faith, heaven forbid, Dominique imagined that she'd be clinging to Jake like white on rice. *But men are different,* she reasoned.

"Mom, we're hungry!" Justin announced, taking Dominique's mind off worry and, for the time being, placing it on food. She was glad for the distraction.

"What's wrong?" As soon as Faith saw Dominique's face, she knew there was trouble.

"It's Jake's brother," Dominique said, eyeing Aaron, Michael, and Justin as they walked inside the comfortable Inglewood residence while the sisters remained outside. "Yesterday, he had a heart attack."

"Oh, no." Faith immediately reached out for Dominique, giving her a nice, long hug. "I'm sorry, sister."

Dominique welcomed the embrace. "Me, too," she said, hugging her back.

"If you need to go down there, don't worry about Justin. We'll take care of him. He can miss a few days of school without a problem."

"Thanks, sister, but right now, Jake wants me to hold tight. They don't know whether Harold is going to make it and quite frankly I'm not sure Jake wants me to see him in this frame of mind."

"But you're the woman who loves him. Where else would you be than by his side?"

"I feel the same way," Dominique replied as the two made their way up the sidewalk and into the house. "And even though it goes totally against my nature, I'm trying to let Jake take the lead."

Over the next three days, calls from Jake were sporadic. Dominique's days were busy, spent planning the issue that would feature her life and profile as the lead story. But not busy enough not to notice that Jake seemed more and more distant. The pain of his brother's life hanging in the balance was evident every time she heard his voice. Dominique recalled the brothers and their closeness, how Jake had looked up to Harold as a father figure when their father had died. *Please let him live,* Dominique found herself praying. *Please don't let Jake lose his brother. Not now, not when we have just found love.*

By Thursday evening, Jake was still in Alabama. His brother's condition still remained critical. Everyone still prayed.

"Where's Jake?" Justin asked, shortly after they'd eaten dinner and Tessa had left.

"He's still in Birmingham, honey," Dominique replied. The day following Harold's attack, Dominique had explained to Justin what had happened, that Jake's brother had gotten very sick and had surgery, and that Jake had flown to Alabama to be by his side.

"Is his brother going to die?"

Dominique swallowed past the lump of fear in her throat as she formed an answer. "We sure hope not, baby," she said, rubbing Justin's arm and then squeezing his hand. She saw the look of worry in his eyes and continued. "A heart attack is very serious. But they got to the hospital quickly, so that increased Harold's chances of getting better. So let's just think really positive thoughts about Jake and his brother, and I think that will help them feel better. Okay?"

Justin nodded his head. But his eyes remained sad.

Dominique clasped his hands in hers. "What is it? What's bothering you, Justin?"

Justin's look was haunted as he locked eyes with his mother. "Is Jake coming back?"

Dominique bit her lip to keep it from trembling. *Of course he's coming back.* That's what she wanted to say but in this moment, faced with the question head on, she experienced a wave of doubt. *Why wouldn't he come back? He's got to come back.* Their recent, static conversations played in her head. He didn't want her to come down. He didn't know when he'd be back. Then she thought of other times when men had walked out of Justin's life: the time when she assured Justin that Leland would return, and he didn't, or when she acknowledged that Kevin was gone for good and the pain that truthful answer had caused.

She looked at Justin, whose eyes continued to bore into hers for an answer. So she gave him the only one in which she could absolutely be sure. "I hope so."

50

"Hang all the mistletoe." Dominique bobbed her head to the timeless Donny Hathaway classic as she twirled the stick of peppermint around in the drink that Aaron had made for her. He told her it was his girly holiday original: vodka, milk, peppermint schnapps, and Baileys Irish Cream poured over crushed ice. It was Christmas Eve and everyone had gathered at Anita's house. The kids were downstairs watching movies and playing games. Anita and some of her friends were in the kitchen cooking. Aaron's two sisters were sitting around the room either singing or humming to the music and Dominique sat alone, watching her brother-in-law dance Faith around the room. "A very special Christmas for me . . ."

Or so she'd thought. In reality, Christmas was turning out to be nothing like she'd imagined. Last week, she thought she'd be dancing in the arms of her man, spending Christmas with her own family before bringing the New Year in with Jake's family. She'd looked forward to spending her favorite holiday with a man she cared about for the first time in years, watching *It's a Wonderful Life*, hearing silver bells, and laughing as Michael sang about seeing Mommy kissing Santa Claus. Instead, she sat with a smile on her face that didn't reach her heart, trying to be happy. She wasn't. Misery and loneliness hung like garlands around her.

Halfway through the drink, Dominique set it on the bar. She'd never been a heavy drinker and the deceptively shakelike drink was going straight to her head and adding to her melancholy. The last time she'd talked to Jake was when she'd reached him at the hospital and he said he'd call her back. That was two days ago. Her calls from yesterday and today had gone to voicemail. *What is going on?*

Donny's melodious voice trailed off and soon James Brown was admonishing Santa to go straight to the ghetto. This lively number brought Aaron's sister and her date to their feet. Even Anita came out of the kitchen, waving her hand like she was in church. Soon some of the kids came up from downstairs, laughing at the adults while mocking their dances. James took a break and the Temptations slid right in, singing "Hey, Rudolph!" The CD changed and now the Chipmunks were dashing through the snow, grandma was getting run over by a reindeer, and Paul McCartney was simply having a wonderful Christmastime. *Well, I'm not,* Dominique thought, as the party became more and more boisterous. Anita and her friends brought out hors d'oeuvres. Soon honey-glazed, barbequed, and fried chicken wings were being waved in the air, and plates were being filled with potato salad, baked beans, and coleslaw to soak up the now free-flowing libations. By the time Mr. Cole's chestnuts began roasting on an open fire,

Dominique had had enough. As quietly as possible, she slipped out of the living room, up the stairs, and through the first door she came to. It was Faith's daughter Alexis's room. With only the Frog Princess night-light to guide her way, Dominique walked around the room that so embodied her niece's frilliness: the pink, lacy comforter covering a white, canopied bed. Rows of dolls lined the Princess dresser, its top cluttered with an open box filled with plastic jewelry, its now-still ballerina poised for the next windup.

Dominique walked over and sat on the bed. She'd never thought much about having another child but now recalled one seemingly innocuous comment when Jake had mentioned the joy brought by little girls. When she'd pressed and asked if he wanted children, Jake had shaken his head. "Too risky," he'd said cryptically. "I'd never want to take the chance of having my child grow up without me." Dominique didn't realize that she was crying until a tear plopped on her arm and rolled down her wrist.

"Nikki, you in here?" Faith eased the door open and seeing her sister sitting on the bed, hurriedly closed the door and walked over. Dominique tried to quickly wipe away tears, but Faith had seen them and knew their cause. She sat down on the bed. "He still hasn't called?"

Dominique shook her head.

"I'm sorry, Nikki."

"Me, too."

"Do you think you should try and call him again?"

"I think two days of unreturned phone calls is a loud enough message."

Faith had no answer for this comeback, and remained silent.

Dominique lay down on Alexis's bed.

"I'll go get your cell phone, bring it up in case he calls." Faith reached for the colorful afghan at the end of the bed and pulled it up over her sister. "The kids are all crashing on air mattresses downstairs. You can sleep in here tonight."

An hour after Faith had brought Dominique's phone to her, it rang. Her heart beat an erratic rhythm as she eyed the caller ID. "Hello?"

"Hey, Dominique." Jake's voice was heavy.

Dominique's heart jumped to her throat. "How's Harold?"

Long pause. "He had a bad day yesterday, some kind of infection. He's getting antibiotics intravenously. The doctors are cautiously optimistic but it's still an uphill battle."

Dominique released the breath she'd been holding. "How are you, baby?"

"To tell you the truth, I've been better."

Dominique sat up against the wall and hugged her niece's large, stuffed animal to her, wishing she could hug Jake instead. "You want to talk?"

Longer pause.

For a while, Dominique wondered if he'd hung up. But she remained silent.

"This situation . . . the waiting, the hospital smell, the nurses . . . it brings it all back . . . when my dad died."

More silence.

Is he crying? So many thoughts ran through Dominique's mind, but she voiced none of them. What should she say? Don't worry? Keep the faith? Everything sounded so cliché and useless.

"I don't know what I'll do if I lose him, Nick . . ."

"Then let's stay positive," Dominique blurted before she could stop herself. "Keep praying that he'll be okay."

"Yeah, that's what they told me when I was twelve years old, to keep praying. I wore my knees out praying that my father would make it. That he'd open his eyes just one more time. It's my biggest fear, Dominique. That like my dad, I won't see my fifty-fifth birthday. I think that underneath it all it's why I never had kids. I never want to put a child through what I went through."

Again Dominique felt at a loss for words. Everything she could think of to utter could be thrown back in her face. Still, she had to try. "Jake," she said softly, "you've said yourself that the heart problems in your family are due largely to diet and lack of exercise. Baby, you eat right and are in great shape. There is nothing to say that you won't live a long, healthy life."

"And there is nothing saying I will."

"Tomorrow's not promised to any of us." After a lengthy silence, Dominique changed the subject. "Justin has asked about you. He wants to know when you're coming home. So does his mom," she finished in a whisper.

"See, that's just it, Nick. Already Justin has grown attached to me, and if something ever happened . . ."

"Please, baby. Please don't think this way. Whatever is in our future, let's face it together."

"I don't know if I can."

Dominique thought her own heart had stopped. "What does that mean?"

Again, silence.

"Jake?" Dominique felt as if the moment were surreal, that she was observing herself in an unfolding drama. Surely what sounded like was happening couldn't be happening.

"I love you, Dominique. And I love Justin. I don't want to hurt y'all."

"Then don't!"

"But can't you see, baby? The longer we hang out, the harder it will be if something happens."

"That's a chance I'm willing to take!" *This is nonsense!* She wanted to scream. *This is crazy!*

"I'm going to stay here a while, make sure my brother pulls all the way through. In this time, I think that maybe you ought to think about a life without me in it."

Dominique was stunned, floored. She felt like a Mike Tyson left hook had come from nowhere and laid her smoothly out.

"Merry Christmas, Nick. I love you."

Ten minutes after he'd said good-bye, Dominique was still holding the phone, staring at the wall, dumbfounded. This Christmas wasn't merry at all.

51

Somehow, Dominique made it through the night without pulling out her hair. For Justin's sake, she knew she had to keep it together. Faith was a big help. She tried to get Dominique to look at the bright side.

"He's going through a lot right now," Faith suggested. "And probably saying things that he doesn't mean."

"But what if he does mean them?" Dominique countered. "What if he decides that he doesn't want a relationship after all?"

"Then we'll do what we have to," she finally answered. "If I can lose a child and come back, you can survive this."

"Thank God we didn't tell Justin that we were a couple. He'll be devastated enough as it is."

When Dominique left the next morning, she let Justin stay with Faith. He'd noticed how quiet she was last night, when she'd finally rejoined the family downstairs. When he'd asked her what was wrong, she'd been honest. "I miss Jake, and I'm worried about his brother." They were going to San Diego and returning on New Year's Eve. Dominique hoped that she would have it together by then.

Today, the day after Christmas, Dominique sat in the otherwise empty offices of *Capricious* magazine. She'd returned to the one thing that had been the constant in her life the last ten years besides her son—work. The issue they'd been working on had been put to bed before the holidays so Dominique plunged herself into the summer issue that would feature her story. "My story," she grumbled, as she pored over pictures of possible locations for her photo shoot. At the moment, Dominique couldn't imagine anybody being interested in her sad tale.

Two hours later Dominique stopped and stretched her back, now feeling the pain of being humped over a viewing table for two hours. She'd gone to the photo gallery, pulled some of the shots rejected from past publications, and gone through them to see if there was a gem she'd missed. She also realized that for the first time since Jake had wished her Merry Christmas, she actually had an appetite. She walked to her desk, pulled out a half dozen takeout menus and, after flipping through them quickly, reached for her phone.

"Yes, I'd like a double cheeseburger with everything on it," she said, after the young girl answered the phone and took her phone number, which pulled up the company's address. "An order of onion rings and an order of fries." Dominique waited as the girl pushed buttons. "Yes, a strawberry shake. No, large." She hung up the phone and felt a twinge of guilt at what she knew was emotional eating. The bad feeling deepened when she thought of Harold and the fact that too many meals like this were partly why he was lying in a hospital. But Dominique was hurting and, right now, a double cheese and starchy potatoes sounded like the perfect antidote. She shook off the guilt and refused to feel bad. *I'll eat a salad tomorrow.*

With food on its way, Dominique reached for another batch of pictures. When her phone rang, she thought about not answering it, but it was probably her mother, sister, or son, so she reached for her phone. She looked at the caller ID and was a bit surprised to see an unknown number. She quickly silenced the ringer and put the phone down. *It's a shame they have telemarketers working through the holiday.* True, she was at work also, but it was her choice. She returned to the stack of pictures, paying particular attention to a shoot that had been performed in Griffith Park. A bike trail laden with greenery and a bridge across a stream of water caught her eye. She could see herself, decked to the nines—the complexity of fashion set against the simplistic backdrop of nature. *Fabulous.*

Then another thought came before she could stop it. Of the last time she'd taken in trees, wild flowers, and boulders stacked against a stark, blue sky. It was when she and Jake had taken a drive down a winding road near the ocean in Palos Verdes and later stopped at Wayfarers Chapel, a building made of mostly glass. With hands entwined, they'd taken in the beauty of the well-tended garden and stopped for a passionate kiss between the irises and azaleas. Dominique dropped the pictures and leaned back in her red leather chair. This evoked another memory: Jake and the passionate love they'd made. She leaped from the chair as if on fire, walked quickly to the minifridge and retrieved a cold bottle of sparkling water. She had been a faucet of dripping tears for most of the previous evening. *I'm done crying,* she told herself. *I can do this.*

But the truth of the matter was she was tired of doing this: being strong, starting over, surviving heartbreaks.

Her message indicator beeped.

The unknown caller left a message?

Dominique crossed the room and picked up her phone. Walking to the window, she tapped the screen to retrieve the message and after the automated voice informed her that she had one new message, she was all ears.

"Hey, Dominique, this is Cynthia, Johnny's wife. We, uh, we talked to Jake and heard what happened. We're thinking about you and wondering how you're doing. Johnny wants to talk to you. Give us a call, sis. We love you."

What happened? What had they heard? Dominique had barely absorbed the shock of this phone call when the downstairs buzzer sounded. Dominique's appetite was gone. She went downstairs, paid the delivery guy, and walked enough food to feed three people back to her office. She walked over to the table, pushed aside a stack of photos, and set down the aluminum container designed to keep her delivery piping hot. She pulled out the burger and fries. The smell of ground round and sautéed onions wafted up to her nostrils. She absentmindedly reached for a fry and chewed on it as she walked back to the window.

Cynthia called. Johnny wants to talk to me. Jake's family is thinking about me. But what about Jake?

Dominique tossed the half-eaten fry in the trash and walked purposefully to the phone on her desk. Before giving herself time to think, she scrolled to the 205 area code and hit redial. At the sound of Johnny's voice, her heart clenched. He sounded so much like Jake.

"Hi Johnny, it's Dominique."

"Hey, sis."

"How's Harold?

"He's doing a little better," Jake said, hope evident in his voice. "If things keep going the way they are, they'll change his status from critical to serious in the next few days."

"That's great, Jake. I mean . . . Johnny. Sorry."

"That's all right, Dominique. Look here, Jake told me that he'd . . . you know . . . put the brakes on y'all and what not."

That's what he's doing? Letting me down easy?

"I watched y'all at Thanksgiving and know you've got feelings for him. How are you doing, Dominique?"

"That's a good question," Dominique answered, sinking into her red leather chair. "Because evidently he's told y'all more than he's told me." Dominique took a breath to quell her growing anger. "I just don't get it, Johnny. One minute we're having the best time ever and the next minute he's 'putting on the brakes' as you say. I understand this is a stressful time but usually that's when people want those they love close to them."

"Trust me, he loves you."

"Oh really? I can't tell."

"That's why I had Cynthia call you, Dominique."

"I mean, his reasoning is totally irrational! He says that because heart disease runs in your family he doesn't want to get any closer to me and Justin. Does that make sense to you?"

"It does . . . but only because I know him, and know what he's been through." Johnny waited, and when Dominique remained silent, he went on. "Jake's a big dude; he gets your attention when he walks into a room. That's why he's able to hide the little boy that is still there, just under the surface. Jake has had to deal with a lot in his lifetime, a lot of heartache, a lot of death. Jake took Dad's death harder than any of us," Johnny went on, his voice soft, reflective. "He worshipped the ground the old man walked on and when he left . . . it's like a part of Jake went with him. Like I said, he's a big dude but underneath all that muscle and bravado is a great big, soft heart."

"I've seen it," Dominique said, her voice almost a whisper as she remembered Jake's sensitivity toward both her and her son. "But what does it matter if he wants to keep it hidden behind fear?" As she said this, she realized how Jake must have felt when she kept pushing him away because she was afraid. "I can't say that I can relate to what he's feeling because I can't. I just don't know what I'm supposed to do."

"Give him time, sis," Johnny answered immediately. "He's pushing you away, but that's not what he wants."

"It hurts, Johnny." Dominique paused, swallowed, aware of the gravity of her next words. "Maybe it's best that I . . . give him some room."

"I understand," Johnny responded. "But there are two things that I need to tell you, to help you understand what Jake is going through right now."

"What's that?"

"We lost Daddy around this same time, just before Christmas. And when he had his heart attack . . . Jake is the one who found him."

52

It was the second day of January and Jake was still in Alabama. He'd spent New Year's Eve at Harold's bedside, happy that they'd finally upgraded his condition from critical to serious, and that they'd moved him out of the ICU. He'd been staying at Harold and Susie's house, but on New Year's Day he'd gone over to Miss Bernie's for the prerequisite serving of greens and black-eyed peas—good luck for the New Year. And today, when he'd wanted to do nothing more than sit in his mother's guest room and let the TV watch him (since he'd stared at it off and on for three days and couldn't put two sentences together about what he'd watched), he sat in Harold and Susie's living room with Johnny, Cynthia, Mike, and Lillian, who were busy trash-talking in a high-spirited game of bid whist. His mother had insisted that he get out of her house. Jake thought it was because she was tired of seeing him mope around. But his brothers were in on the real reason. Shortly after the card game ended, the women decided to go shopping while Johnny and

Mike grabbed beers before joining Jake in the living room.

"You want one?" Mike asked. Jake shook his head and Mike sat down.

For a moment the brothers were silent, staring at a TV on mute.

Johnny set down his beer and leaned forward with his hands on his knees, eyeing his brother intently. "You call her yet?"

Jake thought about feigning ignorance but that idea was quickly doused. His twin had known everything about him since they'd been born. They could read each other's thoughts and finish each other's sentences. "No," he finally replied.

"Why not?" Mike asked, exasperation showing in his voice. Clearly, he was not as patient as his younger brother.

"It's better this way." Jake responded.

Johnny pressed. "Better for whom?"

Belatedly Jake realized that, since it was obvious he was in for a grilling, an ice-cold beer may have been a good choice after all. Then again, he reasoned, having a clear head may be the best bet. He sat back and said nothing. He figured they'd tire of talking to a wall and then leave him alone.

"I spoke to her," said Johnny.

The wall talked. "You what?"

"Cynthia suggested it, bro, and she was right. We'd both seen how she looked at you when she was here for Thanksgiving; all the love that sistah has for you, man. We were concerned about her and knowing you like I do, I couldn't be sure that you'd been in contact." Johnny went on despite the frown on

Jake's face. "She's family, Jake. And we wanted her to know that we were thinking about her."

Even though he didn't like his brother all up in his business, Jake's anger dissipated behind Johnny's words. He sat back and let what his brother said sink in. It was true. From the time Dominique first stepped foot in his mother's house, she seemed part of the family. Everyone had told him how much they enjoyed her and shortly after returning from this vacation, his sisters-in-law had called him to say they'd received the latest issue of *Capricious* along with a complimentary, one-year subscription. As if to underscore her presence in their lives, he glanced down and saw *Capricious* magazines on the coffee table's bottom ledge, wedged between *Essence* and *Time.*

"How was she?" Jake finally asked.

"Beside herself," was Johnny's quick reply. "Confused, angry, trying to understand why you're shutting her out when all she wants to do is support you in your hour of need."

The anger came back. *Yes, this feels good. This helps me feel better about the shitty way I've been treating the love of my life.* "It wasn't your place, dude."

Johnny shrugged. "I made it my place."

"What goes on between me and Nick is none of your business!" Jake bellowed, before standing up and dramatically walking out of the room.

Mike and Johnny watched dispassionately as he left.

Mike took a long, satisfying swig of beer. The quietest of the brothers, he'd been fine with letting Johnny handle the conversation while it was his comment to Cynthia that had gotten the whole complicated ball rolling all along. "Do you think we pissed him off enough so he'll call her?"

"Hard to tell," Johnny answered, drinking the last of his brew. "Jake can be stubborn when he wants to. But I have a feeling that Dominique is the kind of woman who won't let go of something she wants without a fight."

Later that evening, Jake sent a message to the principal at Middleton Prep, saying that he'd be back the following week. He'd initially said his leave would be indefinite. But Harold's health was improving and more than that, it had become obvious in the past few hours that his brothers had made it their mission to be a royal pain in his backside. Jake had decided that getting back to work was probably the best thing that he could do. He refused to contact Dominique to help himself, but he could drown himself in the lives of his students. That way, at least, he could help somebody.

Two days later, Jake touched down at Burbank Airport. He took a deep breath as he exited the terminal, before stepping into the town car that awaited him. He loved spending time with his family and was over the moon that Harold's health had steadily improved. But the fact of the matter was he'd missed California. Had missed the school and working with the kids. And while he wouldn't acknowledge it, the truth of the matter was . . . he missed Dominique.

53

"Coach!" Justin ran up to Jake and threw himself in the older man's arms. It was the second week after the holidays and just the two of them were in the players' locker room. Justin had gone there to retrieve the backpack he'd left before the holidays, and Jake had gone there to inventory the various sports equipment.

"Hey, son." Jake winced at the noun, even though he often addressed his players in this manner. But given the precarious nature of his relationship with this particular student, Jake wished he could have taken back the word. "How are you doing?"

"Fine," Justin said with a shrug of his shoulders, once again in control of his emotions and a bit embarrassed at the excited bear hug that he knew Michael would have labeled as "totally uncool."

"Did you have a good Christmas?"

Justin nodded.

An uncomfortable silence filled the room. Big, questioning eyes looked into hooded, pained ones.

"How's your mother?" Jake asked, clearing his

throat of the hoarseness that had accompanied the question.

"She's fine."

"Good," Jake said, checking the air pressure of a basketball and trying to ignore the bad feeling gathering at the pit of his stomach. "What about you?"

"I'm okay," Justin replied, looking down at the floor.

"You know we could have really used you on the basketball team. I wish you'd taken my advice and signed up."

"I'm too big for that game, Coach."

"Man, what are you talking about? You're quick and you have good hand to eye coordination. You'd make a good center. You should try out next year."

Justin shifted his weight from one foot to the other but remained silent.

Jake could see that the boy had something else on his mind but he was no more ready to have that conversation than the child was. "Think about it," he said as he placed the ball in the large storage basket and reached for another one.

"All right, Coach." Justin had almost reached the door when he stopped and turned around. "You don't like my mama no more?"

Jake's head shot up and silence filled the room as he weighed his answer. "I love your mom," he honestly replied.

"Then you should call her." That said, Justin walked out the door.

Across town, Dominique was also reconnecting with someone she hadn't seen in a while. During his rigorous holiday partying, Reggie had gotten the flu. He'd been out for a couple weeks but now, back at his post, he'd just sat two large lattes down on Dominique's desk and sat opposite her.

"Girl, I thought that bug was going to kill me!" Reggie said to Dominique in typically dramatic Reggie-like fashion.

"But you still made your New Year's Eve party, I see," Dominique responded sarcastically, though the smile on her face belied the seriousness of her words.

"Nothing but death could keep me from it!" Reggie responded with a hand to his chest, mimicking Nettie from *The Color Purple*. "But if I'd known my two men would get to fighting over me, I would have stayed my sick butt at home."

"A fight?" Dominique asked, reaching for her coffee. "You're kidding, right?"

"I wish I was lying but it went down! See, the Jockstrap Bar was packed with revelers, but me and Alex got waved past the line because we had a reserved table. I thought I saw Quinn in the line, but as soon as I sat down they started pouring the bubbly and I forgot all about it. That's until we got ready to count down to the New Year."

"Then what happened?"

"Miss Dom, it was pitiful," Reggie responded, deadpan. But his eyes were twinkling. "Quinn came up to the table demanding to talk to me. Alex stood up and said, 'Over my dead body,' and then Quinn told him that that could be arranged. One thing led to another and the next thing I knew my baby coldcocked Quinn upside the head with a full bottle of Cristal."

"No!"

"Yes, girlfriend. Quinn went down and then it was a countdown all right but we weren't looking at the clock. We all stood over his passed-out ass hoping he'd wake up. He came to just in time to hear 'Auld Lang Syne.'"

"Ha! Reggie, you are a mess."

"What about you, Miss Dom," Reggie continued, his voice turning serious. The last time he was in the office, Dominique had had very little contact with Jake, and his brother was hanging on by a wing and a prayer.

"I'm doing okay," Dominique answered, her voice subdued.

"Have you talked to Jake?"

Dominique shook her head. "I've been in pretty constant contact with his twin brother, though, Johnny, and his wife, Cynthia. They've kept me posted on Harold's progress. Thank God, Jake's oldest brother is out of the woods and doing better."

"Did they say how Jake is doing?"

Dominique took a few sips of coffee, thinking. "All right I guess, though they said he'd been pretty quiet . . . about everything. He took Harold's heart attack pretty hard; especially when he thought they'd lose him. It brought up a lot of bad memories."

"So what are you going to do, Miss Dom? I've been your assistant for five years and in all this time have never seen you so happy."

"Not much I can do about that now," Dominique replied. "It takes two people to write a happy ending."

"Sometimes we have to fight for what we want, Miss Dom."

Dominique arched her brow. "Like Quinn fought over you?"

Reggie preened like a freshly plucked chicken. "Between you and me, even though hot-blooded Alejandro clearly won the fight, Quinn's brazen act made an impression on me." Reggie leaned forward and whispered conspiratorially. "I've started seeing him again."

"You broke up with Alejandro?"

"Girl, I could never give up that caramel cutie!"

"You're dating both Quinn *and* Alejandro?"

"I don't want to hurt anyone's feelings," Reggie explained, as if this statement made perfect sense. "I love them both. Does that sound crazy?"

Dominique looked at Reggie without flinching. "Yes."

"Maybe," Reggie answered, reaching for his drink and standing. "But so does letting the best thing that ever happened to you waltz out of your life. Maybe you need to take a champagne bottle and knock some sense into Jake McDonald's head." When he reached the door he paused and added, "I'm just sayin' . . ."

54

Dominique accepted the plate that Faith had fixed her. Anita was spending the weekend in Vegas with some of her girls, so Dominique had accepted her sister's invite to share Sunday dinner. "Thanks, sis," she said, savoring the aromas arising from her plate of lasagna. "This smells delicious."

"Thank your brother-in-law," Faith replied, taking her seat. "This is Aaron's special recipe."

"Aaron cooked?"

Faith shrugged. "Girl, you don't even know. He's trying to go all Bobby Flay on me."

Aaron came around the corner. "Bobby has nothing on me, Dominique."

"From the smells wafting from the kitchen, I believe it."

"Except several restaurants and a few million dollars," he added.

Everyone laughed.

In fifteen minutes the family enjoyed a meal that had taken an hour to prepare. Shortly afterwards, Alexis retreated to her room and the phone, Justin and Michael resumed their Wii game, and Aaron went out to join his frat brothers for male bonding. Dominique and Faith found themselves alone in the kitchen, putting away leftovers and cleaning up the mess.

"Faith," Dominique began as she placed leftover lasagna into the refrigerator, "I bet you would have never guessed in a million years that Aaron would have turned into the man that he is."

Faith smiled. "I saw snatches of brilliance. Like when he rescued Nell from my window ledge."

"That cat was always psycho."

"And he always remembered my birthday, and the anniversary of our first date."

"That's pretty special, I must admit." Dominique watched Faith place the last of the dishes into the dishwasher, add detergent, and turn it on. "Never take it for granted, Faith," she said as she folded a dish towel and placed it on its holder. "The husband, home, dog, and picket fence . . ."

"Sometimes it's not a fairy tale," Faith insisted.

"But it's there, in your life and your heart. I'm not making light of the work it takes to have a successful family, Faith. I'm just saying to never lose sight of what a blessing it is."

Faith nodded, and took the whistling teakettle off the fire. After fixing mugs for both of them, they settled into the living room. Faith lazily stirred honey into her mug, looked at Dominique, and laughed. "Remember your first boyfriend?"

"William? How can I forget?"

"No, the one before him, the dude in junior high with the long, greasy Jheri curl."

"Ha! That was Greg Sutton. Girl, I haven't

thought of him in years." Dominique smiled at the memory. "Couldn't nobody tell that fool that he didn't look like El DeBarge?"

"Couldn't nobody tell him to stop flinging that hair around either, doing the running man, and spraying everybody with activator?"

"Girl, please. We all had that mess dripping down our necks and ruining clothes." Dominique laughed at the memories. "But Greg was my first crush; William was my first boyfriend."

"If you say so. But I remember Greg because he was the first secret you kept from me."

"I told you eventually."

"Ha! Only after I found y'all's love letters hidden under your mattress."

"I thought I was so in love," Dominique said with a smile, recalling this memorable eighth-grade moment that lasted all of two months. "And then Mama found out that I'd gone with him to the skating rink instead of to the Pizza Hut with my girl-friends." Her smile turned bittersweet. The thought of skating reminded her of Jake.

"And it was over!" Faith said, laughing.

"And if Anita's punishment wasn't enough to slow my role, then Miss Tiffany certainly was." Both women shook their heads as they thought about the most popular girl in Dominique's eighth-grade class, the one who stole Greg's affections while Domi-nique was on punishment.

"Did I tell you that I ran into her the other day?"

"Tiffany?" Dominique asked in surprise.

"The one and only," Faith responded. "She and Greg have four children and eight grandchildren."

"Stop it," Dominique exclaimed. "Did she speak

to you?" She couldn't help but remember that Tiffany treated those around her merely as pawns on her chessboard of life.

"More than that," Faith replied. "She actually hugged me and showed me pictures. Amazing what twenty-five years and about fifty extra pounds can do."

"No . . ." Dominique whispered.

"Girl, she's not the petite princess she used to be, but she looks good. And she's one of your most ardent subscribers. She says she's been a *Capricious* woman since the first issue came out."

Dominique shook her head in wonder.

"A lot of people look up to you, Dominique," Faith continued. "More people than you even realize are watching you, and cheering you on. You have a great career . . ."

Dominique snorted.

"And a wonderful son. You'll get through this," Faith finally added, addressing the elephant in the room that they'd been tiptoeing around all day. "You're strong and—"

"You know what, Faith?" Dominique interrupted. "I'm tired of being the strong one, able to pick up the pieces of my broken heart every time it's shattered! I'm tired of being the one who has to make all of the decisions and put on the brave face. I'm tired of being by myself. I'm just tired!" The tears came, and Dominique didn't try to hide them.

"Call him," Faith said, rushing to Dominique's side and hugging her firmly. "He's probably hurting just as much as you."

Dominique shook her head. "I've left several messages. I'm not calling him again."

Faith rubbed her sister's back. Words of comfort

failed her. She'd been there when Leland had left
Dominique, and when Kevin had stolen her money.
Both of those times, Dominique had been strong.
"For my son's sake," Dominique had told her. She
understood why her older, always-together sister was
tired of keeping it together.

Faith took Dominique's face in her hands, forced
her sister to look her in the eye. "It's going to be all
right, Nikki, do you hear me? No matter what happens, you have people around you who love you:
Mama, me, Aaron, our kids. I know you're hurting
and you have a right. But together, we'll get through
this."

On the way home, Dominique noticed that her
normally chatty son was quiet. "Did you kids have
fun?" she asked.

"Yeah," Justin replied.

"What?"

"Yes," he corrected himself.

"What did you do?"

"Just movies and stuff." Justin paused a moment.
"Did Jake call you?"

Where did that come from? "Why do you ask, baby?"

"I told you I saw him back at school."

"Yes . . . and?"

"Nothing."

Dominique glanced over at her son. "Justin, is
there something that you want to talk to me about?"
When he didn't respond, she continued. "Baby, I
don't want you to worry about me and Jake. He's
been really concerned about his brother, and work
is keeping me busy."

"But y'all still like each other, right?"

This is the very reason why I didn't want Justin to know about this relationship . . . to have him know that another one has bitten the proverbial dust.

"Huh, Mom? You still like him, right?"

"Don't concern yourself with grown folks' business, Justin," Dominique replied brusquely, even though she understood why Justin thought it was his business as well. "No matter what happens between Jake and me . . . Mommy will be fine."

The look on Justin's face suggested that he wasn't buying Dominique's story. She couldn't blame him. She didn't buy it either.

55

The next morning, Dominique entered the *Capricious* offices with a determined stride. She'd barely slept the night before and the simple question that had robbed her of sleep, the one her son had asked, still plagued her. *Did Jake call you?* Asked, Justin had said, because he'd seen Jake at school. *What did they talk about? Was it about me? And if so, did Jake tell Justin something that made him think I'd get a phone call?* At one point, Dominique had almost gone to Justin's room to find out exactly what Jake had said. But as she'd told him in the car—this was grown folks' business. Any conversation about their relationship needed to be between her and Jake, not between her and Justin and most definitely not between Justin and Jake.

Dominique had told Faith that she wasn't going to call Jake again. And she'd meant it. That's why as soon as she left the office today she was going to his house. She'd wait at his door, camp out all night if she had to. But before her head hit the pillow,

Dominique determined, she and Jake were going to have a conversation . . . and she was not taking no for an answer!

Across town, Jake sat in his office thinking about Dominique—but he didn't have talking in mind. It had been a month since he'd squeezed her lusciousness, too long since he'd glided his fingers along her smooth, soft skin and tasted those sweet lips. *Face it, brothah, you miss her. And you've probably lost her because you're scared.* A bittersweet smile crossed Jake's face at the irony: in the beginning it was Dominique who'd shied away from their having a relationship. Now he was running for the border.

Jake shuffled a few papers and tried to take his mind off of his misery. But the effort was futile at best. Since returning from Alabama, he'd tried not to think about Dominique. He'd convinced himself that their breaking things off was probably for the best, that she was angry and probably wouldn't want him back. But the harder he tried to forget her, the more intense were his thoughts about her. And the guilt. Jake remembered the words he'd uttered when trying to convince Dominique that all men weren't the same, and to give their love a chance. *You were with senseless jerks!* Now he was the one being insensitive and uncommunicative. Lately, his twin had talked to Dominique more than he had, and Jake knew that wasn't right. His mother had raised him better than to ignore a woman who clearly deserved to hear from him. Jake threw down the report that he wasn't reading and reached for the phone.

Dominique was deep in thought as she left the conference room and headed for her office. The meeting with the sales team hadn't quite gone the way she'd expected. In fact, it had basically gone to hell in a hand basket. When she'd pushed the execs to double their efforts and try for longer contracts and more full-page ads, one of the top producers had responded by tendering his resignation. After the meeting, the sales manager had pulled her aside to assure her that what she'd said had nothing to do with their colleague leaving. The seemingly unhappy employee had been wooed away from *Capricious*, and was going to work for the new, competing magazine. Dominique only hoped that this was the end of the exodus of good employees, and not the beginning.

"Whew, Miss Dom," Reggie said as soon as she'd entered their offices. "You look like you're ready to kick some butt!"

"I could go a round or two and hold my own," Dominique admitted, walking to his desk to retrieve messages.

"Well, girl, something is getting ready to put a smile on your face."

Dominique looked up from the papers. "What?"

Reggie's eyes twinkled. "Just go into your office and find out."

Jake's here? Dominique's heartbeat quickened as she walked toward her closed office door. She opened it, entered her office and looked around. No one. She walked to her desk, and didn't see anything unusual, saw nothing that wasn't on it when she'd left an hour ago. "What is he talking about?" she asked aloud as she rounded the corner to where the ten-seat conference table and buffet were placed. That's when she saw it: a huge, beautiful bouquet of flowers.

Her feelings were mixed as she walked toward the display. There was no doubt in her mind about who'd sent them. But that she'd received flowers instead of a phone call didn't exactly make her feel all warm and fuzzy inside. In fact, a part of her was downright peeved. What did he think a bouquet of flowers would do? Make up for the unreturned phone calls, or the fact that he'd been MIA from her life for weeks?

She walked over to the bouquet, and the scent of orchids, lilies, and star gazers assailed her nostrils. She touched the silky white and pink petals dotted with black, leaned in and inhaled. The smell was heavenly and her frown somewhat lessened as she reached for the card.

> *Nick,*
>   *I've been the senseless jerk that I warned you about, and I'm sorry. I know that we need to talk. I'll be at our restaurant at six o'clock. Hope you can meet me there.*
>   *Jake*

Dominique read the card a second time before she folded it and walked to her desk. Now that a conversation she swore would happen today was about to take place, Dominique wasn't sure she was ready for it. What if he wanted to meet to officially break things off? Or as important, what if he didn't? Was she willing to continue with someone haunted by his father's death and the heart disease that ran in their family? What if Harold had another heart attack, or worse? Would Jake run away again? Dominique placed the card in her purse and turned to her computer. There were a few hours left in her workday and she needed to stay focused. She'd have the answers regarding Jake McDonald soon enough.

At exactly six PM, Dominique handed her car over to the valet at the cozy Italian eatery in her and Jake's neighborhood. She hadn't eaten there since running into him there months ago and was immediately filled with thoughts of that evening. The flutter that often happened when he was near began in the pit of her stomach. Dominique took a breath, reached for the door, and walked inside.

She saw him right away, sitting at the booth where they'd shared dinner. He looked up immediately. Their eyes met and held. Dominique lifted her chin, quelled her nerves, and walked back to where he was seated.

Jake stood as she approached. He wanted to take her into his arms and kiss her senseless, but he could tell from the look on her face that that probably wasn't a good idea. So instead, he said simply, "Dominique."

"Jake," she said, sitting on the other side of the booth.

Jake sat as well. "You look beautiful."

And you look fine as hell. "Thanks."

An awkward silence followed, ended by the waiter who came over to take drink orders. Jake ordered a beer; Dominique, a white wine.

Eyes met and held again.

More silence.

"I owe you an apology," Jake finally began. "For how I've acted since Harold's heart attack and for not returning your calls. You don't deserve how I've treated you and . . . I'm sorry."

"You're right, Jake. I don't deserve it." And then, "Why didn't you call me?"

Jake sighed. "I don't know."

"You don't know?"

"I mean . . . look, I know you're angry but . . . chill out a little, all right? This isn't easy for me—"

"And you think I'm skipping to my Lou?"

"But I want to tell you everything; I need to try and make you understand."

Jake was right. Dominique was angry. Still, she remembered what Johnny had told her about the little boy who still lived inside this massive man sitting in front of her. So she took a breath, uncrossed her arms, and waited.

After the waiter had placed down their drinks, Jake continued. "Something happened that day in the skating rink parking lot when I heard about Harold's heart attack. I went into shut down mode, much like I did when Daddy died. Back then I buried my feelings, stuffed all of that hurt and anger and anguish deep inside me and basically tried to ignore how bad I felt. Over the years, I never dealt with it. When Robin died, I did the same thing—buried the hurt under work and a string of casual affairs. But that day, that phone call pulled the scab off the wound and all of that pain came rushing back full force.

"From the time I was twelve, losing the people

around me that I love has been my biggest fear, even bigger than the fear of my dying young. But that fear, that belief, that I wouldn't live to see my fiftieth or sixtieth birthday, is probably the reason I waited too late to have children with Robin. I never want to put a child through what happened to me.

"When I sat in that hospital with Harold clinging to life, all I could think about was Justin, and how he'd feel if I died. I remember what you said about Kevin, and how hard it was for Justin when that man left his life. I thought about you," Jake continued, looking deeply into Dominique's eyes, "and how hard it would be for you, too."

Dominique swallowed past the lump in her throat. "But you left me anyway."

"I didn't mean to; I didn't want to. But can't you see that I was only trying to protect you? To keep you and Justin from being hurt?"

"But you *did* hurt me!" Dominique said, her voice rising along with her ire. She got why Jake had been afraid but he didn't seem to get that his argument was seriously flawed. "You're hurting me now, with this . . . explanation that, while understandable, makes no sense! Justin is wondering why you don't come over, I'm at home with no clue as to what you're thinking, and Johnny is telling me to give you time. Your father died when you were twelve, Jake," Dominique continued, her voice softening. "You're almost forty years old! How much more time will you need to move past the fear of what happened when you were a boy, and be able to love completely?"

She meant well, but Dominique's words angered Jake. "How much time did you take to let me in after what had happened to you because you were hurt by that thief? I'm not the only one with issues at this table!"

"I never said I was perfect," Dominique replied heatedly. "But I was woman enough to not let the relationships of the past affect my future."

"And I'm man enough to be sitting here right now, Dominique, trying to do the same thing!"

A few patrons looked in the direction of the back booth, but neither Jake nor Dominique noticed. They were staring down each other, the air fairly crackling between them.

The waiter who'd brought their drinks hesitantly approached the table. "Would you like to order appetizers now?" he asked.

"No," Jake said as he stood, reached into his pocket, and threw a twenty-dollar bill on the table. "We're leaving." He turned to Dominique. "Let's go."

Dominique raised a brow. "Excuse me?"

"You heard me. We need to finish this conversation, but not here."

"I'm not sure I want to go anywhere with you, Jake."

"I didn't ask you. I'm telling you. We're leaving. Now."

Without waiting for an answer, Jake reached over, firmly gripped Dominique's arm and pulled her up. To resist would have been futile; plus, Dominique didn't want to cause a scene. Jake was probably the one person in California who was more stubborn than she was.

"Wait, Jake," she said when he continued out the door and began walking them to the parking lot. "I valeted my car."

"I'll call them later, have someone drop it off at the house," Jake said, ushering her into the passenger seat of his car. There was no way he was taking the chance of Dominique getting in her car and making a beeline for her house. He took a deep breath before starting the car and easing into the heavy, rush-hour traffic. He had handled things poorly; he acknowledged that. Dominique had a right to be angry. He acknowledged that, too. But he was determined to get through to her, resolute about trying to bring back what they had. By the end of the evening, Dominique might decide to end the relationship. *But if you think I'm letting you go without a fight, baby girl, then you are totally misinformed.*

56

The five-minute ride to Jake's house was a quiet one. The silence continued as they walked to his front door and entered the home.

Once inside, Dominique turned to him. "Okay, we're alone. What else do you want to tell me?"

Jake looked at her, noted her eyes, bright with anger, her pouty lips, and heaving breasts. The breasts he'd missed and longed to touch. "I love you," he answered simply.

"I love you, too, Jake."

"Then can we sit and talk to each other calmly, listen to each other, and work this out?"

Dominique heaved a sigh and walked toward the couch. "We can try," she said, sitting down.

"I'm sorry," Jake said again.

Dominique's response was not what he expected. "Tell me about your father."

Jake did that, and more. He bore his soul, sharing experiences that he hadn't discussed in years. When he talked about finding his father slumped over, tears came to his eyes. "I know he died a long time ago," he said. "But it still hurts."

Jake's tears washed away Dominique's anger. She listened as he shared his pain, and his fears. Dominique then shared her thoughts and desires, including how she hoped Jake would seek counseling for the grief he still carried. To her surprise and delight, Jake agreed. For the next hour, they had a true heart-to-heart and when it was over, both felt depleted yet relieved.

After a companionable silence, where they simply held hands and absorbed what had just transpired, Jake asked, "So . . . are we cool? Am I forgiven?"

Dominique smiled, remembering that these same words were the ones she'd uttered before, when she'd refused to let Justin go to Oakland. "I'll think about it," she responded, which had been Jake's answer.

Jake nodded, even as he turned toward Dominique and looked in her eyes. "I've missed you," he whispered. "I've missed these." He leaned over, licking his lips before pressing them slowly, gently against Dominique's. The kiss was soft and tender. He kissed her again, and then looked into her eyes. "Have you missed me?"

Dominique nodded, and looked at his lips. "I've missed these." She leaned over and swiped her tongue against his lips.

When she would have leaned back, Jake stopped her, wrapping his arms around her and deepening the kiss. His hand slid from her back to the juicy fruit that for weeks he'd dreamed of touching. He tweaked her nipple before sliding his hand beneath her blouse. Dominique moaned her appreciation, even as her hand slid to the shaft that brought so much pleasure. Jake was already hard; about to bust out of his slacks.

"Come on," he commanded, taking her hand. "I want to make love to you."

They walked upstairs to Jake's master bedroom. When they reached it, Dominique took off her shoes, then reached for the buttons on her blouse.

"No, I'll do it," Jake said. His eyes never left hers as, one by one, he slowly unbuttoned her blouse. He pulled back the fabric, kissing her lips, neck and the delectable chocolate mounds spilling out over the top of her black, lacy bra. He reached for the front clasp, undid it, and was quickly rewarded as Dominique's girls waved their greeting. He buried his head between them before taking one nipple into his mouth, twirling the other with his fingers into a hardened peak. He walked behind Dominique, unzipped her skirt, and admired her plump, round booty as he eased the fabric over her panties and down her big, strong thighs. The skirt pooled at Dominique's feet and once she stepped out of it, Jake hugged her to his chest, running his hands all over her body. He made quick work of shedding his clothes and then reached for his pants and pulled out his cell phone.

"Call Tessa and tell her you're going to be late."

Dominique looked at her watch. "But it's just seven-thirty. She doesn't leave until nine."

"Baby, you won't be home by then."

"Why not?"

"Because," he said, lazily running a finger down her arm before clutching her backside. "I have several things I'm going to do to you, and I'm not going to rush. In fact, judging by the way I feel right now, we're probably going to be busy all night long."

Dominique had barely finished the call when Jake reached for her panties and took them off. He picked her up and walked them over to his large, custom-made bed, rubbing her body against his as he put her down.

"Sit down."

She did. Jake kneeled in front of her paradise, spread her legs and begin kissing the inside of her thighs. Dominique closed her eyes and lay back. Jake kissed her nether lips and then ran his tongue along her already wet folds. Dominique shivered and clutched the sheets. Jake used his fingers to play a melody on her love box, teasing her nub as he licked and stroked and nipped and teased. His strokes were strong and purposeful as he lapped up her nectar, his tongue making love to her, skilled and precise. It had been weeks since they'd enjoyed each other and before long, Dominique cried out in ecstasy, her whole body shaking with the intensity of her climax. But Jake wasn't finished. He was just getting started. He crawled on to the bed and lay beside her, reaching for her hand and placing it on his manhood. They kissed, and he started to get on top of her. But Dominique had something else in mind.

"Lay back," she commanded, her voice husky with desire. She kissed him on the mouth, long and wet, before working her way down his body: neck, arms, chest, and stomach. When she reached his navel, she swirled her tongue around it, massaging Jake's massive erection as she did so. When she raked her fingernails along his inner thighs, he hissed and raised his hips off the bed. Dominique smiled. She knew exactly what he wanted. It was what she wanted, too. She ran her fingers along his mushroom tip before following that same trail with her tongue. Jake was very thick, but Dominique still managed to enthusiastically worship at his nine-inch shrine. She took her time, licking, nibbling, whipping Jake into an erotic frenzy. "Damn, baby," he whispered. And then again, "Damn."

Finally, he could take no more. He got to his knees, positioned himself behind Dominique and sank deeply within her with one powerful stroke. He reached around and fondled her breasts as he set up a slow, lazy rhythm—pulling out to the tip before plunging in again and again. He picked up the pace, and felt Dominique's walls clutch around his shaft. He rotated his hips, making sure that she felt all of him, everywhere. She pushed back against him, demanding even more. Jake couldn't seem to get enough of her, but for hour after hour, in position after position, he tried and all the while, he branded her body with his own.

In the early dawn hours, after waking up and making love yet again, Dominique kissed Jake and said the three words that put their relationship firmly back on track: "I forgive you."

57

That weekend, Dominique and Justin were once again at Faith's house. But this time, Jake accompanied them. Since the meeting that began at the restaurant and ended at Jake's house, Dominique and Jake had been together every night. Justin was often included in their outings. They'd informed him that they were dating, and that they loved each other. Justin was thrilled, and asked if they were going to get married. Dominique had truthfully answered, "Son, we're taking this relationship one day at a time."

"Sister, I didn't think it could get any better," Dominique said, as she and Faith enjoyed an after-dinner walk around the block.

"You don't need to tell me," Faith said. "The afterglow is all over your face."

"Really?" Dominique put a hand to her cheek. "It's that obvious?"

"It is to the sister who's known you her entire life. I'm so happy things are working out for you and

Jake. He's a good guy. Aaron and I are rooting for y'all."

"Speaking of the guys, shouldn't they be back by now?"

"Girl, please. If I know Aaron, him showing Jake the golf course probably turned into them playing a few holes. I hope you're okay with hanging out a while."

Jake took his time, lined up his shot, and swung. The golf ball sailed through the air before banking left near a grouping of bushes. "Damn!"

Aaron laughed. "Better luck next time, man." They walked a ways to Aaron's ball. He swung and fared much better.

"You know you're a bad influence, keeping us away from the house this long. I'm surprised Dominique hasn't called me by now."

"Faith probably talked her out of it. She knows how important it is for us to hang out, you know, male bonding and all. And I've got to tell you, man, after being surrounded by so many women all these years, I'm sure glad to welcome another man into the family."

Jake looked up from where he was studying his next shot. "Aren't you getting a bit ahead of yourself?"

"What? You're saying that your intentions aren't honorable where my sister-in-law is concerned?"

"Ha! No, man, I'm not saying that at all."

"Well all right, then. Y'all better get to setting a date. Neither one of you is getting any younger."

"What is this, Aaron, a conspiracy? Have you been talking to my brothers?"

"I don't even know your brothers," Aaron said, laughing. "So why would you think that?"

"Because the last time I talked to Harold, he pretty much said the same thing."

58

The sold-out Oakland Coliseum cheered as the Raiders left the field for the halftime show. That they'd gotten to the playoffs was amazing in itself but that they were ahead of the Vikings by fourteen had the fans starting the celebration early. Justin was beside himself with glee.

"Hold on, partner," Jake admonished. "There's still a lot of game left."

"Yeah, but—"

"Yes, Justin . . ." Dominique interrupted

"We're on fire!" Justin continued. "And now that their quarterback is injured . . ."

"He may sit out a few plays, but he'll be back in the game," Jake replied. "But trust me, it would take him breaking something to not get back on that field."

As the boys continued to talk, Dominique was happy to take in the halftime show and the jubilant fans around her. Never one who'd embraced sports, she now saw how one could get addicted to this atmosphere filled with camaraderie and excitement.

She watched Jake and Justin conversing and felt warm all over. His ongoing presence and attentiveness continued to have a very positive effect on her son.

"And now," the announcer began as the band marched off the field, "we'd like to say a special hello to one of our all-time favorite Raider players . . . the Big Mac man himself . . . Jake McDonald!"

A camera zoomed in on Jake and soon Justin and Dominique were staring at his face on the big screen. Jake waved to the roaring crowd.

"And we'd also like to welcome the special lady in his life who is also the editor in chief of *Capricious* magazine . . . Dominique Clark!"

Dominique's eyes widened as she looked questionably at Jake.

"Stand up and wave, baby," Jake insisted.

Dominique made a fuss, but finally stood up and waved to the crowd.

"Dominique," the announcer continued, "Jake has allowed us to be a part of some exciting times in his life. He's made some of his best plays right here in this stadium. But I think, and folks, you'll probably agree with me, that this is the best one of all."

The announcer stopped talking. Dominique looked at Jake. Jake shrugged.

Dominique turned to look at Jake. "What is he talking about, Jake? What play did you make?"

Jake pointed to the screen. "That one."

Dominique looked at the screen. Her mouth dropped open as she read the words: Will you marry me?

The crowd started cheering. Jake's heart thudded as he awaited Dominique's answer. Dominique's eyes filled with tears as she looked from Jake to Justin, who was grinning from ear to ear.

"Answer him, Mom!" Justin finally shouted.

Dominique couldn't talk for the lump in her throat. So she simply nodded before throwing her arms around him. "Yes," she whispered in his ear.

Once again, the screens filled with images of Jake, just in time to see Dominique plant a soft, loving kiss on his juicy lips. He raised his hand and gave a thumbs up. The crowd cheered again.

"Well, folks," the announcer boomed in his signature deep voice, "it seems that while the Raiders have been keeping the ball in play, our own Jake McDonald has been putting *love* in play."

The cameras zoomed in on Jake and Dominique, as he sealed their engagement with a longer, scorching kiss. Justin jumped up and down. The crowd went wild. "Love in play!" somebody shouted. The chant was picked up by those in their section and before long, almost sixty-three thousand fans were chanting: "Love in play, love in play!"

The lopsided grin that his mother loved spread across Justin's face. Dominique leaned over and hugged him. "I'm glad you said *yes*, Mom."

Dominique laughed at how Justin emphasized the correct pronunciation. "Yeah," she answered with a wink, hugging him again. "Me too."

That night, as they lay in each other's arms after a round of slow, tantalizing lovemaking, Dominique and Jake recounted their journey, the ups and the downs, and how both looked forward to a future together.

"Do you want children?" Dominique asked. "You know I'm almost forty years old."

"It would be kinda nice to have a daughter to go along with our son," Jake answered.

Our son. Dominique liked the sound of that. It had been made clear that while Leland Clark was the biological father, Jake fully intended to serve as Justin's full-time dad. "You know what, baby?"

"Hum."

"I agree with that announcer. I think today's was one of the best plays you ever made."

"Without a doubt," Jake responded, wrapping his arms around Dominique. "Now aren't you glad we decided to get back in the game?"

"Absolutely," Dominique replied, as Jake ran a hand down to her backside and gave it a squeeze. "I especially like those touchdowns."

"That's good," Jake replied, as his hand ran along Dominique's hip, settled in between her thighs, and dipped inside her satin pj's. "Because I'm getting ready to score again."

Want more? Check out

LOVIN' BLUE

Available now wherever books are sold

Turn the page for an excerpt from *Lovin' Blue*. . . .

1

The police! Eden Anderson's heart leaped into her throat as she pulled behind the police cruiser parked in front of her brother's Baldwin Hills residence in Southern California. "What's going on, Michael?" she whispered as she fumbled with her seatbelt, then the lock button, before scrambling out of her packed Acura SUV and rushing to the front door. Her concern had been growing for the past three days—ever since her phone calls and e-mails to her older brother had gone unreturned.

At first she'd shrugged off her worry. After all, her brother, Michael "Big Mike" Anderson, was trying to make a name for himself in the music game. He'd produced a couple B-level acts while working for a major record label. His work often went late into the night, and reaching him wasn't always easy. But when Eden had left two "call me right now" messages, followed by texts marked with the same urgency, she'd experienced the first twinges of fear. And now, looking at the black-and-white squad car sitting at the curb of her brother's front door, Eden's anxiety went into full throttle.

Eden knocked on the front door. No response. She repeatedly rang the doorbell but didn't hear the chimes that usually sounded when the button was pushed. Eden knocked harder, first on the door, then on the window. The living room was dark; she could detect no movement. But lights were on upstairs. Eden's fear increased.

You've got a key. Out of her panic came a voice that reminded Eden she had a key to her brother's house. He'd given it to her months ago, when she'd come house hunting and stayed at his place. She'd meant to give it back but hadn't. Remembering that she'd placed it in the zipper compartment of her large Junior Drake purse, Eden walked purposefully back to her car to retrieve it. Her steps were measured and much slower than before. Eden wasn't sure she wanted to find out what was happening on the other side of the door.

Jansen McKnight turned off the shower. *Did I hear a knock?* He waited a beat, and then another, before turning the water back on and finishing the long, hot shower. He turned to let the water pound against the knots in his shoulders. *I need to see Dakkar,* he thought dispassionately. Dakkar was the masseuse trained in Swedish massage who had rubbed away tension, stress, and frustration from Jansen's body for years. For now, however, the near-scalding hot water pulsating from the heavy-duty showerhead was serving as a viable alternative. Jansen rested a large palm on either side of the stall, hung his head, and let the water work its magic.

A loud thud interrupted Jansen's serenity. His just relaxed muscles tensed, his entire body rigid in alert. He lessened the water pressure, straining to hear beyond the guest bathroom he'd used since agreeing to house sit for Michael the previous week, and beyond the stereo playing in the bedroom across the hall.

Thump. There it was again, unmistakable this time. Either the sound of footsteps, or something being dragged across the floor, or both. Jansen's officer instinct went into auto mode, and for good reason. A recent rash of burglaries in the upscale, central Los Angeles neighborhood was why Michael had asked his friend to house sit. Jansen loved the comfort of his home in Gardena, and agreed to his best friend's pleas only after Michael promised that a home security system would be installed immediately upon his return. *Well, brothah,* Jansen thought with a resigned sigh, *looks like I'm getting ready to earn my keep.*

With the stealth of a panther, Jansen turned the shower back to full blast, eased out of the stall, soundlessly wrapped a towel around his waist, and reached for the 9mm Glock that was never far from his reach. Tonight he'd unstrapped and rested it on the closed toilet seat, before the rest of his navy uniform ended up in a heap on the bathroom floor.

Thunk.

Jansen eased the gun out of its holster and crept down the short hallway to the top of the stairs.

Taking a deep breath, he placed his foot on the top step and prayed the old maple wood wouldn't creak under his weight.

Eden walked into the living room and dropped another load onto the hardwood floor. Her first thought had been to leave everything in the car until morning, but a chance glance at a crime-watch sign nailed to a post nixed that idea. Even in what she felt was a fairly safe neighborhood, a car packed with clearly visible goods may be too much for either a hardened criminal or a bored teen to pass up. So with the last ounces of energy she could summon after driving for ten hours, she walked in with her beloved stereo system—the final load.

Jansen kept his back against the wall as he noted the shadow passing along the living room's far wall. *Whoever this fool is has a lot of nerve.* Normally, especially when it was obvious that someone was home, a burglar would do one quick, thorough sweep—get in and out. But Jansen wanted to catch this perpetrator, believing that in doing so he may nab the person or ring of persons behind this neighborhood's woes. That's why he'd left the shower running, to give the thief a false sense of security. The criminal had obviously taken the bait and made himself at home. *You may be nervy, but you're not too bright, son.* Jansen quietly cocked his weapon. It was about to go down.

Eden gingerly sat her stereo on the coffee table and then reached for the suitcases she'd tossed on the couch. She couldn't wait to get in the shower.

Her head hurt; her hair—stuffed under an Orioles baseball cap—was in desperate need of shampoo, and the secret that was strong enough for a man but made for a woman was about to become public news. *Oh, I'm funky,* she thought as she used the sleeve of her long-sleeved Bison Blue T-shirt to wipe her face. As she did so, her earring caught on the sleeve and came out of her ear. She'd planned to replace the clasp on her favorite hoops before leaving DC, but like many other plans she'd made in the past two weeks, these, too, had changed. Ever since resigning her job on Capitol Hill, her life had been a series of unexpected interruptions. Part of what she was hoping for with this move back home was a life without surprises.

"Freeze! Don't move!" Jansen eased off the last step onto the floor, assumed a strong, wide-legged stance, and pointed his gun at the back of the scrawny, ball-capped thief who'd been wreaking havoc on the neighborhood. "Get your hands up and slowly turn around."

Eden stood frozen, unable to speak or move. *What's going on? Where's Michael?* After hearing the music, and the water running, Eden had assumed it was Michael upstairs. But these strong, authoritative commands had definitely not been uttered from her brother's lips, and her womanly intuition, along with a rapidly beating heart, told her this was not a joke.

"Do it now!" Jansen took another step toward his suspect.

Eden began to shake as she slowly turned around. She took one look at the huge man whose face was

hidden in the darkness, noted the gun that—unlike
his countenance—was clearly visible from his
outstretched hands, and did what any normal, law-
abiding citizen would do under such dire circumstances. She fainted.

2

Jansen frowned as he slowly eased his finger off the trigger. He'd seen a lot of reactions from suspects in his near-decade of life as a cop, but he had to admit—this was a first. *Are you bluffing? Huh? We'll soon find out.* "Stay on the floor. Don't move," Jansen commanded, even though it seemed quite clear that the suspect had no intention of changing positions. Jansen moved the coffee table with his foot and, with the gun in his left hand still trained on his target, used his right hand to turn over the intruder so he could see his face. As he did so, the baseball cap came off, and a head of long black hair cascaded over the hand clutching the suspect's shoulder. Jansen's frown deepened. He kept his weapon trained on the unconscious female and hurried over to turn on the overhead light. As the harsh, bright light flooded the room, the suspect groaned and opened her eyes.

Eden! Jansen's heart clutched in his throat. He'd thought often of Michael's younger sister in the past few days, especially since staying here at her

brother's house. Michael had told him that Eden
was moving back to Los Angeles, but he'd mentioned nothing about her staying at the house. In
fact, he'd assured him that they'd probably not cross
paths at all because the condo she'd found was in a
totally different part of town—Santa Monica, an area
Jansen rarely frequented. Yet here she was, sprawled
on the floor. Jansen hadn't seen the girl-turned-
woman he used to mercilessly harass in at least ten
years, and he quickly took in the curves he'd missed
in the heat of the moment, and the onion that
begged to be peeled. Jansen had to admit . . . she
looked good lying down.

"Girl, you sure know how to make an entrance,"
Jansen scolded to cover his concern and unexpected
attraction, even as he hurried to her side to help her
up. "Breaking into someone else's home, even your
brother's, is a good way to get shot!"

Eden's eyes narrowed as reality dawned. She
hadn't seen Jansen, otherwise known as her childhood tormentor, in ages, probably since marrying
her college sweetheart. After the divorce, she'd
buried herself in work, and her trips back home
became infrequent. Except for the house-hunting
trip, Eden hadn't been back to LA in three years,
ever since her mother relocated to Phoenix. The
last she'd heard of Jansen, he was married and
living in Chicago. She also remembered Michael
saying he'd become a police officer. But still . . .
what was he doing here? And why was he one towel
shy of being naked?

"You!" Eden spat, her ire part anger, part chagrin,
but mostly relief. "What are you doing here?"

"Well, now, little sis," Jansen responded, his voice soft but firm. "I could ask you the same question." He assumed his favorite wide-legged stance, crossed arms across a massive chest, and noted Eden's eyes were larger and more almond-shaped than he remembered. And were her lips always so full and luscious?

Jansen's arm-folding action caused Eden's heart to flutter a bit as she watched his pecs ripple with the movement. Her eyes slid to the wide, muscled shoulders, down the six-pack to a narrowed waist, inverted navel, and over the strong powerful legs that held up a man she determined had gotten finer with age. And why was she imagining what lay just beyond the beige-colored towel shielding his manhood? Eden closed her eyes and licked suddenly dry lips.

A lazy, knowing smile crept across Jansen's face. "Liking the view?" he asked cockily as he leaned against the stair banister. "I can part the, um, *curtain,* if you'd like."

"Still arrogant, I see," Eden said, turning away from him and reaching for her suitcases—just for something to do.

"Arrogance is when a person thinks he's all that," Jansen shot back. "Confidence is when he knows it."

Eden ignored Jansen's comment. *Dang, I was looking at him like he was a piece of chicken, and I was the colonel getting ready to fry.* She picked up the ball cap from the floor and placed it back on her head, feeling a semblance of composure coming back. After all, this was her brother's best friend, the one she'd known since she was five years old. The one who had stuttered as a child, squashed bugs, and then picked up their remains and chased her with them. Who had collected the most Halloween candy but still stole the mini Snickers bars Eden received. Who had refused to take off his "Thriller" jacket Christmas gift for a whole week, but later scared the bejeebers out of her by donning a monster mask and jumping out of her bedroom closet. This was "germy Jansen"— the name she'd called him when they'd gotten older and Jansen and Michael had begun to play sports. They'd come home sweaty and funky, and Jansen would insist on nabbing a hug, giving Eden the willies. This was Jansen all grown up . . . but Eden tried not to think about that now.

"What are you doing here?" she asked again. "Where's Michael? And can you put that . . . thing away?"

"Are you sure you want me to?" Jansen asked, wriggling his eyebrows. Eden huffed. "Oh, you mean the gun." The Glock was almost an extension of himself. Jansen had forgotten he was holding it. He placed it on the third step, where Eden couldn't see it. "Is that better?"

Eden nodded. "A little. Where's Michael?"

"Out of town. Actually, out of the country." Jansen tightened the towel around his waist. "He asked me to watch the place."

Oh, so that's why I couldn't reach Michael. And why the police car is out there. "Well, if you're just patrolling the area, why are you taking a shower in his house?"

"I believe the official term for what I'm doing is 'house sitting.'"

"You're staying here?" Eden was surprised to hear a trace of panic in her voice.

"Yeah, why? Are you? I thought you got a condo over there in prime-real-estate Santa Monica."

"I did. I mean, I do. But there's a problem. It's not ready. . . ." Eden's voice trailed off as her exhausted mind tried to process her predicament. When the contractor had begun the kitchen makeover, mold had been found under the sink and behind the refrigerator that had come with the house. Further inspection confirmed it had spread underneath the hardwood flooring and under the baseboards. The job that was supposed to take three days would now take two weeks to finish. Eden had planned to save her money by staying with her brother. But now . . . "I can't stay here," she finally said, sighing, the thought of getting back into her car and looking for a hotel tiring her out more than she already was. Once again, she reached for her luggage.

"Don't be ridiculous. You can sleep in Mike's bedroom."

"Don't try to tell me what to do!" Eden snapped, feeling ten again.

"Eden, it looks like you drove here. That means you're probably exhausted, which is why you passed out."

"No, I passed out because I saw the shadow of the Incredible Hulk pointing a gun at my chest."

"Sorry about that, baby, but I thought you were a burglar. There's been a rash of them in the area, which is why I'm here at Mike's house. I'm sleeping in the guest room. You can either sleep in your brother's room or on the futon in the weight room.

C'mon, now. You know you want to stay and soak up the charm of the knight."

"You are so full of yourself."

Jansen chuckled. "I'm just messing with you, girl. But on the real tip though . . . you know you can't resist me."

"I'm going to take a shower." Eden grabbed her purse and began pulling her luggage toward the staircase.

Jansen raced to her side, quickly picking up the gun Eden eyed with disdain. "Don't worry, it won't bite you. Here, let me get that."

Eden batted away his hand. "I can get it myself."

"Oh, it's like that? See, I'm trying to be a gentleman, and you're acting all independent and whatnot. But I understand, baby girl. Things happen when I get too close to a woman, and even in that raggedy T-shirt and jeans, I can see that Mike's little sis is definitely all grown up!"

Eden hoisted the suitcase onto the first step and then the second. By the fourth step, her strength was drained. *Why didn't I think to just get out what I needed and leave the datgum case downstairs?* Now Eden felt she'd put herself in the position to prove that she could indeed carry the suitcase up the entire flight. She took a deep breath, grabbed the handle . . . and suddenly felt the weight of nothingness as Jansen took the case from her and effortlessly mounted the stairs.

Eden raised her head to deliver a sarcastic comment but just as quickly lowered it. The towel around Jansen's waist was a short one that perfectly outlined his round, hard buns. Two more steps, and Eden knew there was a good chance that she'd be able to see the package Jansen was working with. And even though they would be under the same roof for only one night . . . Eden knew life would be easier if she didn't know.